When Josiah agreed to become the coyote alpha, he knew it was a bad idea, and he was right. No matter how hard he tries, the band doesn't respect him, and he doesn't know how to change that. With humans sticking their noses all over the forest, he has to solve that problem, but how?

Luther might be in the forest to keep an eye on the shifters who live here, but that doesn't mean he's enjoying it. He has to follow orders, even when he disagrees with them, which in this case, he does. Shifters shouldn't be locked up, and they should have the same rights as humans.

Josiah doesn't know why Luther seems so interested in him, but he can't chalk it up to Luther doing his job for long. When it becomes obvious there's more between them, Josiah tries to keep his distance, because Luther is human, and eventually, he'll leave.

But Luther doesn't want to leave. He's in love with Josiah and will do pretty much anything for him, including trying to find a way to be allowed to stay.

Luther's superior has plans, though, and there's still a shooter on the loose in the forest. Then there's Josiah's problem with the band, which he knows will become worse once they find out he's pregnant. Can Josiah and Luther find a way to make things work, even an imperfect one, or are they doomed to be wrenched apart by circumstances?

Perfectly Imperfect
Copyright © 2021 Catherine Lievens
ISBN: 978-1-4874-3281-2
Cover art by Angela Waters

Published by eXtasy Books Inc or
Devine Destinies, an imprint of eXtasy Books Inc

Look for us online at:
www.eXtasybooks.com or www.devinedestinies.com

Perfectly Imperfect
Allegheny Shifters 8

By

Catherine Lievens

CHAPTER ONE

Josiah stared at the piece of paper in front of him on the desk. It was supposed to have a list of names written on it, but instead, it was empty. He had no candidates to fill his beta spot, and he knew better than to think he ever would, at least when it came to the coyotes.

So far, he hadn't been doing a good job as the new alpha. He barely knew where to start, but he did know he needed a beta. The problem was that no one wanted to work with him.

He snorted to himself and leaned back in the chair that had once belonged to his father. It wasn't only that no one wanted to work with him. No coyote respected him, either, which made things even harder. He didn't know how to break through that, or even if he could.

Maybe he shouldn't have accepted the alpha position. He understood why the council had needed him, and if it kept the humans off their back for a while, he was willing to continue, but he doubted he could actually do this. Shifters had to respect their alpha, and they didn't when it came to him.

He couldn't blame them. How could anyone respect him after what his father and his brother had done and the way they'd treated him in front of everyone? They believed what their old alpha had told them, which was that since Josiah was a carrier, he wasn't fit to become anything, least of all an alpha. It just wasn't done anywhere in the forest.

But things were changing. Josiah had never imagined he would be the first alpha carrier in the forest, yet here he was. In a few years, he wouldn't be the only one anymore. In the meantime, though, the position was unique to him, and he didn't know what to do.

He could ask for help. The council and Thomas, the badger alpha, had offered to help any way they could. Josiah wasn't proud enough to say no, but he didn't think they could do anything in this situation. He needed a beta, and it would be better if that beta was a coyote. Of course, it would be a problem if the band respected his beta more than they respected him, but he supposed he would deal with that problem if it ever happened. In the meantime, he was trying to deal with the band on his own, and they were ignoring him.

That was going to become a problem soon, and Josiah had no idea how to solve it.

He grabbed his cell phone from the desk and opened the messaging app. *I want to go home,* he wrote.

Nico's answer came only a few moments later, as if he'd been waiting with his phone in hand. That was surprising, since he was training with his father to become the next alpha. His twin brother had thrown him and their father for a loop when he'd decided to step down from the role and move in with the badgers, but Nico was more than happy to take Chris's place.

Isn't that what we all want? Nico answered.

Josiah frowned. *I thought you wanted to become the next alpha.*

I did. I DO. It's more complicated than I thought, that's all.

Tell me about it. Nico had been there every step of the way for Josiah, and Josiah was grateful. Now that they didn't live together anymore, he missed his best friend something fierce. He wished Nico could move in with him and maybe become his beta, but it just wasn't possible.

What's going on?

Josiah sighed. He didn't want to dump all his problems on Nico, especially not since Nico seemed to have his own. *Nothing much.*

Bullshit. Talk to me, Joe.

Josiah glared at the screen. *I told you not to call me that.*

Fine. Talk to me, JOSIAH.

Josiah rolled his eyes. *I still haven't found a beta.* If he couldn't tell Nico about this, then who could he tell? Thomas would listen to anything Josiah had to say, but he didn't want to burden the older alpha. The man already felt guilty enough that he'd pushed Josiah to accept this role. He wasn't wrong, though. Josiah wouldn't have accepted if Thomas hadn't asked. But Josiah owed Thomas everything, and if there was even one thing he could do to thank the man, he would do it.

Even if the thing was becoming alpha to people who hated him.

Has no one volunteered? Nico asked.

You know better than to think anyone would.

The three dots on the screen danced as Josiah waited for Nico to answer. He startled when his phone started ringing instead of a text appearing on the screen, but since it was Nico, he answered. "You should be working," he said.

"Yes, well, I'm not the only one. What's going on?"

"Nothing different than what was already going on before."

"Are they still ignoring you?"

"On the good days. On the bad ones, they snap at me and tell me I should never have become the alpha."

"They should be punished for that."

That word made Josiah cringe, because it reminded him of his father. Nico wasn't wrong, though. "And who's going to punish them?"

"You're the alpha. You ought to do it, or at the very least, order it."

"Me and what army? You know they're not going to care. They don't respect my authority, and I don't think they ever will. My father saw to that."

"Your father was a dick." Nico sounded fierce.

Josiah's heart swelled. Once, he hadn't thought he would

ever have a best friend. Hell, he'd thought he wouldn't be alive past his twenties. His father and his brother had abused him, and there had been nothing he could do about it. But he'd survived, and here he was, at twenty-three years old, a carrier and an alpha.

This was nothing like the life he'd expected to have, but in many ways, it was better. He wasn't alone anymore. He had people he cared about and who cared about him. He didn't have a lover, and he wasn't planning on finding one anytime soon, but he was young. He had time for that. Right now, he needed to focus on the band. If he didn't manage to get them under control, the humans would step in, and no one wanted that to happen.

Maybe that was what Josiah should tell the coyotes. He could make sure they knew what was going to happen if they didn't listen to him. He didn't understand why they didn't. Both his brother and his father had been abusive, and not only to him. They'd been bad alphas, and he didn't understand how the band wasn't relieved that they were gone and happy to have a decent alpha.

Not that it took a lot to be a decent alpha, considering whose shoes Josiah was filling, but he supposed that doing nothing was better than what his brother and his father had done.

"I guess we should be grateful they're not making too much of a fuss," he told Nico.

"They don't want the council to know they don't accept you."

"I don't want the council to know, either. You know what's going on. We can't afford to attract even more attention from the humans." The band was already in the spotlight.

The humans had visited, and Josiah didn't know what to think of them, especially their leader. That man had the band's future in his hands, but he hadn't told Josiah anything.

He'd just looked around with his intense gaze, taking everything in.

"And you're *sure* no one will agree to become your beta?"

Josiah sighed. "I already asked the older band members. The ones who stayed with me long enough to listen to what I had to say laughed in my face. The others took one look at me and turned around to leave."

"I wish I could do more to help you."

"Knowing I can call you anytime to whine is enough. I don't know what I would do if I didn't have you."

"You'll never have to find out, because I'm not going anywhere. You can do this, Josiah. I know you can, and so does the council. They wouldn't have asked you to become the alpha otherwise. You'll find a way around it. I know it."

Josiah hoped Nico's faith in him wasn't misplaced. God knew Nico trusted him more than he trusted himself.

Luther sat at the head of the table and looked down its length. It was strange to see an empty seat, but he was also relieved it was empty. He'd never liked Randy, and now he knew why.

Luther wished there was more he could do to Randy. He wanted to punish him for going against his orders, but unfortunately for him, Randy had been following other orders, coming from people higher up than Luther in the hierarchy. That was why the only thing Luther had been able to do was to kick his ass out of the team, and he knew he was going to pay for it sooner rather than later. In the meantime, both his mission and the forest were safe.

"Who do we still have on our list?" he asked.

He knew the answer to that, but it wouldn't be a bad thing to go over the territories they'd already visited and the ones still missing.

"The deer, the bats, and the raccoons," Dean said.

Luther nodded. "Any of those who might cause trouble?"

"Not as far as I know. I'm not the right person to ask, though."

But Chris and Jacob weren't here, and they weren't part of the team. No matter how much Luther trusted them, they were still shifters, which meant they were part of the people he and his team were investigating.

"Possibly the raccoons," Suzanne said.

"What have you heard?"

"Nothing much, just a whisper here and there."

"That's not a lot to work with."

"What about the coyotes?" Miriam asked. "Aren't we supposed to visit that territory again?"

Luther leaned back in his chair. They *were* supposed to visit the band again, but he wasn't looking forward to it.

The coyotes were the problem child in this situation. Their alpha was young, and from what Luther had seen, the band didn't respect him. So far, it hadn't been a problem, but he doubted it would last long. He should have written that in his reports, but instead, he'd kept it secret.

He knew why.

For some reason, Luther was fascinated by Josiah. More importantly, he liked him, and he hoped Josiah would be able to keep the coyotes under control. He'd just become the alpha, and Luther wanted to give him time to settle into the role and earn the coyotes' respect.

It was a problem waiting to happen, though. From what Luther had heard around the forest, the coyotes were hard to deal with. It all stemmed from the way Josiah's father and brother had led the band, and they hadn't left Josiah easy shoes to fill. They'd both been abusive assholes, and it was obvious the band was used to dealing with that kind of alpha. They probably didn't know what to do with Josiah, and the fact that he was a carrier didn't help matters.

Luther tapped his fingertips on the table. He needed to write up another report. His superior was becoming impatient, and he wanted Luther to get to the point and make a decision. It wasn't an easy one to make, though, especially because Luther didn't want the forest and the shifters who lived here to have to change the way they lived. As far as it looked, even though there had been a fight a little while ago, they had everything under control.

"We'll visit them again," he agreed. "Once we're done with the others." That would give Josiah time to try to get the coyotes under control. Luther didn't even care if it was only a façade. As long as everyone was respectful and appeared to follow Josiah's orders when he and his team visited the band, he would be happy to put that in his report and go on his way.

"I can't wait to go home," Miriam said.

She had a baby girl at home, so Josiah wasn't surprised.

"I'm more than happy here," Marlow answered. He'd been quiet until now, but then he always was.

"That's because you like living in the forest. I'm sure the shifters can't wait for us to leave, though."

That was probably the truth. No one liked having people sticking their noses in their business, but especially not when those people were humans who were supposed to decide your fate. Luther wasn't looking forward to going home like Miriam was, but then he didn't have anyone waiting for him there. His apartment was empty. He didn't have a family or a significant other. He had his parents and his sister, of course, but they had their own lives. Luther didn't see them anywhere near as often as he wanted, but it made sense.

"I don't know," Marlow said. "I think that a lot of them are curious about us and wouldn't mind if we stayed."

That was news to Luther. He wasn't blind, and he'd seen the distrust and sometimes hatred aimed at them. "Wouldn't they?" he asked.

Marlow shrugged. "You might not realize that, since you're our team leader, but I know it for sure. I've been talking to a lot of people."

"On your own?"

"I promise I was careful and that I didn't put myself in more danger than I could deal with. These shifters are just people, though. They want the same things we do."

"Except you can't turn into a badger," Suzanne pointed out.

"So? It doesn't make me more human than they are. They're good people, just like we are."

"The coyotes wouldn't be in this situation if their alpha had been a good person."

Marlow waved Suzanne's words away. "There are bad humans, too. It's the same everywhere. It doesn't mean that the entire forest wants to kill us. I wish you could see that."

Luther wished the same. He hadn't known what to expect when he'd accepted this job, but now he was glad he had. Just like a lot of humans, he'd always wondered what happened in the forests. That was where shifters had been relegated after the war and where they had been locked in since then. What he'd found was very different than what most people thought happened here, and he still didn't know how to deal with it. These people weren't just animals like a lot of people thought. Like Marlow had said, they were humans, and they deserved to be treated as such.

The way they were locked up in forests didn't sit right with Luther, but he was only one man. How was he supposed to change that on his own?

"Maybe you should stick around," Suzanne said.

"I would if I could," Marlow responded. "I like these people more than I like my own family, so it wouldn't be a problem."

Luther cleared his throat to get everyone's attention again. As much as he enjoyed listening to his team talking, they had work to do. "Who do you think we should start with?"

Suzanne turned her attention back to her phone. "I don't think it makes a difference. Since I heard people talking, though, maybe the raccoons? The deer and bats should be easy enough, and once that's done, we can go back to the coyotes."

"What about the skunks?" Dean asked.

"What about them?"

"They weren't happy to see us when we went."

"Not being happy to see us doesn't mean we have to visit them again. I didn't see anything that gave me doubts when we did. Did you?" Luther asked.

Dean shook his head. "Not see, but I talked with the future alpha. His father isn't happy about our presence in the forest, and while he played nice while we were there, it might not last."

Luther was surprised to find out that Dean had talked to a shifter on his own, too. What was happening to his team? "Who did you say you talked to?"

To Luther's surprise, Dean's cheeks turned pink, and he looked away. "The future alpha. His name is Jasper. He's Alpha Rhodes' son."

Luther remembered him. He hadn't been happy to find out what the skunks had done to their carriers, but he didn't have any authority over them, and his superior wouldn't care because carriers were shifters. "Did he mention his father was planning something?"

"No, but he's worried."

Luther nodded. "We'll add the surfeit to our list, then. We can visit them after the coyotes." Maybe in the meantime, Luther would find out what Dean knew about Jasper and his father.

Josiah needed advice. He wished he didn't have to go running back to Thomas, but the badger alpha had been more of a father to him than his own father ever had. He'd told Josiah to call whenever he needed help, and Josiah did. He had no idea what he was doing when it came to being the alpha, and it was starting to show.

Besides, Josiah was more than happy to be away from the band for a bit. When he was there, he spent most of his time in his cabin. It wasn't because he wanted to, but rather because he'd had enough of people staring at him and talking about him as if he wasn't even there. He hated being talked about, even though he was used to it. It had happened since he was a child, and he knew why. He'd been an oddity, a carrier born to the alpha. His father had hated that, and he'd made sure everyone knew. He hadn't wanted people to think he was weak because he had a carrier son, and he'd taken it out on Josiah.

Even though his father wasn't there anymore, the abuse was still happening. No one in the band would raise a hand to Josiah, but the gossiping and the way they were ignoring his orders came close. They were showing him they didn't respect him, and there was nothing he could do about it.

So he was always happy to be able to leave band territory, especially when it came to visiting the badgers. They'd saved him, and the weeks he'd spent with them had been the happiest of his life. He hoped that would change eventually, but for now, he wanted to go back and finally have the opportunity to relax a bit.

He wished he could still live with the badgers without a care in the world like he had before. Well, Josiah had never felt like he didn't have a care in the world. The time he'd spent with the badgers was the closest to that, though. He'd been away from his father and his brother, with no one abusing him. He'd been able to focus on licking his wounds and healing from what they'd done to him. It hadn't been easy, and he was still dealing with the aftermath, which was one more reason the band didn't trust him.

He had nightmares. Sometimes he woke up screaming in the middle of the night, and he knew the others heard him. It never took much for information to make the rounds, so everyone knew what he was dealing with. They might have been able to accept the fact that he was a carrier, but his trauma was something they held against him.

He sighed. No matter how much he wished he could just stop being the alpha, move back with the badgers, and forget all about this, he also knew he was doing the right thing. No one else could take his place at the head of the band, and he would have to learn to deal with it.

He was relieved when he finally parked his car in front of Thomas's house. He turned the engine off and closed his eyes, taking a moment to breathe. He was tense every second he spent with the band, but he was starting to relax now. His shoulders didn't feel as tight as they had an hour ago, and even though it wasn't going to last long, Josiah would make the most out of it.

He hopped out of his car and smiled when he saw that Alex and Seamus were sitting on the porch. Seamus had given birth recently, and he was holding his baby against his chest. Both he and Alex were looking at Josiah, and Seamus waved with his free hand.

The sight of them made Josiah's chest feel tight. Seamus was a friend, and Josiah wished him all the happiness in the world. He suspected Seamus was close to having that now that he had his baby and was married to the man he loved. Seeing them together made Josiah wonder if he ever would be able to have that.

No matter how many times he'd been told that being able to have a child made him weak, he knew that wasn't the truth. He'd seen enough carriers have children and be the strongest men he'd ever known. It had taken him a while to wrap his mind around that, but now he knew that even if he had a child, it wouldn't change how capable he was. It wouldn't change the fact that he was an alpha.

He was young still, and he didn't have anyone in his life, but he wanted children. Now would be the worst moment for him to have any, of course, but that didn't stop the yearning. His family had been a disaster, and he wanted that to change. He wanted children he could love, a man standing by his side. He'd never have loving parents or siblings, but this, he *could* have.

But having children would mess up his new role as the alpha, at least for now. The band already disrespected him. It would be worse if he got pregnant. They'd accepted him because they didn't have a choice, but having a pregnant alpha would be the last straw. The coyotes wouldn't accept it, and Josiah didn't know what would happen then.

All of that was pointless, since he didn't have a boyfriend.

"Josiah," Alex said with a smile. "Were we expecting you?"

Josiah shook his head and climbed the porch steps. He made a beeline for Seamus, leaning down to see his daughter. "No one knew I was coming. I need to talk to your father." One day, Josiah and Alex would work together as alphas. For now, Alex was free to spend time with his family without a care in the world. He spent time with his father, learning how to become an alpha, but he wasn't one yet, not like Josiah.

"He's in his office. You know the way."

"You don't want to spend some time with us?" Seamus asked.

"I wish I could," Josiah answered. He was pretty sure Seamus could hear the yearning in his voice. He'd always been perceptive.

Seamus frowned. "Did something happen?"

"Nothing that hasn't happened before. I'm fine. I promise."

"You don't sound fine."

"It's nothing." Josiah didn't want to burden Seamus with his problems. Seamus needed to focus on his daughter, and besides, even if Josiah told him about the band, there was nothing he could do.

There was nothing anyone could do. Josiah needed to find a beta, but he didn't know where or how. Everyone he'd asked had laughed at him and slammed their doors in his face. He doubted that was going to change anytime soon, no matter who he talked to.

He was stuck. He didn't know how to go forward, and he couldn't go back. No matter how many orders he gave, the coyotes didn't listen to him. He needed a beta who could take things in hand, but what would happen if the band respected his beta more than they respected him?

He didn't have answers to those questions, and he wouldn't find them until he found a beta. Where he would get that person, he didn't know, but he *would* find a way.

Josiah might be a carrier, and he might never have been supposed to become the alpha, but he was. It ran in his veins, which was why the coyotes hadn't been able to say no when the council had asked him to take charge. Josiah was strong, stronger than anyone thought, including himself. He could do this, and he would, even if it killed him.

He just hoped it wouldn't come down to that.

CHAPTER TWO

Josiah was still thinking about his conversation with Thomas a few days later. He was tempted to accept Thomas's offer of sending a badger or another shifter from the council to help as his temporary beta, but he was afraid it would only make things worse. He needed help, but antagonizing the coyotes wasn't going to help anyone, especially not him.

They didn't trust Josiah. Having another kind of shifter as their beta would make that worse, and if there was even one chance for him to become a real alpha to the band, that would ruin it.

No. If he wanted a beta, he was going to have to find one himself, and preferably a coyote. He had no idea where to start, which was yet another problem. He'd already asked the oldest people in the band, thinking that they would want the best for the band and would agree to help, if not for him, for the coyotes.

They'd all said no.

Josiah wanted to think it had nothing to do with his father, but he wasn't an idiot. The entire band might not believe what his father had told them about carriers, but some did, and others, even if they didn't believe it, couldn't risk it. Agreeing to help Josiah and step up as his beta would put anyone who did it in the spotlight. They would have to deal with recriminations, possibly accusations of betraying the band and the old alpha.

Sometimes, Josiah wished his father were still alive so he could get his hands on him and strangle him.

He sighed. Most of the time, he was happy his father and his brother were out of the picture. He would never have to deal with them again, which was a relief, but it didn't help him in this situation. They might be out of his life, but their presence was still very much hovering over the band and making things harder for him.

Nico poked at Josiah's thigh with his bare foot. "You have to stop moping."

Josiah playfully glared at him. He could never be angry at Nico. "I'm not moping. I'm thinking."

Nico folded his legs under himself. "What are you thinking about?"

"Thomas offered to send me one of his badgers as a beta."

Nico grimaced. "I know it's tempting to accept, but I don't think it would be a good idea."

Josiah was relieved he wasn't the only one to think that. "I know. I told him I'd think about it, and I am, but I suspect it would make things worse."

Nico nodded. "They don't trust you now. It won't get better if you allow another kind of shifter to have power over them. I don't think it would work."

"I don't, either, but what else can I do? They won't listen to me. When they see me, they turn around and leave, when they don't outright spit on the ground in front of me. I should be punishing all of them, but I'm only one man." And he wasn't as cruel as his father and his brother had been. He'd thought that would be a good thing, and he never wanted to become like them, but it would be easier for him to control the coyotes if they were afraid of him.

A knock on the door interrupted them before Nico could answer. They looked at each other, and Nico looked as surprised as Josiah felt.

"Are you expecting someone?" he asked.

Josiah shook his head. "I don't know who it could be."

Maybe a coyote who wanted to tell him how bad he was. It wouldn't be the first time. Usually, they avoided him, but a few had come up to his door to tell him what they thought about him becoming their alpha.

Josiah wasn't looking forward to having to listen to that again, but he couldn't ignore the knock and whoever was on the other side of the door, no matter how much he wanted to. If the band needed him, he had to be there for them.

He got to his feet and padded to the front door. The cabin was still more crowded than he liked with old furniture and knickknacks, but he hadn't had the time to throw out everything yet. When he did, he would need help to get most of the furniture out, and while normally an alpha would count on his people to help, Josiah couldn't. He would have to call Nico and Chris and other people. The coyotes wouldn't be happy, and they would make sure he knew it.

He didn't know what they wanted. They didn't want him to be the alpha, but when he did something he shouldn't be doing as the alpha, they got angry at him.

He opened the door and blinked at Luther. He'd met the human before, and he'd been looking forward to talking to him again, but he hadn't expected him to come around today, and more importantly, he hadn't expected him to come around on his own.

He looked around. "Is your team exploring the territory?"

Luther shook his head. "They're not here."

"You're alone." That confirmed Josiah's thoughts, but he didn't understand *why* Luther had come on his own.

"I am."

Something had happened, hadn't it? There was no other explanation for Luther's presence here. "What's going on?"

Before Luther could answer, Nico was there, pushing past Josiah. When Josiah looked down, he saw that Nico had put his shoes on. "I need to go home," his best friend declared.

Josiah frowned. "Why? Did your father call?"

Nico narrowed his eyes at Josiah. He looked amused, and Josiah didn't understand why. "Not yet, but he's going to soon. I don't think he likes having me out of his sight, not after what happened with Chris."

"He can't lock you in your house."

Nico laughed. "He can certainly try, but he won't manage. I'm not Chris, and I'm not afraid to stand up to him." He kissed Josiah's cheek. "Call me tonight, all right? We can talk some more."

That was a way for him to ask for Josiah to tell him everything that was about to happen with Luther. Josiah would probably need it. He didn't know how to act with Luther, and it didn't have anything to do with the fact that Luther was human.

It had *everything* to do with the fact that Josiah found him attractive, and that sometimes when he didn't have nightmares, he dreamt about him.

Josiah watched Nico walk to his car. Once Nico was inside, Josiah turned his attention back to Luther. "Sorry about that. You were saying?"

"That I'm here on my own and that you don't have to worry, because it's not an official visit."

Josiah stepped aside to let Luther in. Luther might not be here officially, but that didn't mean Josiah shouldn't treat him as the human envoy he was. "Would you like something to drink?"

Luther rubbed the back of his neck. "I wanted to talk to you."

"You can do that while sipping on some lemonade. Or would you rather have coffee?" Josiah needed a moment to gather his thoughts and be ready to face Luther. No matter what Luther was saying, he had a reason to be here, and Josiah couldn't think of one, especially not one that didn't have to do with his job.

Luther smiled.

It made him look softer and less dangerous, and Josiah had to remind himself of who Luther was.

"Lemonade would be perfect."

Josiah led the way to the kitchen. He grabbed the pitcher of lemonade from the fridge, two glasses from the cupboard, and put them on the table. He sat on the other side of it, facing Luther, and filled both glasses. He drank half of his before Luther even took a sip, but he was nervous.

"I want to help," Luther said after a few moments.

"I'm not sure I understand what you're talking about."

Luther ran his fingertip on the condensation on the surface of his glass. "I know about your problems when it comes to the band."

"I'm pretty sure everyone knows about my problems."

"You're probably right. I wasn't given any details, but I know enough to realize how bad it is. That's what I want to help you with."

This wasn't what Josiah had expected. "That's not your job."

"It's not," Luther confirmed. "I realize you see me as a human who's encroaching on your territory, but that's not everything I am. I have orders to follow, but it doesn't mean I can't help you, or at the very least, try to."

"Why would you do that?" It was the first question Josiah thought to ask, even though it might be the wrong one. He needed the answer before he could accept or decline Luther's offer, though.

Luther hadn't missed the way Nico had looked at him as he left. He wasn't sure what the look meant, but he made a mental note to ask Nico when he next saw him — if he did. Luther saw Chris almost every day, because Chris was assigned to follow him around and smooth things out with the shifters in the forest. Luther knew Nico because he was Chris's twin, but he didn't think they'd ever talked in private.

He was curious, though, and he was pretty sure Nico wouldn't hesitate to tell him what he wanted to know. He was more open than Chris, and from what Luther knew, he would be honest.

First, though, he needed to answer Josiah's question. It would be easier to do if he knew why he was here exactly, but he didn't. He also wasn't sure why he'd offered to help Josiah. Luther doubted there was anything he could do to help. No matter how much he wanted to, he wasn't a shifter, and he didn't know how things worked in the forest. He'd been told about the situation, but it wasn't the same.

"Luther?" Josiah asked.

Luther shook himself and looked at the man in front of him. "Because I don't think any of this is right," he murmured.

Josiah's back was ramrod straight. "I swear I'm doing my best to keep the band under control. I don't have a beta yet, but I'm looking for one, and I know I'll find someone soon. That will help."

Luther realized Josiah thought he was blaming him for the mess they were all in. There couldn't be anything further from the truth. Luther hadn't been talking about that when he'd said he didn't think it was right. Still, the fact that Josiah didn't have a beta was worrying, and it could be a trigger for his boss. The man wanted to rain hell on the forest, and he was only waiting for the right excuse to make that happen.

Luther leaned forward. "That's not what I was talking about. Like I said, I was told about your situation, and I'm not surprised you're having trouble. I don't blame you for it, and I have faith that you'll find a beta and keep everything under control."

"What do you mean, then?"

Luther wanted to tell Josiah everything, but he couldn't. No matter how much he wanted to, this was his job. "You know why I was sent here," he started, trying to find a way to tell Josiah what he meant without actually telling him.

"Everyone in the forest knows about that."

"Right. So we're here to keep the shifters in the forest under control and make sure a war doesn't start between the various groups. We're supposed to keep humans safe from you."

Josiah frowned. "I don't see how we could be a danger to humans. We're locked up in the forest."

With how young Josiah was, he wouldn't have known anything different from the forest. It didn't seem like a bad place to grow up, but freedom was important, too. Besides, even though the forest was beautiful, some of the people who lived in it weren't. Josiah's father was a prime example of that.

Luther needed to take a chance. "And that's not right," he said. He stared at Josiah as he said the words.

"What do you mean?" Josiah sounded cautious, and Luther didn't blame him.

"I have to obey orders, even when I disagree with them. That includes keeping shifters locked up in their forests."

"You think we should be free?"

"You're as human as I am. The fact that you can turn into a coyote doesn't change that. I'm not the one making decisions, though. I *have* to obey orders, even when I don't like them. In this case, my orders are to keep an eye on shifters, to make sure we don't have a war about to start on our hands, and that all of you are safely locked in here."

"I still don't understand what it has to do with you helping me."

Luther drank the rest of his lemonade as he tried to find a way to answer. "With the way the coyotes are behaving, it would be easy for some people to start a war between them and other shifters. Some people might take advantage of that. Most humans don't want a war with shifters, but some are eager for one." Including Luther's boss, but he wasn't about to say that out loud.

No matter how much he wanted to trust Josiah, he didn't know if he could, and he couldn't risk it.

Josiah frowned. "Why would they want that?"

"To have an excuse to kill as many shifters as they can. I don't know how much history you're aware of, but some humans wanted all shifters to be killed after the war. Luckily, they didn't win, but it was a close thing."

"Which is why we ended up locked up in here."

"Exactly. Some of these people are still alive. Unfortunately, they view you as little more than animals who need to be put down. There are other people trying to protect you as much as possible, but it's a thin line to walk. That's why we can't afford for anything to happen here. It would give the people after you an excuse to do what they've been planning."

Josiah slowly nodded. "I believe you. This is too much for me to wrap my mind around, though. I already have enough problems with the band. I can only imagine what's happening outside the forest, and to be honest, I don't *want* to think about it. It feels too big, and there's nothing I can do to change it."

"You don't have to think about that. Leave it to me." Luther was used to dealing with humans, after all. "But I'd like you to believe me when I say I'll do everything I can to help you. I might not be able to free you and your people from the forest, but I can make sure you're as safe as possible."

"I don't think there's anything you can do to help me, though. Not even the council can help, and they're shifters who know everything there is to know about my situation."

Luther had been afraid of that, but it didn't mean he was

giving up. What shifters were forced to do, the fact that they were prisoners, wasn't right. They should have the same rights as humans to move around the country, and while Luther didn't think there was anything he could do to change that, he *would* do everything he could to help keep the shifters in the forest safe.

Josiah wanted to believe Luther. He was saying all the right words, but he was the first human Josiah had met. Josiah might like him, but how could he be sure that his trust wasn't misplaced?

He couldn't. That was always the case, wasn't it? Josiah could either trust Luther or decide he didn't and ask him to leave. Luther sounded honest, but that didn't mean he was. Still, he wanted to help, and even though there was nothing he could do, maybe he would want to listen to Josiah's problems.

That was why he was here. The humans wanted him and his team to find out about the forest and the shifters who lived here. They wanted to know whether or not they would have a war on their hands, and Josiah could give him that answer.

"The coyotes won't start a war," he told him.

"I didn't think they would."

"You did, but that's okay. I realize you don't know us. There aren't enough coyotes to be dangerous to the rest of the forest, but more importantly, I don't think they'd even try. They're not organized, and I doubt they will be anytime soon."

Josiah could feel Luther's gaze on him. He kept his focus on the glass he was still clutching, even though it was empty.

"You're still having problems," Luther said.

Josiah had to swallow before he could answer. "That's an understatement." He had no idea what he was doing, but he hoped he could trust Luther. "You know my situation. I'm young, and I don't have experience when it comes to being an alpha. Even worse, I'm a carrier. In any other circumstance, in any other shifter group, I would have a beta who could help me learn how to do this. It would be someone with experience and that the band could respect."

"But you don't have a beta."

Josiah leaned back. He stared at the ceiling, wondering if he had to talk about this one more time. It would be a problem until he solved it, and he knew better than to avoid it. "Not for lack of trying," he admitted. "I feel like I've asked everyone in the band if they wanted to be my beta. All of them said no."

"Because you're a carrier."

Josiah shrugged. "In part. In part, though, it's because of my father. He was the alpha for years. Decades, really. He had a long time to convince the band that he was right about everything and that even if he wasn't, they better not go against him if they wanted to live. He used fear and cruelty to guide the band, and he made sure everyone knew that he didn't consider me his son or worthy of anything. As soon as he found out I was a carrier, I became scum to him. It started long before then, though."

"You don't have to talk about this if you don't want to do."

"Everyone knows, even the shifters who belong to other shifter groups. By now, I'm pretty sure the entire forest knows what my father and my brother did to me." It was still hard to talk about it, but Josiah didn't want to hide. He had no fault in what had been done to him. He'd survived, and he wasn't going to hide how bad his father had been.

"That doesn't mean you have to tell me." Luther's voice was soft and gentle.

It made Josiah's heart feel like it was going to break. He didn't want people to think he was fragile and had to be coddled. "My father never liked me, not even when I was a child. He thought I was weak, and when he realized I was a carrier, it was a confirmation for him. He beat me regularly. He told me that I couldn't be his son, that I was an error of nature. He's never really bought into the idea that was going around that children born from carriers are stronger, and he loathed the fact that I might get pregnant."

That was probably the only time Josiah's father had been right. Who you were born from didn't matter, or at least, Josiah hoped it didn't. He'd been born from a monster.

"He made sure the entire band knew why he hated me," Josiah continued. "He allowed them to bully me. He didn't care, even though I was his son. The fact that I was helped a bit, though. It meant that most of the band didn't want to hurt me, just in case my father changed his mind or believed he was the only one who *could* hurt me. But they all saw how he treated me. They never learned to respect me, and now, it's a problem."

Luther twisted his glass around on the table. It was almost as if he couldn't stay still, which Josiah understood. He wanted to run into the forest screaming instead of having this conversation.

"You were never supposed to be the alpha."

Josiah shook his head. "Even if I hadn't been a carrier, I was a second son. My brother was supposed to take my father's place, and he did."

"And he used the band to attack the badgers."

That was the reason Luther and his people were here. "He did. He paid for it, and now I'm stuck in his role. I'm doing everything I can, but it's not easy when the band won't even look me in the face. I don't know how to make them see that my father was wrong about me."

Luther sighed, and his shoulders slumped. "I don't think you can, not if they don't want to see it. It'll take time. Once they realize you're making the right choices for the band and that you're trying to protect them, they'll have to admit that you're not a bad alpha."

Josiah suspected they would try not to. He'd always known this wasn't going to be easy, but he hadn't expected it to be hell.

"And you said no one will step up to help you?" Luther asked.

"I've asked pretty much everyone in the band. I'd hoped that one of the older members would agree to help me, but they all refused. I don't think it's because they hate me, at least not all of them, but they don't want to be seen helping me."

"How about another kind of shifter? I know it's not done, at least from what I've seen since I arrived, but it might be a solution."

"That's what the council offered, but I don't think it would work. The band might hate me even more for bringing a stranger into it."

"Sooner or later, you're going to have to make decisions not based on what the band wants. If this is the best for the band, you might have to do it, whatever they think."

Josiah sighed. "I hope it won't come to that."

Luther hesitated. "What's going to happen if you can't get the band under control? Do they realize what's at stake here?"

"I tried to talk to them about it. I organized a band meeting, but only a few people came, and when they saw they were the only ones there, they left. Everyone knows what's going on with you and your people, though. It's why even alphas who never wanted you around allowed you to explore their territories. They know what's at stake, and they're not willing to jeopardize their people and the forest. It should be enough to keep the band under control." But for how long?

"I came here to help you, but I'm afraid there's not much I can do," Luther murmured.

Josiah found himself smiling. "But you already knew that. I'm glad you offered, though. Not a lot of people did, and even though it's such a small thing, it makes me feel better." It didn't help his crush on Luther, but he suspected nothing would.

He liked Luther even more now that he'd seen a hint of the man under the uniform. Spending more time with him would be a disaster waiting to happen, but as long as Josiah kept his feelings to himself, it would be okay.

It had to be.

Luther should have known better than to think he could do anything. He realized that it was an excuse, though. He'd wanted to see Josiah and to talk to him alone, and he had.

Josiah was even sweeter than Luther had thought. When he and the others had visited band territory, Josiah had been stiff and anxious. Luther couldn't blame him for that, and he'd made sure to stay away from the alpha. He'd seen Josiah other times, but there had always been other people around, and Josiah had been burdened and busy.

He still was. There was no denying that, but now that they were alone, Josiah appeared more relaxed. Luther didn't know if that was the case or if he'd caught Josiah in the right moment, but he wanted to help more.

The problem was that he couldn't.

He was useless when it came to shifters and how they behaved. He wanted to take on the band for Josiah, but it would be a disaster.

He tapped his fingertips on the scarred wood of the table. "So the only solution is to have a coyote by your side," he said.

Josiah nodded. "If I could convince one, yes."

"Maybe you should try having a band meeting again."

"Why? No one would come."

"How about calling in the council and the people who work for them? They could force your band into a meeting. It might be the only way to get them to listen and for them to grasp how complicated and vital the situation is. Maybe once they realize what will happen if they don't allow you to lead, they will, even if only begrudgingly."

Josiah sighed and rubbed his face. "I don't want things to come to that, but they might have to. But I wouldn't count on the fact that they'll relent once they realize what it could mean."

Luther wanted to find every single coyote in the forest and beat them to a pulp for what they were doing to Josiah. It wasn't enough that his brother and his father had been abusive. It wasn't enough that Josiah had been forced to accept being the alpha. No one here realized how much Josiah was sacrificing or how much pain he'd gone through in his life.

No matter how many times Josiah told this story, Luther doubted anyone could understand entirely. Josiah's life had been hard, and it would have been his right to say no when the council asked him to take the band in hand. Instead, at only twenty-three, he'd agreed to take his father's place. He'd known things wouldn't be easy, yet he hadn't turned his back on the people who had abused him all his life.

Luther was in awe. Josiah was one of the strongest men he'd ever known, and whatever happened, he would do everything he could to help. "Is there any other way for them to gain respect for you? Even if they don't like you, you're still the alpha."

Josiah shrugged. "I doubt it. In other circumstances, I could marry someone and have their help."

Luther frowned. "What do you mean?"

"You know Thomas, right?"

"The badger alpha. Yes."

"And you also know Morris, the bear alpha. Their sons are

married, which means that the sleuth and the cete are allied. They're much closer than any other shifter group in the forest. That has as much to do with the kind of people Thomas and Morris are than with their sons' marriage. That's what alphas do, though. They create alliances so they'll have support when they need it."

"So you could marry one of Thomas's sons and have his support."

Josiah laughed. "I could if they weren't all already in a relationship." His expression turned more serious. "And if I wasn't a carrier. I don't think marriage would work for me. To the band, I would always be the weakest man in my marriage because of what I can do."

"I don't understand how being able to carry a child makes you different from any other man in everything else."

"That's because you're human, and you haven't lived here for decades. I'm honestly surprised at how easily you accepted the fact that I could become pregnant. But my father hammered into everyone's head that being able to do that made me weak, and they believe it. If I were to get married, even if it was to an alpha's son, they would see me at the weakest. They would expect him to be the one to lead the band, and they wouldn't respect him. Sure, I could use the help when it comes to manpower, and I would have people I trust to talk to about this, but I already have that."

"How about a woman? What would happen if you married a woman?"

Josiah blinked. "You think anyone would believe it was a real marriage?"

"Why not? Are all carriers gay?"

"You know, I'm not sure. I suppose they're not, but there aren't many of us around. That's not the point, though. I don't want to marry someone for the good of the band. I've already had to give up much of my life to my father and now, to this.

I don't want to give up love, too. If I ever get married, I want it to be for that reason."

But that probably wouldn't go down well with the band. It wasn't right, especially not after everything Josiah had gone through. His life had been hell before his father and brother died, and he shouldn't have to be the alpha, especially not to people who hated him.

But Josiah knew the situation better than Luther. No doubt he'd already thought about every solution, and nothing Luther could say would help.

He wanted to protect Josiah. He wasn't an idiot, and he couldn't lie to himself. He didn't want to, either. He liked Josiah, and he was attracted to him. There could be nothing between them, no matter how much he wanted it. Even if Josiah had feelings for him — which Luther wasn't sure of — the situation was already complicated enough without adding a relationship with a human. Besides, Luther would leave eventually. He didn't have a place in the forest, no matter how much he enjoyed spending time here. Josiah had to think of the band first and his own life second. The same went for Luther and his job.

"So I bothered you for nothing," Luther said.

Josiah's smile was kind. "I wouldn't say it was for nothing. I realize you're here to police us, but you want to learn more about us."

"I do."

"And you don't think it's right for us to be trapped in the forest. You want to change things, which not a lot of people do."

"It doesn't matter how much I want that. I doubt I'll be able to do anything to help."

"Sometimes, what you want to do matters as much as what you can do. I enjoyed talking to you, and even though we couldn't find a solution to my problems, it felt nice to talk about them with someone who doesn't know what's going on."

But it wasn't enough. Josiah thought he'd be able to keep the coyotes under control, but Luther wasn't too sure about that. What would happen if the coyotes rebelled? They would be squashed, as they should be, but would Josiah pay for it?

The council had put him in charge, and as far as Luther could see, they expected him to solve their problem. What were they doing to help him, though? What would they do if he couldn't get the band under control like they expected him to?

Luther didn't have answers to those questions, and he wasn't sure he would get any, but until he was a hundred percent sure the coyotes wouldn't rebel, he'd stay in the forest. He would keep an eye on everything, but things wouldn't end well for anyone if his superior had anything to say about it.

And Luther wasn't sure there was anything he could do to protect the forest and Josiah from that.

CHAPTER THREE

When Josiah opened his front door a few days later, he wasn't surprised to see Luther standing there. He'd been thinking a lot about the conversation they'd had, even though he'd avoided mentioning it to Nico. Nico had been teasing, and he was the only one who knew that Josiah was attracted to Luther—and who would ever know, because Josiah wasn't about to broadcast his feelings.

He didn't want Luther to find out about them. He didn't want to appear weak in the humans' eyes.

But having feelings wasn't a weakness. Josiah never wanted to become like his father, who had only known hatred and contempt and had never allowed himself to love. Josiah didn't think he had wanted to. If anything, his father had been happy not to love. He wanted control and power, and he'd had it.

That hadn't turned out to be good for him in the end.

"Am I bothering you?" Luther asked.

Josiah shook his head and stepped aside to let him in. He didn't miss the way the few coyotes around were staring, but he didn't care. If they had a problem with what he was doing, they could come to him and talk about it. It was what anyone else would do, but so far, unless he'd been the one to push, no coyote had come anywhere near him.

"You're alone again?" he asked.

Luther nodded as he looked around. "What about you? Where's Nico?"

"With his father. He's been complaining by texts, but he

actually loves it."

"While Chris doesn't."

Josiah closed the door and nodded. "He never wanted to be alpha, apparently, and he has a choice. It's good that his father allowed him to make it." Whereas Josiah hadn't had one.

Even though Thomas and the council had made it sound like he didn't have to say yes when they'd asked him to take charge of the coyotes, he knew better. They would have been lost if he'd refused, and it would have been a problem with the humans. Now that Josiah knew Luther, he realized it wouldn't have been, but he didn't regret saying yes, at least most of the time. He just didn't know if there was anything he could do.

Being an alpha was his legacy, and he was fucking things up. It could mean the band would have to be dissolved and the coyotes taken care of in other ways, but he didn't want to think about that yet—hopefully not ever.

"I just wanted to check in," Luther said, turning to face Josiah. He'd been looking around, probably curious about the house.

"I'm fine," Josiah said. "You don't have to worry about me. I'm sure you have more than enough work and things to worry about without adding me to the pile."

Luther grimaced. "You're not wrong there. I don't think I can ever be busy enough not to worry about you, though."

Josiah sucked in a breath. He hadn't been sure Luther was interested in him, but now he wondered. Or maybe Luther was just a good person who cared about what happened to Josiah. His interest didn't have to be sexual or romantic, and Josiah needed to keep that in mind.

He already had enough on his plate without adding a crush on a human who probably wouldn't see him that way after what he'd told him and who would leave once his mission was over.

Josiah knew he wasn't weak and that being a carrier didn't change who he was, but it had been pounded into his head that he would never amount to anything. He wanted to show everyone that wasn't the case, but sometimes it was hard to ignore the voices in the back of his mind. They sounded suspiciously like his father and his brother, and if they weren't dead, Josiah would want to kill them himself.

"Well, like I said, I'm fine. I still haven't found a solution, if that's what you're asking, but I'm sure I will eventually."

"I know you will. But you shouldn't have to do this on your own."

"I'm not. I can call Thomas or the council anytime I need something."

"But can they do anything for you?"

"They're doing what they can." And it should be enough.

But it wasn't. Josiah had to focus on the band, on finding a beta and a council member. The council had called him a few days ago to point out that he couldn't continue being his own council member, and he agreed. Who could he choose when no one even wanted to be his beta, though?

There was no coyote he trusted enough to have the band's best interest at heart when it came to the council. The coyotes were selfish, even more than a lot of other shifters in the forest. The deer and the bobcats, the badgers and bears—all wanted the forest to be safe. They didn't want a war with anyone, and they weren't afraid to give up some of the power they could earn by being cruel assholes.

Josiah's father had enjoyed being cruel. He'd used the fear he created in the coyotes to control them. He'd used the band council member as a way to earn even more power throughout the forest. That wasn't what Josiah wanted, which meant he needed to find the perfect person to represent the band on the council.

Where was he supposed to find that person, though?

"So you still haven't found a solution?" Luther asked.

There was no scorn in his voice. He truly was asking because he wanted to know, not because he was implying that Josiah wasn't strong enough. "I've tried, but so far, no. I found the registers of every member of the band, and I've been going over them in case I missed someone."

Luther frowned. "How can you miss someone?"

Josiah gestured at the couch and sat on the edge of it without waiting for Luther to move. "It's not as hard as you think. Since you visited this territory, you know how big it is and how easy it would be for someone to isolate themselves in the forest. It's easier for coyotes to stick around the alpha house, but not everyone wants it. A lot of coyotes had built their homes away from it, probably to run away from my father."

"So you think there might be some coyotes hiding in the forest who could become your beta?"

"I'm hoping so." But it was Josiah's last hope. If he didn't find anyone, he was going to have to accept Thomas's offer of sending someone else to help. He wasn't looking forward to it because he knew it would make things worse when it came to him and the way the band saw him. But did he have a choice?

"I probably shouldn't have come," Luther said. "I don't want to distract you from your work."

"I'm glad to see you," Josiah told him in a rush. He didn't want Luther to leave, not yet.

Luther smiled tentatively. "Really?"

"Really. Can we talk about something else? I understand why this is important to you, but apart from promising you that I'm doing everything I can, there's not much more I can tell you." Josiah paused. "But of course, this is your job. It's why you're here." Why would Luther want to stick around Josiah if he didn't have to?

"It is, but it's not the only reason," Luther murmured. "I could have called you or even asked the council what was going on. There's a reason I came to talk to you in person and alone."

Josiah's heart raced. "There is?"

"I like you, Josiah. You're a good person, someone who was dealt a horrible hand by life and who's making the best he can with it. You're awe-inspiring, and I'm surprised you don't realize that."

Josiah's shoulders slumped. This wasn't what he'd expected or what he'd hoped for. He supposed it was better than the alternative of Luther checking in on him because he didn't trust him, though. "Thank you," he murmured.

"You have nothing to thank me for. I realize that it's probably strange for you to think we could be friends, but that's how I see you."

But that wasn't how Josiah saw Luther.

Luther had just lied. He didn't see Josiah as a friend, or at least, not merely. He was attracted to Josiah. Josiah was strong and beautiful, and Luther didn't understand how anyone could resist him. He was a mixture of fragility and strength—something Luther had never seen in anyone else.

But Luther knew better than be honest when it came to his feelings. Josiah was dealing with a lot, including his past and what had been done to him by his father and his brother. He didn't have time to waste on Luther, and Luther shouldn't have come.

He was human. He was in a position of power when it came to Josiah and every other shifter in the forest. He would have to go back home soon, even though he wasn't looking forward to it. He couldn't demand anything from Josiah, and he didn't want to put Josiah in a place where he would be uncomfortable spending time with him.

"It's strange," Josiah said. "I never thought I would be friends with a human."

"But you think you could be?"

Josiah's smile was gentle. "I think I already am. We haven't solved anything by talking, but it feels good to have someone from the outside to talk to. You don't have the same thoughts as another shifter would have, or the same preconceptions. You have a different way of looking at life, and it might come in handy."

"Well, if you ever need anything, you know where to find me."

Josiah grinned. "You're staying in Northwood?"

"We thought it would be for the best. That way, we're truly neutral."

"But you're not. I know you like Thomas and Morris. Besides, you told me yourself that you think shifters should be free. That's not being neutral."

Luther shrugged. "As neutral as possible, then." He realized there was no such thing as not having thoughts about what was going on. He had them, and they were strong.

"Do you miss home?"

Luther blinked at the unexpected question. "You mean my home outside the forest?"

Josiah arched a brow. "Why? Do you have a home in the forest?"

Luther had to look away. He wanted to say yes to that question, but he couldn't. No matter how much he enjoyed being in the forest and how much he disliked thinking about going back to his empty apartment, he couldn't stay. He wouldn't be allowed to.

No human had ever lived with shifters, not officially. Luther was sure that in a few places, some humans had managed to sneak into the national forests and make their life with the shifters who lived there, but Luther wasn't just someone. He worked for the government, which meant he wouldn't be allowed to do something like that.

"You know I don't," he told Josiah. "But I don't have a lot to go back to. This is the most interesting job I've worked in a long time, and I can honestly say I'm not looking forward to going back."

Josiah frowned. "What about your family? Do you have one?" He hesitated and briefly looked down at Luther's hands. "Are you married?"

Luther shook his head. "I'm not married, and I don't have anyone important in my life. I only have my parents and my sister, but they all have their own lives, and I don't see them often. As for my personal life, well, I don't really have one. I'm more focused on my job."

Josiah slowly nodded. "I see. So you enjoy this job."

Luther wasn't sure how to answer. Once, he *had* enjoyed it. He had a new superior now, though, and he didn't like the man. He also didn't like most of his orders, but there was nothing he could do about that. "Sometimes," he said as a compromise.

"But sometimes, you don't?"

Luther wasn't sure that talking about this was the best idea, especially not with Josiah. He didn't think Josiah would go around talking about what they were saying, but he didn't know if he should risk it. "That's the case with every job, isn't it?" he asked instead of answering.

"I wouldn't know. This is the first job I've ever had."

"Let's just say that it depends on what kind of jobs me and the team are sent on. This isn't one of my favorites."

"You mean babysitting shifters?"

"I mean playing sheriff."

"I'm not sure what you're saying."

Luther sighed. "When I started this job, I did it because I

wanted to help people. I did, for a long time, and sometimes, I still do. But this job, in particular, is different. The team and I were sent here to keep an eye on shifters and make sure they behaved the way they should. If they don't, we have to punish them. It's not just babysitting. I don't want to punish anyone, especially not for something I feel they have every right to do."

"But the forest would be a mess if everyone did what they wanted."

"You're not wrong. But humans have locked up shifters in the forests. They should have no say in what happens in them."

"But you said you were sent to make sure we wouldn't threaten humans."

This was getting too deep into things Luther didn't want to talk about. He had suspicions, but he'd never told anyone, and he didn't want to burden Josiah more than he already was. "I don't think you'd threaten humans, whatever happens."

"I don't know. I wouldn't be too sure about some people. They really don't like humans, and they see you guys as the reason we're here."

"That's not wrong. We *are* the reason you're locked up."

"Exactly. Can you trust every single shifter who lives in this forest not to try anything? To be honest, I'm surprised only one team was sent. I don't understand how you and your people don't feel threatened, especially when you visit some territories."

Luther *had* felt threatened, but thankfully, no alpha had done anything against him and his team. They probably realized that while Luther and his people were only one team, they had the force of the entire government behind them. If something happened to them, it wouldn't go unpunished.

Josiah got to his feet, startling Luther. "Why don't you

come with me?" he asked.

"Where are we going?" Luther would follow Josiah anywhere, but he wouldn't mind knowing what was about to happen.

"I'm sure you're curious about the band. You visited this territory, but you haven't seen a lot of people and how they behave with me."

And Luther didn't want to start now. It was enough for him to have heard Josiah explain what was going on. He didn't want to see him being mistreated, although maybe his presence would help with that. "What's the band going to think about having a human walking around with their alpha?" he asked, following Josiah to the door.

Josiah shrugged. "Do you really care?"

"I don't want you to be in trouble."

"I can't be in trouble. I'm the alpha, remember? And maybe it's time to stop hiding in this house and show the band what it means. If they have something to say, they can come to me, and we'll talk about it. They can't continue treating me both as a pariah and like I'm doing everything wrong when it comes to being their alpha. If they truly don't want me to be in charge, they're going to have to come up with someone else."

"That doesn't sound like a good idea, considering what I know about the band."

"It probably wouldn't be. I want to believe that not all band members are evil like my father and brother were and that some of them would be good alphas. Maybe that's the best solution. I was never meant to be an alpha. I became one because the council asked me to, but if the band wants something different, it might be best to try to accommodate them instead of pushing an alpha they never wanted on them."

Josiah hadn't wanted to think about that solution, but he should have a while ago. He'd never wanted to be the alpha, so why did he feel so bad at the thought of stepping down?

As long as the band was under control, it didn't matter who was the alpha. The only reason the council had asked him to do it was that it had been natural. He was his father's son, and after his brother had been killed, he was the only one left in the family. The council had hoped that the fact that Josiah's father had been the alpha before him meant that the band would accept him more easily, but Josiah had known that wouldn't be the case.

The thought that he could go back to his life before agreeing to this was overwhelming, yet it also made him feel guilty. The time he'd spent with the badgers, living in the Bishop house, had been the happiest of his life. He hadn't wanted to give it up, but he had because Thomas had asked.

Now that he was the alpha, though, stepping down from the role felt like he was giving up. He'd thought it was what he wanted, but he wasn't so sure anymore.

The problem was that he still couldn't think of another solution. This might be the easiest for everyone. If he couldn't find a beta, eventually, he wouldn't be able to keep the band under control any longer.

He wasn't stupid. He realized that the only reason he had managed was that the band had allowed him to. It wouldn't take much for them to get rid of him. They knew where he slept, and he didn't have guards. No one wanted to be his guard. If any band member wished to hurt or kill him, they would have an easy time of it. Josiah might want to do this, but not if it meant giving up his life for it.

Thinking about giving up the alpha position created complicated feelings in Josiah. It wasn't easy to deal with his feelings and thoughts about his past, so instead, he focused on Luther.

They walked around the forest, and Josiah pointed out houses and explained who lived where. He didn't know much about his people, but he shouldn't be afraid of the band. An alpha should never be afraid of the people he was supposed to guide.

Josiah had never been an alpha. He'd never been taught by his father how to behave. He was doing this entirely in the dark, and he didn't know if anything he could do would help light his way.

"And you've talked to everyone?" Luther asked.

"I think so. I'm still going over to the list I found, and I hope I manage to find someone who knows what they're doing when it comes to this and who'll agree to help me, but I'm not holding my breath."

Luther nodded. He was looking around, and Josiah wished he knew what the man was thinking.

"Everything seems to be under control," Luther said eventually.

"For now. I think the band is still regrouping after losing my father. It's not going to last forever, but I guess we'll see what the future holds."

Josiah was tired. For just one moment, he wanted to stop thinking about the band and what they were planning. He wanted to stop trying to find a way to make this work. He'd never asked to be the alpha, and after seeing his father do it for so many years, he'd never wanted to be. He'd accepted the role only because Thomas had asked him, and he owed Thomas his life. It would feel like giving up if he stopped now, but maybe it was the best choice for him. Maybe it was the best choice for everyone.

"I should go," Luther said once they reached Josiah's house again.

They'd spent a couple hours together, and Josiah had felt more at peace during those hours than he had in a long time.

He didn't want to let Luther go, and he didn't want to be alone. "Do you want to stay for dinner?" he asked.

Luther looked surprised. "You want me to stay?"

"I wouldn't have asked if I didn't."

"I thought you didn't like me much, considering who I am and what I'm doing here. I realize I've been pushing you to spend time with me when you probably don't want to."

"That's not true. I appreciate the thought you're putting into your job and how worried you are about me. I never thought about it, but now that we've talked, I realize you don't want to be here, or at the very least, that you don't want to be here to do what you're doing. I think it's a pity that you have to follow orders, but it doesn't mean your time here has to be bad. I'm not going to force you to stay for dinner, though."

Luther smiled. "You wouldn't be forcing me. I accept your offer for dinner as long as you allow me to help you cook."

"I won't say no to that." After his father found out that he was a carrier, Josiah had been relegated to doing housework, including cooking. He'd become quite good at it, but it had never been fun for him. He'd come to hate cooking, and now that he was on his own, he often didn't and limited himself to eating what was in the fridge. Nico had noticed, and he often brought leftovers, but it would be good for Josiah to cook for once, especially when he wasn't doing it on his own.

He and Luther couldn't be together. There was no future for them, not with everything that was going on. He didn't even know if Luther liked him that way. He had a crush on the man, but it didn't have to become more. It *couldn't* become more.

Josiah couldn't afford to be distracted. Luther had to focus on his job. Josiah could imagine what would happen if Luther's superiors found out he was friends with shifters, let alone having a relationship with one.

So no, they couldn't be together, no matter how much Josiah wished they could. That didn't mean they couldn't be friends. Josiah had several friends now, and he didn't need Luther, but he wanted the man in his life.

It would probably be a disaster. Josiah could see himself falling in love with Luther easily, especially after the conversations they'd shared. As long as he hid his feelings, everything would be okay, or at least, that was what he was trying to convince himself of. Spending more time with Luther might become torture, but Josiah would deal with it if things got bad. In the meantime, he would enjoy his time with his friend.

Luther brought a particular point of view in Josiah's life, something no one else could. Everyone Josiah knew was a shifter, but Luther wasn't. He could tell Josiah about the world outside the forest, and he could try to help him solve his problem with the band. Maybe not being a shifter would help him see something Josiah and the others couldn't.

And even if it didn't and the only thing Luther brought to Josiah's life was a friendly chat over dinner, that was okay. Josiah had a lot of time to make up for when it came to relationships, including friendly ones. He'd started with Nico and Chris and other carriers, and having a human friend was fascinating.

If only Josiah didn't want to climb Luther like a tree.

Luther hadn't expected the dinner invitation, but he wasn't about to say no. He wanted to spend more time with Josiah, and this was a perfect way to do it. Maybe they would finally be able to talk about something that wasn't the band or what Luther was doing in the forest.

Luther wasn't holding his breath. He understood that this didn't mean anything. Josiah was lonely, and Luther was convenient. They could keep each other company for a bit, and hopefully, once dinner was over, Josiah would feel better.

"What did you have in mind?" he asked once they were in the kitchen. He looked around, smiling at the neatness of it.

"I'm not sure what's in the fridge, so we'll have to see. Nico often brings me leftovers from his mom, and they're good. I haven't cooked for myself in a while." He opened the fridge and stuck his head in it.

"Don't you like to cook?" Luther asked.

"I have contrasting feelings about cooking. When my brother and my father were still alive, my mother and I were forced to cook for them. Once I didn't have to, I stopped because I could. I haven't started again."

Luther nodded. "I see. Well, you don't have to cook if you don't want to."

"I don't mind. I'm just not sure what I'll be able to put on your plate."

"Leftovers are fine with me."

Josiah leaned back and smiled. "Good, because there's not much here. Or I could make eggs? Maybe a frittata. I have peppers and tomatoes. I could pair that with some bread."

"It sounds perfect." It truly did. Luther was only interested in spending time with Josiah, and he didn't care what they did. If there wasn't enough food, he could eat once he was back with his team.

Josiah took out the vegetables from the fridge and put them onto the counter. "You want to start chopping? I'll take care of the eggs."

"Just hand me a knife, and I'll be your man."

Josiah's cheeks flushed, which pleased Luther. He had no idea what he and Josiah were doing, but it felt like they were dancing around each other and ignoring the elephant in the room. He was pretty sure by now that Josiah wanted him as much as he wanted Josiah, but since Josiah hadn't brought it

44

up, he wasn't going to, either. If anything happened between them, it would be Josiah's choice, and it would be at his pace.

They worked in silence for a while, but it didn't last long. Luther was surprised when Josiah started talking.

"My mother used to cook this a lot," he murmured.

Luther hadn't yet heard anything about Josiah's mother. He didn't even know if she was alive or dead. "Do you want to talk about her?"

Josiah sighed. "Not really. I guess that since I brought her up, though, I should."

"You don't have to do anything you don't want to, and that includes talking about your mother." Considering what he knew of Josiah's past, Luther realized it couldn't be easy to talk about any part of it.

"She still lives with the band. She moved out of the house I grew up in, though. She refuses to have anything to do with it."

That wasn't what Luther had expected. He wasn't sure why, but knowing about Josiah's father, he'd imagined his mother would be much of the same. "I imagine that very few people would want to live in that house."

Josiah nodded. "I certainly didn't want to, which is why I moved here. This house belonged to my grandparents, my mother's parents."

"Yet you're the one living here?"

"It's complicated, and I'm not kidding when I say that. I know my mother was abused as much as I was. She never wanted to marry my father, but it just wasn't done to go against an alpha's orders back then. I guess it wasn't done in recent times, either, at least until I became alpha. When my father decided he wanted her, her parents couldn't say anything, and neither could she. She was forced to marry him and to give him two sons."

Luther wanted to find Josiah's father and tear him apart, so it was a good thing the man was dead. It would have gotten Luther in trouble, but he doubted he would have cared.

"My father blamed her for what I was," Josiah continued. "For as long as I can remember, he told her it was her fault if I was weak and a carrier. He said that she wanted a girl, and she made me like this because of that. I understand why she didn't stand up to the abuse my father put me through. I don't know if I would have in her place. It's hard to spend time with her because of that, though. Every time I see her, I think about my father."

"I can only imagine what you're going through." Luther wanted to do so much to help Josiah, but he didn't know where to start. He'd never been abused. For all that he and his parents were distant now, they'd been a decent family when Luther had been a child. They'd never hit him or insulted him and his sister, and even now, when they talked, they always told Luther they loved him.

How would his life have been if he'd been in Josiah's place? It was impossible to think of, so Luther didn't even try.

"I hope that eventually we'll be able to talk to each other again," Josiah said. "I know why she never tried to stop my father, but part of me is angry."

"I doubt she would blame you for that."

"Probably not." Josiah shook himself. "But I don't want to talk about her tonight. I invited you over for dinner, yet here I am, talking about my parents and how fucked up my life was. That's not why you're here."

Luther put the knife down and caught one of Josiah's wrists. He waited until Josiah looked at him, and when he did, he smiled. "I'm here to spend time with you. If that means talking about your parents, I'm more than happy to listen to you."

"You shouldn't have to. No one wants to listen to what my father did to me."

"I do, if it makes you feel better or if that's what you need. I can't say it's a pleasant topic of conversation, but it doesn't mean we should avoid it."

Josiah nodded, but when he opened his mouth again, he didn't talk about his parents. Instead, he talked about the friends he'd made when he'd been with the badgers, and Luther let go of him and focused on his vegetables.

Listening to Josiah talk about his friends made Luther wonder. He enjoyed living in the forest, and he could see himself doing it easily. He was human, though. He had no idea what these people had gone through and were still going through. No matter how many times they told him about it, no matter what Josiah said, he would never understand.

That didn't mean he didn't have a place here.

But life in the forest was so different from life outside of it. He wished he could take Josiah out, allow him to see the world. No one should be locked up anywhere, not even in a vast national forest. It wasn't right, especially when shifters hadn't had a say. But Luther was only one man. What could he do against the government and the hatred against shifters?

But not everyone hated shifters. A lot of people fought for them, and he wasn't sure the shifters realized that. They had access to cell phones and the Internet, so probably. They might not understand what it meant, though.

In the past few years, people had started pushing for the forests to be open. Some of them had family there, and they wanted to be able to see them. Luther suspected that eventually, something would break, but he didn't know what or when. That was kind of terrifying, especially now.

Before, he hadn't had a stake in what was going on. He hadn't known shifters, and he hadn't thought he ever would. Now, though, he had Josiah and a lot of other people. He liked Chris and Jacob, as well as Thomas. He wanted to do right by them, but it didn't fit in with his job. Eventually, he would have to make a choice, and he wasn't sure which way he would go—the right one or the one that would keep his life the way it was.

CHAPTER FOUR

Luther's phone vibrated on his nightstand. He finished rubbing his damp hair and stared at it, knowing he had to answer and not wanting to. The name that had appeared on the screen made him groan, and he reached for the phone. Delaying it wasn't going to help. If anything, it would make things worse, which was the last thing he wanted.

"Sir?" he said as he answered.

"I want an update," Hawley snapped.

Luther swallowed. He should have called a few days ago, but he hadn't. He'd hoped things wouldn't come to this. He'd been wrong. "I don't have anything new, sir."

"How is that possible? I sent you to that forest to take care of the shifters. What are you doing in there?"

"You sent me here to make sure a war wouldn't start between the shifters. I'm still visiting territories, but I can tell you that I don't think it will. The forest is as peaceful as possible considering the circumstances."

There was a pause. "What circumstances?"

Luther almost groaned. Did the man even read his reports? "The coyotes attacked the badgers before we got here. It's why my team was sent. The coyotes are under control now. They have a new alpha, and while things are complicated, he's working hard to make sure that won't happen again. The coyotes — or any of the shifters — aren't a danger for humans." That was one thing Luther was sure of. Shifters might be dangerous to each other, but as far as he could see, none of them was planning on invading the human world. He wasn't sure if that was what his boss was afraid of, and he suspected it was an excuse. For what, he didn't know, but he was going to find out eventually.

He had to.

"How can you say they're not a danger to humans? We should be creating new laws and rules for them, not allowing them to do what they want."

That was new. "You can't create new laws, sir."

"I know that. I *can* create rules, though, and make sure they follow them." He paused again. "And if they don't, well, I can make sure they're punished."

This was the first time Hawley talked so plainly about what he wanted. Luther didn't like being manipulated, and he liked that he'd been sent here for that reason even less. In theory, he had to obey orders. In practice, though, he'd already decided he wouldn't do anything that went against what he thought was right. He might lose his job, but at least he wouldn't lose his soul.

"I want you to find a reason for me to create those rules," Hawley continued.

"I'm not sure what you're asking. You already have my reports. You know everything there is to know about this place."

"Dig deeper. I'm sure some of the shifters want humans to die."

Luther suspected he was right, but that didn't mean those shifters should be punished for what they thought. If they were humans, there would be an uproar about something like that.

The problem was that they *weren't* humans and that Luther's boss was an asshole. He had to be careful about what he said and how he said it. He didn't want his team to be called back, not when he felt he had to stick around to make sure the shifters and Josiah were safe. "I can continue digging if you want me to, but I can't promise I'll find anything. Like I said, while not every alpha gets along with each other, they're pretty good at working together to make sure we leave them alone."

"Even that new one? The coyote?"

Luther's chest squeezed. "He's young, but he's managing."

"Look deeper there. Talk to some of those coyotes and find out everything about their alpha. Maybe you can find something that'll help me."

"Sir. I'm not sure you should be doing this on your own." It was probably a mistake to bring it up, but anyone would have, and Luther didn't want his boss to find out that he knew what was going on, or at the very least, that he suspected. "When the shifters were put in the forests, a panel decided what rules they would be following. Shouldn't the same happen here?"

"That was decades ago. There's no need for a panel anymore. What are you insinuating?"

"Nothing, sir. I was just wondering if it's the right thing to do."

"It is. They're animals. They're a danger to humanity, and we have to make sure nothing happens. Find out what's going on. I'll expect a phone call soon."

He hung up without adding anything, and Luther threw his phone on the bed, disgusted.

Hawley wouldn't allow anything to get in his way to permanently remove shifters or, at the very least, to make their lives miserable. Luther wanted to avoid that, but could he? The only way to make it happen would be to show his boss and the people above him that everything in the forest was fine.

The problem was that it wasn't the case.

Josiah still didn't have a beta, and his people didn't respect him. Luther felt that this was the next step to make sure the government stayed away from shifters. He couldn't help with that, though. No matter how hard he tried, there was nothing he could do to help Josiah.

But he could talk to the council again. They might not have anything for him, so he didn't want to make it official. Maybe it would be better to talk to Thomas, then.

The badger alpha had always been honest with Luther as far as Luther knew. He was the main reason Josiah had agreed to become alpha to the coyotes, and Luther disliked him for that, but at the same time, he liked him. Thomas was doing what he could to keep the forest and his people safe. Unlike Josiah's father, he loved his sons and his family. He would do anything to keep them safe, and so would Luther.

Luther got to his feet. What he was doing, or rather, what he was planning on doing, could mean he would lose his job. A few months ago, that would have been unthinkable. Now, he would eagerly sacrifice his job if it meant saving Josiah and the people who lived in the forest.

He didn't know if there was anything he could do, but he was going to try. If it meant losing his job, then he would deal with the consequences when they happened. In the meantime, he was in charge of his team. He couldn't go against direct orders, but he could take his time obeying them. He hoped to find a way around what his boss wanted eventually, but he couldn't count on it.

That didn't mean he was going to sit on his ass and do nothing.

Josiah stared at the man in front of him. "What did you just say?" he asked. He was forcing himself to stay calm, but it was hard.

The man stood up straighter. He was taller than Josiah, and Josiah was kind of terrified, but he stood his ground. He was the alpha, dammit, and he wanted people to treat him like one.

"You heard me. Your father and your brother wouldn't be dead if it weren't for you. You don't deserve to be our alpha or to live with us."

Josiah breathed through his nose. He tried to remember the man's name, but he couldn't. It wasn't like he'd introduced himself when he'd walked up to him as Josiah stood on his porch. He'd gone straight to the point, and he'd told Josiah the words he'd just repeated.

"I had nothing to do with their deaths," Josiah said through gritted teeth.

"The badgers killed your father for you. You allowed them to invade our territory."

"You should remember that I wasn't the alpha back then."

The man spat on the ground in front of Josiah. "And you still aren't. No one wants you here."

Josiah was angry, but he knew better than to show how displeased he was. Instead, he squeezed his hands into fists, welcoming the pain of his nails digging into his palms. "Do you have a better idea? Do *you* want to be the alpha?" he asked.

That seemed to startle the man, and he took a step back. "I never said that."

"All right. Do you know anyone who would want to take my place, then?"

"Anyone would be better than you."

He probably was right. "Then give me a name. I would be more than happy to step down from the role. Do you think I *wanted* to become your alpha? You're a bunch of abusive assholes, and if I could never come back here, I would." Josiah snapped his mouth shut and took a deep breath.

He couldn't do this. No matter what he wanted to say, he'd agreed to be the alpha, and he had to act like one.

"This isn't right," the man said, but he didn't sound as convinced as he had before. "You never should have been the alpha. Your father wouldn't have allowed you to."

"Yes, well, my father is dead, so there's nothing he can say about it. We wouldn't be in this situation if it weren't for him and my brother, so maybe you should start thinking about that instead of berating me for trying to do the right thing."

Josiah turned around and headed for his house. He was going to do something he would regret if he didn't, and it was better for him to step away while he could.

He slammed the door behind himself and leaned against it, closing his eyes. He tried to breathe through the anger and pain, but it was hard.

He'd reached the end of his patience. He wanted to scream and say fuck it, to leave and never come back, but he would lose the little respect he had with the band. Like he'd told that guy, there was no one else who could do this apart from him. He was the alpha, willing or not, and no one could change that.

He groaned and slid onto the floor, covering his face with both his hands. He needed a beta, dammit. He had to find someone before he exploded and made a mess out of things.

Even though he wanted to stay on the floor and never get back to his feet, he did it. He headed to his office, grateful he didn't have to work where his father had. He'd had to move a few things from his father's house to this one, so unfortunately, he had bad memories from some of the furniture, but it was fairly easy to ignore them.

He sat behind the desk and grabbed the list he had of the band members. He'd found nothing the first two times he'd gone over it, but maybe the third time would be a charm. He wasn't even sure that list was complete. He couldn't remember his father working on them, and his brother certainly hadn't. A lot of coyotes had died when his brother had led them to attack the badgers, and Josiah was pretty sure he needed to strike some names from the list. He wasn't about to go around knocking on doors asking people if their fathers and brothers had died in the attack, though.

No. He needed a beta who knew the band, someone the coyotes would agree to talk to without making too much of a fuss. At this point, Josiah wasn't sure he would ever find one. It felt impossible, and as time passed, it became worse. It made Josiah wonder why he'd agreed to this. He knew the answer, but that didn't mean he didn't regret it.

His gaze caught on a name. He tried to remember who Stephen Wright was, but nothing came to mind. Next to the man's name, there was a note that told Josiah he lived in the forest, but it wasn't enough. Where did Stephen live? Who was he?

Josiah leaned back and closed his eyes, hoping it would jog his memories. It took him a moment, but he remembered his mother talking to someone, calling them Stephen. Josiah had been young back then, maybe twelve or thirteen. He'd been sneaking around the house trying to reach the kitchen to get something to eat after his father had told him to go to bed without dinner. When Josiah and his mother had tried protesting, he'd turned violent.

Josiah had frozen when he'd gotten outside the kitchen and heard two people talking. One was his mother, and the other was a man. For a moment, he thought it was his father, but his father never spoke in such a calm voice. The man had told Josiah's mother that she couldn't continue like this and allow her husband to hurt her child. He'd offered to take them away, but Josiah's mother had said no.

Josiah swallowed. He understood why she had. She'd been terrified, and so had he. But he could too easily imagine what his life would have been like if he'd been away from his father. His father had already been abusing him back then, and so had his brother, but Josiah would have been free ten years before the badgers came to him.

Or maybe he wouldn't have been. Maybe his father would have caught him and his mother, and he would have made them pay. Maybe Josiah's life would have been even worse.

He opened his eyes and straightened, his gaze going to the list. How did he know this guy was Stephen Wright? His mother had called him Stephen, but Josiah had nothing else. It didn't mean it was the same person, but what were the chances?

Whoever Stephen was, he'd been worried for Josiah and his mother. He'd been angry at Josiah's father for what he was doing. If he was still alive and lived with the band, maybe there was a chance he could help Josiah.

How was Josiah going to find him?

His stomach churned as he realized he would have to talk to his mother. She might be the only one who would be able to tell him where Stephen was. Josiah didn't know if they'd been friends, but even if they hadn't, Stephen had cared. As far as Josiah knew, he'd been the only one after his grandparents had died. It had to mean something.

Josiah hoped so. For the first time, he thought maybe he could really do this. He needed to talk to someone about all of it, so he got to his feet and strode toward the door. There was one person he went to when he needed help when it came to the band and its future. Hopefully, Thomas wouldn't be busy.

Luther was leaving Thomas's house when Josiah arrived. It was the first time he'd seen Josiah drive a car. The way Josiah seemed to be extremely careful as he parked made Luther smile, and he paused in front of his truck as he waited for his friend to join him.

"I wish I didn't have to do that," Josiah grumbled once he did.

"Do what? Park?"

"Drive. I don't like it. I feel like I'll hurt someone if I make even the smallest mistake." Josiah sighed and pushed his hair out of his eyes. "But I can't avoid it if I want to be able to get around the forest on my own." He looked at Luther. "What are you doing here?"

"I wanted to talk to Thomas."

"Yeah? So do I. He's in?"

"He is, although he was making a phone call when I left. What did you need to talk to him about?" It wasn't Luther's business, but it didn't hurt to ask. If Josiah didn't want to tell him, he wouldn't.

Josiah hesitated. "I found something. Well, it's only a name, really, but it triggered some memories."

"Is there anything I can do?" Josiah had few good memories, so whatever had happened probably hadn't been good.

Josiah shook his head, then nodded. "Maybe? Would you come in with me while I talk to Thomas? It's not that I need the support, but I'd feel better if you were there."

"Of course." Luther would do pretty much anything Josiah asked, and this was minor. If Josiah wanted his support, he had it.

Josiah's smile was sweet. "What about your team? Don't you need to get back to them?"

"Eventually, but they're busy even without me. They're patrolling Northwood and sticking their noses around. I hope they stay out of trouble."

"No one will attack them, if that's what you're afraid of. Even if some shifters wish they could, they know better. Your people would rain hell on the forest if something happened to you."

Luther was pretty sure his boss would celebrate his death

before he did that, but Josiah was right. The man would use it as an excuse to give a harsh response and force the shifters to kneel before him.

Because that was what he wanted. He'd compared shifters to animals, and Luther suspected that was how he saw them. They weren't human, so they shouldn't be treated as such. It was a fucked-up way to think, but unfortunately, it wasn't a new one.

They headed inside, and Luther took a risk and put a hand on the small of Josiah's back. Josiah was startled but didn't pull away, which Luther took as a win. He had to take them where he could, especially when it came to Josiah. He didn't know how long he still had in the forest, but he wanted to get everything he could before he left.

Josiah quickly knocked, then opened the door without waiting for an answer. Luther hadn't done the same, but then, he wasn't at home the way Josiah was. He knew how much Thomas and his people had helped Josiah, so it made sense for him to feel like he belonged.

"Thomas?" Josiah called out as they moved toward the office.

The door was open like Luther had left it, because Thomas asked him to. He could see Thomas behind his desk. The alpha was still on the phone, but he smiled when he saw Josiah and waved them in. They obeyed. Josiah sat on the chair closest to the desk while Luther stood behind him. He could sit, too, but he was too nervous.

He didn't know what was going on, but it made him unsettled.

It only took a few moments for Thomas to be done with the call, and when he hung up, his smile widened. "I'm happy to see you," he told Josiah.

Josiah relaxed in a way Luther hadn't seen him do while they were with the band. That made sense, too, but it shouldn't be that way. Josiah was the alpha, and the band should be his safe place. Instead, the cete was.

"And I'm always happy to come around. I miss this place."

Thomas pressed a hand to his chest. "And here I thought you missed *me*."

Josiah laughed. It was a carefree sound that Luther wanted to hear more often.

"I do miss you, too. I wish I could come back, but . . ."

"But we both know that's impossible." Thomas's expression shifted and became more serious. "What's going on?"

"I had a fight with one of the coyotes this morning. He didn't touch me," Josiah rushed to add when both Thomas and Luther started to move. "But he told me that no one wanted me there as the alpha and that I caused my brother and my father's deaths."

Thomas snorted. "We both know that's not the truth. Your brother caused his own death by attacking my cete, and as for your father, well, we had to kill him to save you. He would have hurt you. He *did* hurt you, much more than anyone should have allowed."

Josiah raised his hands. "I know that. I don't blame you for what you did."

"But you blame yourself."

Thomas had a keen eye. He also knew Josiah better than Luther did, so it wasn't surprising that he could see things Luther couldn't.

Josiah shrugged. "Only in part. I blame myself more because I don't feel sorry that they're dead."

"Nor should you. What they did to you was awful. They should have been punished long before they were. So you had a fight with a coyote. How did you deal with it?"

"I'm not proud to say that I yelled at him. I was angry, and I told him that I never wanted to be the alpha and that as far as I was concerned, he could take my place if he wanted to.

That was enough to shut him up. They all have a lot to say about how I deal with the band, but when it comes to doing something about it, no one wants to step up."

"Being an alpha is harder than a lot of people realize."

"It is. And when I went back inside, I grabbed that list again. I need a beta, and I need one now." Josiah hesitated.

Luther held his breath.

"One of the names reminded me of something. I think this guy was worried about my mother and me. I remember one conversation between them, although I can't be sure it was the same guy. Stephen is a common name, so it could be someone else."

"Why don't you tell us what you remembered." Thomas looked at Luther. "Unless you want to wait until we're alone?"

Luther was glad Thomas wasn't assuming, but he couldn't help but feel a bit offended. He had to remember that only a few people knew that he and Josiah were friends, though, and that Thomas hadn't said anything about his presence until now.

To Luther's surprise, Josiah twisted around to look at him. "I trust Luther. He can stay. He's been trying to help me, so he should probably hear this anyway."

Thomas's eyebrows rose high on his forehead, but he didn't say anything. Instead, he nodded at Josiah to continue.

Josiah cleared his throat. "So I recognized a name, and I think this guy could be a good beta, if only because he tried to help. I don't know where to find him, though, or even if he's still alive. The list doesn't say anything about him dying, but I don't trust my father has been keeping up with it."

"So you need to find this Stephen," Thomas said.

"And the sooner I do it, the better it will be. I might not be able to convince him to be my beta, but at least I'll know."

"You said he was worried about you and your mother,"

Luther said.

Josiah grimaced. "Which means I'm going to have to talk to her. I'm not looking forward to it, but I suppose it's time."

"You don't have to do anything you don't want to," Thomas said.

Josiah's back straightened. "But that's what being an alpha is about, isn't it? You do things because you have to do them, not because you want to."

Thomas stared at Josiah for a moment before nodding. "You're not wrong. I'm proud of you and the man you've become."

Luther was, too, but he didn't say it. It wasn't his place, even though he wished it were.

He wished a lot of things, and all of them were out of his reach.

CHAPTER FIVE

Josiah couldn't stop thinking about Luther. He had so many other things to focus on, yet here he was, daydreaming about the human. What was wrong with him?

He knew what was wrong with him, and he was sure that if he talked to Nico, his best friend would confirm.

Josiah had a crush.

He didn't know what to do with it. It was the first time he'd ever felt this way and the first time he was allowed to. When his father had still been alive, Josiah had been stuck in the house, forbidden to leave and to meet other people. He suspected that even if he had, no coyote would have wanted anything to do with him. They'd been too afraid of his father and maybe disgusted by what he was.

All of that was behind Josiah, though, which meant he had to deal with this. It would become a problem if he didn't, and he couldn't afford for that to happen. He couldn't afford to have feelings for Luther, but it was happening.

Josiah groaned and rubbed his eyes with both his hands. What was he supposed to do? When he was alone in his office like now, everything seemed in reach. He knew he could find a way for him and Luther to be together, and he wanted to do exactly that.

Then reality set back in, and he knew he couldn't. He was an alpha carrier. He couldn't have a boyfriend. Luther, on the other hand, was human and would go back home soon. He would take Josiah's heart with him, something Josiah had started to wrap his mind around. Would it be so bad to be together before he did? Josiah was already in too deep. Being with Luther wouldn't change much.

"Okay, I've had enough. What's going on?" Nico asked. He'd been reading a pack of notes his father had given him. It was part of his studies to take his father's place one day, and he'd been grumpy about it, but at least he didn't have to stay home to read. He'd appeared on Josiah's porch about an hour earlier, pushing past him and telling him that if he had to do this, he was going to do it in a place he actually liked.

Josiah didn't know if it meant he'd fought with his father, but he wouldn't be surprised if that was the case. Nico had always been more assertive than Chris, which was why he would make a better alpha.

"Nothing is going on," he tried.

Nico arched a brow. "Really? Because it doesn't look like it to me." He frowned. "Is it still the beta thing?"

It would be easy to lie to Nico, but Josiah wanted a second opinion. "It's Luther."

Nico grinned. "Finally. I was starting to wonder if I'd seen things wrong."

"It depends. What did you see?"

"That you like him and that he likes you. Why do you think I left the two of you alone that time he came around? I wanted to give you a chance to spend time together."

Josiah resisted the urge to bang his head on his desk. "We shouldn't be spending time together."

"Why not?"

"Because it's going to make everything so much harder. I need to stay away from him."

"Why? Has he said anything? If he hurt you, I'm going to kick his ass."

"He didn't hurt me." Josiah reclined in his chair and tilted his face up to look at the ceiling. "I like him too much. What's going to happen when he goes home?"

"Do you really have to think about that now? There's time."

Josiah looked at his best friend. "Not very much of it. Besides, he's human. Even if he decided he wanted to stay, it couldn't work. I need to focus on the band and being an alpha, not on having a boyfriend."

Nico frowned again. "I don't like that. You didn't have a choice in becoming the alpha, and it's not right. You should be able to live your life, and that includes having a human boyfriend."

Josiah wished he could do that, but they both knew better. "Even if I weren't the alpha, I couldn't be with him. He's part of the government. That's who he works for — the people who keep us in the forest." Even though Luther didn't want that. He'd told Josiah he wished things were different, and so did Josiah.

But they weren't. They had to deal with their lives the way they were and to be realistic about what they could do. Josiah wasn't angry at Luther. There wasn't much he could do to help the shifters in the forest, no matter how much he wished he could.

"But he's not a bad person. I like him, and you do, too," Nico pointed out.

"Even if he wasn't part of the military, he's human. There can be nothing between us."

Nico slammed a hand on top of the desk. "Why not?" he asked, sounding angry. "Humans are not that different from shifters."

"Because shifters aren't with humans. It's just not done."

"Like carriers can't become alphas? Like they have to get married before they reach twenty-six years old because otherwise, the council will choose for them? That's all in the past, Josiah. I realize it's hard to wrap your mind around that, but you have to remember. What happened to us, including the fight between your brother and Thomas, gave us a chance. It's a fresh start for us, but nothing will change if *we* don't. If you want to be with a human, then be with him. People will talk, but then, they're already talking. How different can it be?"

A spark of hope had lit up in Josiah's chest, but he was afraid to give in. "The fact that I like Luther doesn't mean he likes me or that he wants anything with me."

"You won't find out if you don't talk to him. Don't you want to at least try?"

"It's scary." What if Luther didn't want Josiah that way? What if he pushed him away and Josiah lost their friendship?

Nico reached over the desk and took one of Josiah's hands. "I know. But if I learned anything watching my brother being an idiot with Jacob, it's that you'll regret it if you don't talk to him. Give both of you a chance. Tell him how you feel, or try to kiss him, or something like that. Whatever will be good at this point. I'm not saying things will be easy, but the fact that he's human or even that he lives outside the forest doesn't mean the relationship between the two of you is doomed. If you want to be together, you'll find a way. You're not alone anymore. You have many people who are ready to do anything they can to make you happy. I think that includes Luther."

Josiah's heart raced. He could imagine himself with Luther, and it was hard to resist the urge to run out of the office and go find him.

But no matter what happened between them, Josiah had a job, and so did Luther. If they wanted to have a chance to be together, everything around them needed to be as perfect as possible.

That meant Luther had to continue working and that Josiah had to find a beta. Maybe once he had, they could find a way to be with each other.

And if it never happened, well, Josiah couldn't say he

would regret his feelings for Luther. He was the first man Josiah felt free to love, and he didn't want to give that up, no matter the difficulties. Like Nico had said, Josiah wasn't alone anymore, and he knew that if he went to Thomas and asked him for help to find a way for Luther to stay, Thomas would do everything he could to make it happen.

It might not, but could Josiah give up hope when there was a chance it might?

"You've been distracted lately. Bad news from home?" Suzanne asked.

Luther blinked. He *had* been distracted, which was why he wasn't sure what they were talking about right now. "The usual."

Suzanne didn't look convinced. "Yeah?"

"You know you can talk to us if something is wrong, right?" Dean asked. He hesitated, then continued. "I realize you're our team leader and that we have to follow your orders, but it doesn't mean we're not friends. You're the best team leader I've had in a long time, and I don't want that to change."

Luther needed to get his head out of his ass and stop thinking about Josiah every single moment of his day. "It's not going to." Unless he decided he wanted to stick around the forest, but no matter how many times he thought about it, he couldn't find a way to make it work.

He was supposed to leave once he was done with this. No human was allowed to live with shifters, and Luther wasn't sure there was a place for him here. He also wasn't sure there wasn't, though, which was why he was still thinking about it. His boss would have his balls if Luther mentioned it, which was a problem. He wouldn't put it past the man to do something stupid to get revenge.

Luther's answer seemed to appease Suzanne, and she moved ahead to catch up to Miriam and Marlow. Dean stuck around, and Luther was pretty sure they weren't done talking.

Dean was Luther's unofficial second in command. He was always there when Luther needed to talk, be it about the job or something else. They were friends more than coworkers, but Luther hadn't yet confided in him. He didn't know if Josiah would want people to be aware of what was going on between them, or even if something *was* going on.

"I could share your burden," Dean murmured.

"I don't have a burden."

Dean arched a brow. Maybe he wasn't wrong. In the beginning, whatever was between Luther and Josiah had been nothing. Luther had been attracted to him, but that was it. But he was starting to think he could stay in the forest, which meant this was more serious than he'd ever expected it to be. Maybe it would help to talk to someone, and who better than Dean?

Dean was one of those people who had family in the forest. As far as Luther knew, it was distant family, and Dean had never contacted them. He wasn't a shifter, but he had shifter blood, so maybe he could understand better than anyone what Luther was going through.

"I've been spending time with Josiah," Luther started, unsure how to continue.

Dean nodded. He sidestepped someone coming toward them on the sidewalk, but he was back only moments later. "I've noticed that. Well, not that you've been spending time with Josiah, but rather, away from the team."

"That's where I was. With the coyotes."

"You're trying to find a solution about the band."

"That's why I went in the beginning. Now, it's more." Luther swallowed. He'd never been good about talking about his feelings, and it felt strange to put them out there, especially to someone he worked with. "I like Josiah. A lot. I realize I'm human and he's a shifter, but knowing that hasn't been enough to stop my feelings for him from growing."

Dean looked surprised. Luther waited for him to tell him either that he should continue doing what he was doing or that he was totally wrong and that he needed to stop.

"What does he think about that?" he asked instead.

Luther shook his head. "I'm not sure. We haven't talked about it. I don't know if I should even bring it up. I suspect he knows I feel something for him, but he probably doesn't have the time to worry about me. Besides, what good could come out of it? I'll go home soon, and he'll be left alone."

"That's true. It doesn't mean the two of you shouldn't be together while we're still here, though."

"I don't want to break his heart."

Dean snorted. "No offense, but you don't know that you would. Maybe he just likes the way you look. Since you haven't talked to him, you don't know if he wants something serious. It could be only sex."

It wasn't. That much, Luther was sure of, but he didn't say it out loud. "What are you saying?"

"That you might not have to find a way for the two of you to be together once we leave." Dean frowned. "But if you do, there could be a solution."

"What solution? You know that no human can live with shifters. It's just not done. Do you think the shifters here would agree? They tolerate us because they have to. If I decided to move here, they wouldn't anymore, and I don't think they would hesitate telling me. Even if we don't consider that, though, there's no way I'll be allowed to live here."

Dean sighed. "You're not wrong. I'm sorry if I gave you hope, but I can't think of anything."

"Me neither." And that was why Luther was hesitant about

talking to Josiah about his feelings. He wanted to, desperately, and he wanted to find out if Josiah felt the same, but what good would it do?

"You could talk to Hawley," Dean suggested.

Luther snorted. "You know what he would say. He called me the other day and asked me to find a way to punish the shifters. That's all he's in it for, and he can't wait to make me miserable just because he finds it fun. I can't go to him with this." Or to anyone.

Luther supposed he could go over his superior and talk to the man's boss, but Hawley would make sure he regretted it. There was nothing Luther could do, no matter how hard he thought about it or how much he wanted it.

He didn't want to give up. For now, he and Josiah were friends who spent time together. Luther didn't think he would be able to forget the other man when he left, but maybe Dean was right and there really was nothing much between them. Maybe they just were friendly and found each other attractive.

But if that wasn't the case, they would end up with two broken hearts, and Luther didn't want Josiah to be in pain ever again, not even for something like this. Maybe it was time for him to take a step back from Josiah and leave him to live his life without a human sticking his nose into it, but he wasn't sure he could do it. He wanted to be with Josiah, to spend time getting to know him, to make sure he was safe and happy. That didn't make him a bad person, although plenty of people would think it did.

Luther had to make a choice. He wasn't sure he was ready for it, but he didn't have much time left. He needed to think about this, think about how important his job and Josiah were to him. Think about which one he would choose if he had to.

Because soon, he *would* have to choose, and he had no idea which way he would go.

Josiah needed time away from the band. No matter how hard he tried to be a good alpha, nothing was ever good enough for them, and he'd had enough. They might feel like he was abandoning them, and maybe he was. At this point, he didn't care. It wasn't like he was leaving and never coming back. Eventually, he would come home, but for now, he needed to breathe.

He peeked at Nico, who was driving. They were headed toward the badgers, and Josiah could breathe easier now that he was away from the band. Nico hadn't even asked. He'd arrived, taken one look at Josiah's expression, and dragged him out. No one had tried to stop him, but then Josiah hadn't expected them to. The band was probably happier when he wasn't around to mess things up for them.

It also felt good to be able to leave band territory without anyone trying to stop him. Until the badgers had rescued him, Josiah had barely been allowed to leave the house he'd been born in. His father had wanted him in sight every moment of every day, just in case he did something stupid. That was what his father had said, but Josiah suspected the man just loved control. He wanted Josiah to know that he was the one who decided what Josiah could and couldn't do. He even decided if Josiah could continue living or if he should die. No one would have raised a finger to help him if his father had decided to kill him.

Things were different now. Josiah had to remember that, and it was easier when he found the time to leave the band. It wasn't like there was anything for him to do when he stayed anyway. No one wanted to talk to him, and while he'd been taking care of mundane details, with no help from the coyotes, it was getting harder to find work he could do on his own. Josiah was supposed to support and protect the coyotes, but so far, he felt like he was the one who needed that against them.

Thankfully, Nico stayed silent on their way to the cete. He knew better than to try to get Josiah to talk when he was feeling so down, and Josiah was glad to be able to just close his eyes and relax in his seat. Once they reached cete territory, though, Nico looked at him.

"We don't have to talk now, but eventually, we'll have to. I realize I'm not a coyote, but I'm working hard to be able to take my father's place when the time comes, and I feel that maybe I could help you. I realize that not having a coyote as your beta might be a problem and make things worse, but at this point, it's the only thing you haven't tried."

Josiah blinked. "Are you offering yourself to be my second in command?"

Nico shrugged. "You don't have to sound as surprised as you do. Like I said, I know what I'm doing, at least mostly."

"That's not why I was surprised. If I could have you as my beta, I would say yes in a heartbeat. But there's no way the coyotes will accept you. Don't think I didn't see that one guy snarling at you the last time you visited."

Nico's expression flattened. "I can beat his ass if I need to. His, and the ass of everyone who has something to say against you or me. Just say the word, and I'll help you get the band back into shape."

It was tempting to accept, if anything because, that way, Josiah could spend more time with his best friend. Instead, the only thing he could say was, "I'll think about it. Thank you, though."

"Don't worry about it. I wouldn't do it for anyone else, but you're my best friend."

It warmed Josiah's heart to hear that. He'd always been lonely. No coyote had wanted to even try to befriend him once it was obvious that his father hated him. They didn't want to risk it, and Josiah didn't blame them for it. His brother had been as much of an asshole as their father, and Josiah's mother, well, she had her own pain to deal with. She hadn't been able to be there for him, something for which he was still angry, but also something he could understand.

It had taken him a long time to accept that Nico was friends with him because he liked him. He didn't doubt it anymore, and he was glad he had Nico in his life. He would have broken down a long time ago if he didn't.

Nico parked in front of Thomas's house. They smiled at each other before climbing out, and Josiah's smile widened when he noticed a few carriers sitting on the porch, drinking iced tea and talking. Even though carriers weren't in danger anymore, one of Thomas's guards, Raven, was there, too. He was keeping an eye on the small group, although Josiah didn't miss the way he kept staring at Turner.

He grinned. "Did you notice?" he asked, keeping his voice soft.

"That Raven has a massive hard-on for Turner? I think everyone but Turner noticed," Nico answered.

Josiah laughed. This was why he'd wanted to spend time away from the band. There, he couldn't be himself. He couldn't laugh or smile, not without having people stare at him and judge him. Here, he was home, and no one would say anything about him laughing.

The front door banged open, and Thomas stepped out. He smiled when he saw Josiah and Nico, but his smile turned to a frown as they walked closer. "You look tired," he told Josiah when they reached him.

Josiah glared at him. "You've been married for years. Shouldn't you be better at this compliments thing?"

"I would never tell my wife she looks tired, but I'm not married to you." He sighed and looked at the small group.

Nico had joined them, and he was sitting next to Turner,

his arm around Turner's shoulders. He kept peeking at Raven, who looked like he wanted to kill him.

"I wish I'd never convinced you to become the alpha," Thomas murmured.

Josiah's heart lurched. "You didn't have a choice."

"There's always a choice, and I shouldn't have made this one. It was the easiest one considering the humans were coming, but it didn't need to be made."

"You couldn't know that before you met Luther and the others."

"Maybe not, but we could have found another solution. I don't like seeing how tired you are or that you're dealing with the coyotes insulting you and berating you for what you are. It's not right."

Josiah could only agree. "There's nothing we can do about it, though. I agreed to become the alpha, and I did. I'm doing the best with what I have, and I'm going to continue doing that."

"We could try to find a new alpha."

It was tempting to say yes. Josiah wanted to, desperately. He wanted to be able to forget all about the band and the coyotes, to focus on his own life.

He felt like he deserved it. His life before the badgers had freed him had been hell. He'd thought he would finally have a chance to choose the way he wanted to live once the new laws had been passed to protect the carriers in the forest, but instead, Thomas had asked him to do this. Josiah felt like his life had gone from being hell because his father abused him, to him being in limbo while he was at the Bishop house, to him becoming an alpha against his will. He'd never had time for himself, and he didn't think he would anytime soon.

But he wasn't giving up. He wanted to show everyone that a carrier could do this, and more importantly, that *he* could. His father and his brother might be dead, but he wanted to prove them wrong. They'd thought the only thing he was good for was having babies, but here he was, an alpha, while they were gone.

He shook his head. "Not for now. I'm fine."

Thomas didn't look convinced. "Well, come to me if you're not anymore. I'll do everything I can to help you. I hope you know that."

"I do." Josiah leaned back against the porch railing. "And I want to say yes. I can't yet, though. I agreed to do this, and until there's no way for me to do it anymore, I'm going to try. It doesn't matter that the coyotes hate me. They've always hated me. I need to do this for me. I need to show to myself that I'm more than what my father always said I would be."

"You don't need to be the alpha for that. Everyone knows you're more."

Everyone but Josiah. Sometimes, at night, he could still hear his father's voice in his mind. He didn't think it would fade until he took charge of his own destiny, which was what he was trying to do. Whether it would be enough, he didn't know, but he wasn't done trying yet.

Marlow parked the truck in front of the bat alpha's house. Luther looked around. Bat territory didn't look any different from the other territories they'd explored. The alpha's house stood in front of him, a wooden cabin that didn't look out of place in the forest. Luther could see other cabins deeper in the woods, close enough to quickly be reached if something happened, but far enough to give everyone privacy.

The forest was beautiful, just like everywhere else around here, and his heart ached at the thought that he would have to leave soon.

It wasn't only Josiah that made him want to stay. It was also the people he'd gotten to know, like Chris and Jacob. It was the cabins the shifters lived in. It was the way the forest smelled, how it made Luther feel more peaceful.

Another truck stopped next to theirs. Miriam waved from the driver seat, and they all climbed down, following Jacob and Chris's lead, who had arrived just ahead of them.

The cabin's door opened, and a tall, thin man came out. He was fidgeting, which suggested he was nervous. Luther understood that most shifters were nervous about his team's presence, since they'd been sent to the forest to judge whether or not shifters should be left alone, but usually, alphas were better at hiding it. It was refreshing to see that this one wasn't, until Luther realized the alpha wasn't nervous because of his presence.

Chris went to stand in front of him. He glared, and the alpha looked bashful.

"You're an asshole," Chris told him.

The alpha didn't try to protest. "I realize that. You know him, though. You know he's not easy to deal with."

"I don't care. He's a person, and you threw him away. Do you know how that made him feel?"

Luther had no idea what was going on. He moved closer to Jacob, ready to ask. He didn't have to, though, because once he reached Jacob, Jacob said, "That's Ralph Foley. You probably have a hard time believing it because of the way he's cowering, but he's the bat alpha."

"What did he do to Chris to get him to yell at him that way?"

Jacob sighed. "I don't know if you've met Callum. He's a bat shifter, and he's a carrier. I can't say if he was abused by the bats and Alpha Foley, but he wasn't happy when he was here. We had a lot of trouble with him in the beginning, when he first moved into the Bishop house, although things have been going better recently. He was surly and snappish, and everyone knew it was due to what had happened to him here."

"And what happened to him?"

"He never said, not to me anyway, and I doubt he told anyone. It might not have been physical abuse, but that doesn't mean he wasn't hurt." He sucked in a breath. "Well, I should go before Chris tears him a new asshole. It's not why we're here."

It wasn't, but Luther wouldn't be against helping Chris. He could hold down the alpha while Chris hurt him. Luther cared about the shifters much more than he'd expected, which might become a problem. If he became less objective, he wouldn't do a good job.

He wasn't sure he wanted to.

His job here was to find a way to make shifters pay just for living. He hadn't been able to say no when he'd been given his orders, and he hadn't known it would be this bad, but he'd known he needed to protect the shifters in any way he could. If he hadn't said yes, who knew who Hawley would have sent in his place? He might not be enough to protect the shifters, though, and the thought made him more anxious every day.

Luther moved closer to the alpha. The man turned to look at him and offered him his hand. Luther took it and squeezed a bit too hard. The alpha's eyes widened and he tried to take it back, but Luther didn't let go. Instead, he leaned closer. "What's that about you not treating a carrier right?" he murmured.

Alpha Foley dropped Luther's hand as if it were on fire. "What do you know about Callum?"

"Not much, but it's enough for me to be sure I don't like you."

Alpha Foley gaped. "How can you say that? You don't know me. You don't know Callum, because if you did, you'd know why we treated him the way we did."

Chris cleared his throat. He was glaring at Alpha Foley,

and he looked ready to jump the man and strangle him if he had to. Alpha Foley took a step back and gestured at the forest around them.

"You're here to explore. Why don't we do that?"

Luther nodded curtly, and when the alpha started moving, he followed him, along with his team and Chris and Jacob.

Chris fell in line next to him. "I'm impressed," he whispered.

"What about?"

"The fact that you're angry for what he did to Callum."

"I don't know what he did to Callum."

"Maybe not, but you trust me enough to be angry anyway. Not a lot of people care about carriers, and I didn't think you would, since you're human."

Luther shook his head. "Carriers are people. The fact that you can get pregnant doesn't change that, and it doesn't change you. You should have the same rights as everyone else, and you should be treated as any other shifter. Whoever doesn't do it deserves to be threatened at the very least."

It was too easy to imagine Josiah on his own once Luther left. Josiah didn't need Luther to protect him, but after Luther had seen how the coyotes behaved with him, he wanted to.

But he was leaving. He wouldn't be there for Josiah, no matter how much he wanted to. He didn't like that, but so far, he hadn't found a way around it. He wasn't sure he would, but it wouldn't stop him from trying.

"I like you," Chris said.

Luther arched a brow. "Thank you?"

Chris laughed. "You sound like you're not sure whether or not you should thank me."

"That's because I'm not."

"It's a good thing. I didn't think I would when I first met you. You were the enemy, as far as I was concerned, and I didn't want anything to do with you."

"And you didn't want to spend time with us because it meant spending time with Jacob."

When Luther and his team had arrived, Jacob and Chris had been broken up. Luther had heard the stories, though. He knew they'd been together when Chris had been hiding in the Bishop house, and he was glad they'd found their way back to each other. He was also glad that Chris didn't seem to mind his teasing.

"There was some of that, too. But I didn't know what to think of you, and now I'm glad to find out that you're a good person. It doesn't matter that you're human and that you were sent here to babysit us. You won't do anything to hurt us just because you can, which makes you a good person."

Luther wished that wasn't the case. Shifters deserved more than having humans not hurt them just because they could, but he didn't say it out loud. Chris probably thought the same, and neither of them could do anything to solve the problem.

"Yes, well, after I've seen the way some alphas treat their carriers and their people in general, I wish there was more I could do." But that was a problem shifters had to solve. It was why they had a council, and it was none of Luther's business.

Chris shrugged. "We're working on it. It's not going to be a quick solution, but then, this isn't a recent problem. We have to deal with decades of traditions and backward thinking. We'll manage eventually. A lot has already changed in the past few years, and we're not done yet. Carriers have rights now, and we're allowed to roam all over the forest without anyone trying to marry us. I see that as a win."

"You shouldn't have to."

Chris's smile was soft. "Trust me. This is a lot better than what I've had to live through for a long time. Nico and I were lucky not to be abused by our parents, but we still had to be careful. We weren't allowed to leave clowder territory in case someone found out we're carriers. And, of course, there had never been a carrier alpha in the forest before Josiah. Things are changing, even if it's slowly."

But Luther wouldn't be here to see those changes.

CHAPTER SIX

Josiah was struggling, and he had enough of feeling that way. He had enough of the band, of the ungrateful coyotes who were making his life hell, and of his own stubbornness. Why hadn't he accepted Thomas's offer to find someone else to deal with the band? He'd offered the last time Josiah had seen him, and Josiah knew he would do everything he could to make that happen if only Josiah told him it was what he wanted.

He stared at the documents in front of him. The band was broke, and there was no way around that. He should have realized that sooner, but neither his father nor his brother had been great at keeping records, and it had taken him a while to untangle them. Now that he had, he knew the truth.

There was no money set aside to fix the houses that needed fixing. There was no money to help the band members who needed it. There wasn't even money to bulldoze the house Josiah had grown up in.

He sighed and flopped back in his chair. There was no money for anything, and he'd be lucky if he managed to pay the electricity bill when it came. He was going to have to talk to Thomas and the council and find a way around it, but he didn't know if it was even possible.

The coyotes had apparently stopped paying their dues to the band's account when Josiah's brother had died. That was how things worked — the coyotes who worked had to pay a percentage of their wages to the band, which in turn took care of paying pack bills and making sure everything was in top shape. Josiah didn't know if this was how every shifter group worked, but it was how the band did — or had, once.

But his father had stopped caring, or maybe he never had. A lot of the communal buildings, like the kindergarten, had fallen into disrepair, and Josiah didn't know how to fix them. He didn't know how to fix anything.

It was a disaster.

He was sure that some of the coyotes wouldn't have a problem doing the repairs. Several worked together at a construction company, and he was ready to pay them for the labor and the materials. When he'd tried asking, though, they'd ignored him. Didn't they understand it would be good for them, their *children*, if the band had a safe building for kindergarten?

But they'd said no because he'd been the one who'd asked, and Josiah didn't think there was a way out of that. They were stubborn when it came to him being the alpha, and nothing he'd done had changed their minds. At this point, he doubted anything could.

And that wasn't Josiah's only problem.

He'd found out that some of the coyotes were bullying other band members. It brought back bad memories, which was why he hadn't dealt with it yet. He couldn't just ignore it. He knew how much it hurt to be bullied and abused, and he never wanted anyone to go through that, not even coyotes. They might hate him, and they might wish they could do the same to him, but he was their alpha, and he had to act like it. Maybe that way, they would finally see that he was doing his best and that even though he was still learning, he was a better alpha than his father and his brother had been.

Josiah jumped out of his chair. He might not be able to do anything about the repairs, but he could go find the bullied coyotes and talk to them. Maybe it would be enough for them to realize they had someone they could talk to. Maybe it wouldn't, but at least, Josiah would have tried to. He was going to continue until he couldn't, and the moment hadn't come yet.

He left his house and headed toward one of the smallest cabins behind the home he'd grown up in. His father had wanted all the coyotes to be close by, not caring about his privacy but caring about keeping an eye on them. That meant that Josiah could reach any house in band territory within minutes, which was probably the only reason he arrived while this coyote was being bullied.

He heard the sounds first. He recognized them because he'd been punched and kicked too many times to count. He started running. The house finally came into view, and Josiah sucked in a breath.

Two men were fighting in front of it, or rather, one was beating the other. Josiah wasn't surprised to see Gordon reach down for the coyote on the ground, pull him up by his shirt collar, and punch him in the face. The second man—Josiah couldn't recognize him with the blood on his face—dropped back to the ground and curled into a tight ball.

"What the fuck do you think you're doing?" Josiah snapped.

Gordon froze only for a second. He slowly turned to face Josiah, and even though Josiah was terrified, he stood his ground and straightened his back.

Gordon had always been one of the worst. He'd been friends with Josiah's father, but since he hadn't been there when Josiah's brother had attacked the badgers, the council hadn't arrested him. He was still free to hurt anyone he could, which apparently, he hadn't hesitated to do.

"This isn't your business," Gordon said with a growl.

"How is it not? I'm the alpha. You're hurting one of my band members, which means it *is* my business."

Unfortunately, Gordon seemed to find that amusing rather

than scary. "One of your band members, huh?" he asked as he turned around to face Josiah fully. "I never thought I'd see the day you were the alpha. Your father is probably rolling around in his grave right now."

"He can die a second time as far as I'm concerned. Why are you beating him?"

"Because I felt like it. Why don't you fuck off? I don't want to hurt you because your father was a friend, but I'll do it if I have to."

Josiah couldn't help it—he snorted. "You don't want to hurt me because of my father? Are you serious? My father would be happy if he found out you or anyone else is hurting me."

That was probably the wrong thing to say because Gordon smiled. "Yeah? Maybe I should hurt you, then."

He moved away from the man on the ground, for which Josiah was grateful, but the problem was that he moved toward Josiah.

Josiah wasn't a fighter. Fighting back had been beaten out of him. His father would have hurt him even worse if Josiah had tried. But Gordon wasn't Josiah's father, and Josiah wouldn't allow him to hit him without retaliating. He had no doubt he would lose, but he *was* going to try. No matter how scared he was, he was done cowering.

"What's going on here?" a voice asked.

Josiah didn't think he'd ever been so relieved to see Luther. He didn't know why Luther was here, but right now, he didn't care. He was so glad to see the man that he might have kissed him.

Gordon looked at Luther. "You shouldn't be here," he spat out.

Luther crossed his arms over his chest. "Wrong. You see, my job is to make sure that the shifters in the forest are behaving the way they should. I don't think that beating your alpha counts as that. Do you want me to report you?"

"You wouldn't put every shifter in the forest in danger for that." Gordon didn't sound convinced, though.

"I wouldn't have to. You're only one man. I can easily arrest you and make sure you never see the forest again. Just try me."

Gordon stared, and for one moment, Josiah thought he would. Instead, he shook his head, his expression one of disgust. "You won't be here forever, human."

"Maybe not, but Josiah isn't alone. He has friends and the backing of the council. I'd be careful, if I were you. Besides, I'm not going anywhere anytime soon."

Josiah breathed more easily when Gordon walked away. His knees almost buckled, but he managed to turn toward Luther. "Thank you." He might be the alpha, but he was relieved Luther had saved him.

Luther's expression smoothed out, but he still looked worried. "I don't like this."

"Trust me. I don't like it, either, but it's my job, and I'm going to do it."

Luther wanted to go after that guy and beat him into the ground, but Josiah was more important than taking out his anger and disgust on that asshole. "You shouldn't have faced him alone," he said.

Josiah, who had turned toward the bleeding man on the ground, faced Luther again. "I shouldn't have, no, but who was going to have my back? I don't have a beta or guards."

"You could have called me."

Josiah's expression softened. "I didn't have the time, but even if I had, I don't want to get used to having you here when you're not going to stay. What's going to happen the first time I confront someone and you're not there to have my back? I can't rely on you, not because I don't want to, but because I can't."

With that, Josiah turned to the man again. He crouched next to him and reached out, but the man jerked back as if he couldn't get away fast enough. There was a flash of hurt in Josiah's expression, but he quickly smoothed it out. "You're Bennett," he said.

Bennett got to his feet. It looked painful, and Luther wanted to help, but like Josiah had pointed out, he should stay out of it.

"I'm fine," Bennett croaked.

"You're still bleeding, and the bruises on your body tell me it's not the first time something like this has happened. What's going on?"

Bennett shook his head.

Luther couldn't tell much from him because of the blood, but he thought Bennett looked young, maybe as young as Josiah.

"Nothing. I'm fine," Bennett repeated.

Josiah sighed. "I know you don't trust me. No one here does. It doesn't mean I'll turn my back on you if you want to talk about this. I can recognize the signs of abuse, and I don't want anyone in the band to have to go through that."

"And what are you going to do to stop it?" Bennett snapped. He reached up to try to clean some blood from his face, but the only thing he managed to do was to spread it even more.

Josiah raised his hands. "I'm doing everything I can."

"It's not enough!" Bennett stumbled and almost fell, but Josiah was there, keeping him on his feet.

Bennett fought for a moment, trying to push Josiah away, but Josiah didn't move. He stayed where he was, and when Bennett broke down, Josiah was there for him. He gingerly wrapped his arms around Bennett's shoulders and held him as he cried.

"No one can do anything," Bennett said.

"I promise you that I'm doing everything I can. It's not easy, though."

Bennett sniffled and tried to move away, and this time, Josiah allowed him to. "I know it's not easy. But when you became alpha, I hoped that something would finally change. It hasn't."

"It will. I promise you that. I don't know how I'll do it, but I will."

Bennett looked more sad than angry now. "I wish I could believe you, but things never get better. But thank you. The next time Gordon beats me, it's going to be even worse because you intervened, but at least I know that someone cares about me."

When Bennett started walking away, Josiah didn't try to stop him.

Luther didn't, either. He wouldn't have known what to say or do. This wasn't right. No one should be beaten the way Bennett had been, and Josiah should be able to help Bennett. This entire situation was such a mess that Luther couldn't see a way out of it.

But he wanted to. He wanted to stay and help and be there for Josiah when something like this happened. He would never be Josiah's beta, but he didn't have to in order to be with him.

Luther wanted to stay, quit his job, and make a new life for himself in the forest. It wasn't just because of how strong and beautiful and incredible Josiah was. It was because Luther loved living here and because he enjoyed talking with shifters and getting to know them. They were good people, much better than a lot of humans Luther had met.

He wanted to stay.

He was ready to move into the forest permanently, maybe

not with Josiah since they weren't together, but close enough that something could happen between them. He still couldn't see a way to make that happen, no matter how much he wanted to. That was why he didn't say anything as he moved toward Josiah, who was still staring at the small house Bennett had disappeared into.

Luther gently touched Josiah's arm, and when Josiah didn't react, he took his hand and pulled him along. He led Josiah home, his heart feeling like it was about to explode.

He wanted to be there when Josiah needed him. He wanted to guide him if he needed guidance, to fight for him if something like this happened again. He was going to do everything he could to find a way to stay, but until he managed, it would be better for Josiah if he didn't mention anything.

Because Josiah was right. What if he came to rely on Luther, and Luther couldn't stay? It wouldn't be fair, and it would make his life harder, which was the last thing Luther wanted.

Josiah finally got out of his funk when they reached his house. He slammed the front door after they walked inside, then raked his hands through his hair. "How could I allow this to happen? It isn't right. I can't believe something like this was going on and I wasn't aware of it."

"You're only one man," Luther told him. He understood why Josiah was angry, but he didn't want Josiah to think all of this was his fault.

"But I'm the alpha. I should know what's happening in my band. I should have stood up for Bennett much sooner. Did you see the bruises? It wasn't the first time Gordon hurt him, and it won't be the last."

"We'll make sure it doesn't happen again."

Josiah threw his hands in the air. "How? I might be the alpha, but I have no one backing me. I still haven't been able to find that guy, Stephen Wright, and I don't think I will. Every coyote I asked ignored me. I can't tramp around the forest calling for him if I don't even know where to start."

"I'll do everything I can to help you. Just tell me what you need."

"I don't know what I need! I don't know what I can *do*. I want to help Bennett and all the other coyotes who Gordon and his friends are abusing, but even though I'm the alpha, there's nothing I can do." His shoulders slumped. "And the fact that I want to give all of this up makes me feel guilty. Bennett needs me. How can I even think about not being the alpha anymore?"

Luther wanted to hug Josiah, but they'd never done anything like that, and he wasn't sure Josiah would allow it. He stayed away, but he tried to find the right words to help his friend. "Why don't you talk to the council? They put you into this trouble, and you told me they'd promised to help if you needed them to. It looks like you do now. I know you didn't want to upset the band even more, but I think the time for that has come and passed. You need help, and if you can't find it with the band, you're going to need the council to step in. Have them send guards. Have them keep an eye on Gordon and his friends. It's not like the band can hate you more than they already do, but this way, you might be able to send a message and to keep Bennett and the others safe as you do so."

"I hate this. I hate everything about it."

"I know, and I don't blame you. But you already know you can't do this alone, not if you don't want to get hurt. For now, Gordon left, but what's going to happen if I'm not here to help you? He could have hurt you." And the thought was enough to terrify Luther.

Josiah didn't deserve any of this. He didn't deserve the coyotes to be so angry when he tried to do the right thing or to be threatened by them.

What could Luther do to help, though?

Josiah was going to have to deal with Gordon sooner rather than later. Gordon was a danger, to both Bennett and Josiah and probably a lot of other coyotes. Josiah didn't know how he would deal with the man, but he would find a way. He had to. He'd promised Bennett he would do something, and he always tried to keep his promises, even when they were complicated.

Luther was right. Josiah should talk to Thomas again, bring the council in. They'd made promises when Josiah had agreed to become the alpha, and they better keep them.

Luther was also right when he said that Josiah would probably be left alone to deal with Gordon. Even if the council agreed to help, it was Josiah's job, and he had every intention of doing it. He'd feel better if someone had his back while he did, mostly because he suspected he would end up bleeding and broken otherwise, but he'd do it even if it killed him.

Which it probably would.

Josiah didn't want to think about this anymore. He had at least a few hours of reprieve, and Luther was with him. They could spend the rest of the day together, maybe have lunch. Josiah could stop thinking about Gordon and act as if he didn't have a care in the world for a while.

First, he had to reassure Luther, who was still staring at him.

"I promise I won't face Gordon on my own," he said.

Luther arched a brow. "I'm not sure I can believe that."

Josiah should have known better. They were friends, and Luther was one of the few people who knew him fairly well. "I promise I'll be careful, then. I don't want anything to happen to me, but I can't ignore this and hope it will go away."

Luther sighed. "I'm aware of that. And I know you'll do

what's right, even if it hurts you. Just, please, if you need anything, if there's anything I can do, call me. If not me, call someone else, like Thomas or even Nico. I wouldn't face that guy on my own. You shouldn't, either."

Luther wouldn't do it alone because he had his team. That was what Josiah needed — a team of people who had his back and who would stand by him if he had to face someone like Gordon. "I'll do what I can. I don't want Gordon to beat me up. I don't want anyone to do that or to hurt any of my coyotes."

Luther stared for a moment. "This is one of the things I like about you," he murmured.

Josiah's eyes went wide. "What do you mean?" It was the first time Luther told him he liked him. Josiah hoped he meant it in the same way he liked Luther, but he would take it even if it was only friendly.

Luther gestured at Josiah. "You're honorable. You could have told the council to take a hike when they asked you to become the alpha. You could have agreed and then hid in this house without doing much of anything for the band. Both of those solutions would have been easier for you, yet here you are, trying to do the best for a band that doesn't like you."

Josiah snorted. "I'm pretty sure that saying they don't like me is an understatement. Most of them *hate* me."

"They wouldn't if they knew you. But you're a good man, and eventually, they'll realize that. They'll realize that they were lucky you agreed to take their lead, and things will calm down."

"That sounds like a dream."

"It might be, but that's what you're working toward doing, and I know you'll get it eventually. You deserve it."

Josiah swallowed. It was painful, and knowing how much faith Luther had in him was terrifying. What if Josiah failed? He already had, in a way, and he didn't know how to find a way out of it.

That wasn't going to stop him from trying.

He cleared his throat. "Did you already have lunch?"

Luther shook his head. "I haven't. That doesn't mean you have to invite me. I can just head back to Northwood."

"It also doesn't mean I should send you on your way hungry. Besides, I like having meals with you. I don't want to eat alone." Or to be alone right now. Josiah still felt shaky after his confrontation with Gordon, and it would take some time for him to feel better.

"What did you have in mind?"

"Well, I don't have much in the fridge this time, either, but we can make some sandwiches."

They settled on BLT sandwiches. Luther took charge of the bacon while Josiah grabbed the tomatoes to slice them. He was getting used to cooking in this house and kitchen, and it was starting to feel like his. He was surprised to see that Luther seemed to belong, too. They moved around each other, not once bothering the other, and it made Josiah wonder.

Could he have this with Luther?

He realized that even if he could, it would be only temporary, but at this point, he was ready to accept pretty much anything. Even with Nico in his life, even knowing he could go to Thomas at any moment, Josiah was lonely. He wanted someone to love and who would love him, and he suspected he would be happy if that someone was Luther.

"The bacon is done," Luther said after a moment. "I'll set the table. Where are the glasses?"

Josiah gestured at the cupboard above him. He felt Luther move, and before he could react, Luther was behind him. Both of Luther's arms went around him as he reached for the cupboard, and Josiah couldn't help but wonder if he was doing it on purpose. Luther was effectively caging him within his arms, and if Josiah turned around, they would be face to face and closer than they'd ever been.

Josiah sucked in a breath. He *wanted* to turn around. He wanted to kiss Luther and see what happened. He wanted to be brave enough to do it and not be afraid that Luther would reject him. He was pretty sure that wouldn't be the case. There was no reason for Luther to continue coming around to help him besides Luther liking him.

Josiah had never done anything like this. He'd never had a boyfriend, not when his father had been alive, not when he'd been in the Bishop house. He'd never kissed anyone. He wouldn't know where to start, but he wanted to find out.

He put down his knife and turned around.

Luther was already lowering his arms by the time Josiah faced him. He blinked, and Josiah was pretty sure he hadn't intended to be so close to him. He started to move back, holding a glass in both hands, but Josiah stepped forward. Their chests brushed against each other, and it was so easy to slide his arms around Luther's neck, to inch even closer, to press his lips against Luther's.

Luther didn't pull away. Instead, Josiah felt his shoulders sag as if in relief. He wrapped his arms around Josiah, pulling him into the embrace. Josiah could feel the glasses press against his back, but it was still perfect.

He didn't have experience in kissing, but he knew the theory. He kept the first few kisses light and gentle, but once they were plastered against each other, he licked a path around Luther's lips. Luther opened to him, and Josiah delved inside, his heart racing in his chest, his head feeling that it was about to explode.

It was perfect, exactly like he'd expected, yet also so much more. It was like a dream, one Josiah never wanted to stop.

It didn't have to, at least not for a while. Eventually, Luther would have to go back to his team and then back to his home outside of the forest. He would leave, while Josiah would have to stay back.

Josiah didn't want to think about that right now. The only thing he wanted to think about was Luther and how perfect his lips were against his, so he pushed every other thought away and did just that.

Luther wasn't surprised that Josiah had kissed him. He'd wanted to do that almost since the first time he'd met Josiah, and he'd suspected Josiah wanted the same. He hadn't expected Josiah to actually do it, but he was relieved and happy he had. This way, Luther could be sure Josiah wanted this and that it wasn't just a pipe dream he'd built in his mind.

He realized that doing this wasn't the best idea. Josiah had his hands full with the band, and he shouldn't be distracted, especially not by a new relationship with a human. In addition,, Luther still hadn't found a way that would allow him to stay in the forest. He hadn't mentioned anything to Hawley because he already knew what his superior's answer would be, but he wasn't giving up, not yet, and maybe not ever. If he and Josiah could have what he hoped they could have, it would be worth sacrificing a lot, maybe everything.

The only thing Luther wasn't ready to sacrifice was Josiah himself, and he would do everything he could to make sure Josiah was happy, even if he had to go.

Luther couldn't stop kissing Josiah. He wanted him too much. He also wanted Josiah to know he was loved. He hadn't had enough of that in his life, and while he already had a friendly love with Nico and Thomas and the other carriers, Luther was the only one who could give him this kind of love, at least right now.

It hurt to think that eventually Josiah could find someone else. If Luther had to leave, he wouldn't demand that Josiah wait for him. It would be stupid, and Luther would never be that cruel. He didn't want to think about going just yet, though. He wasn't done looking for a way to stay, and he wasn't done kissing Josiah.

Kissing him felt like coming home. It made Luther want never to leave even more. Josiah felt perfect in his arms, wrapped around him as he was, his lips soft and hesitant, yet also firm and enthusiastic. He was putting a lot of himself in the kiss, and Luther did the same. He might not be able to say the words out loud, but he wanted Josiah to know how he felt.

He'd always thought it was stupid to believe that someone could say something with a kiss, but now he found himself hoping it was possible. He wanted Josiah to know how important this was to him, how important *he* was. He was afraid to say it out loud because he didn't know if he'd be able to stay, and he didn't want to hurt both himself and Josiah even more than they already would be.

For now, this had to be enough, and it was.

"I didn't expect this," Josiah murmured.

Luther took advantage of the fact that they weren't kissing anymore to put the glasses on the counter. He was pretty sure he squashed the tomatoes Josiah had been cutting as he did so, but he didn't care, not when it allowed him to touch Josiah's back with his hands.

"You were the one who kissed me," Luther teased.

Josiah's cheeks flushed. "I did, and I don't regret it. I just didn't think it was going to be so good."

He sounded stunned, and Luther knew he wasn't lying.

Josiah had never had much good in his life. His mother might have loved him, but she hadn't been able to show him that. His father certainly hadn't, and as for his brother, Luther suspected it was more of the same. Josiah had been alone for a long time, without love, and Luther wanted to make him forget that. He wanted him to feel cherished, and he knew how to do that.

He had no idea what would happen next, but he hoped that this was the first step to something good for both of them. It wouldn't be easy, but then, nothing worth having ever was. That was why Luther was ready to fight for Josiah and for a place in the forest. This, *all* of this, was worth having. It was also worth the fight.

Josiah leaned closer. They kissed again, and Josiah felt more sure of himself this time. Luther didn't have a problem allowing Josiah to take the lead, so, still holding onto Josiah's waist, he turned them around so he could lean against the counter. Something fell, and when he pressed back, something damp squashed against his body.

He jerked away and turned around to see that one of the slices of tomato had slipped off the cutting board. He lifted it and threw it into the sink. When he turned back to Josiah, Josiah looked amused.

"We should probably have lunch," he said.

"Probably. Are you still hungry?"

Josiah stared at Luther's lips. "I am, although I'm not sure for what."

His words were enough to make Luther's heart beat faster. "We don't have to stop kissing, or we can stop and start again later. We have the rest of the day to be together."

"Don't you have to go back to your team?"

"They can deal on their own. They have been." And they'd noticed something was going on.

Thankfully, none of them had pushed yet. Luther was going to have to find a way to tell them what was happening, because he didn't like keeping secrets from them, not when they were supposed to have his back. He didn't know how to do it, even though he trusted them.

That was a problem for later. Right now, Luther wanted to focus on Josiah and only him.

Josiah looked from Luther's lips to the tomatoes still on the counter. "I suppose we should eat. As long as you promise you're not going anywhere once we're done."

Luther smiled. "I'm not. If you want me here, I'm sticking around."

Josiah's smile twisted for a moment, but it was back soon enough.

It was clear they both knew it might not come down to Luther deciding whether or not he would stay, but neither of them brought it up. They were going to focus on each other and what was happening right now and not what would happen in the future. It would come soon enough, and it would be complicated. They could take these few moments to avoid thinking about it and focus on what they both wanted.

Each other.

CHAPTER SEVEN

Luther and Josiah were holding hands. Luther wasn't usually a handholding guy, but he was charmed by Josiah wanting to do it. He hadn't protested when Josiah had taken his hand and pulled him into the forest, and he wasn't going to.

It had been a few days since their first kiss, and things were proceeding exactly the way Luther wanted them to. They'd been spending even more time together, mostly in Josiah's house, but also exploring band territory. If Luther was going to try to stay, he should know more about this place. Josiah wasn't going anywhere since he was the alpha, and eventually, if they had a relationship, Luther would end up here, too. He could too easily imagine how angry the coyotes would be. They didn't want Josiah as their alpha, and they would want a human by his side even less. That wasn't a problem Luther wanted or was ready to deal with today, and he was relieved he didn't have to. Right now, the only thing he had to deal with was Josiah and how perfect he was.

"I wish some of the coyotes had built their homes a bit farther away from my father's house," Josiah was saying. "But he wanted all of them close so he could keep an eye on them."

"That means they're too close to you."

Josiah nodded. "I suppose I should be grateful I didn't have to stay in my father's house, and I am. I still wish I had more privacy, though. The other morning, I stepped out on the porch bare-chested, and two old ladies were staring at me from their porch. I was embarrassed, but I waved. They just went back inside. It's not enough that they all stare at me all the time, but they still hate me, and I don't know what to do."

Luther's heart broke every time he heard how dejected Josiah was. He couldn't force the band to love Josiah, but damn if he didn't want to try. Since they would probably laugh in his face, it was easier for him to focus on Josiah. Josiah would be embarrassed if he knew how much Luther thought about him, so Luther didn't say anything. Instead, he asked questions about the one thing that was important to Josiah.

The band.

As much as Josiah hated dealing with the band members, he loved his territory. As soon as they'd stepped away from the houses, he'd relaxed, and now, as they were walking in the forest, he looked happy and at home. Luther couldn't be a hundred percent sure that was the case, and he didn't want to ask because he didn't want to ruin the moment, but this was what Josiah should have. He should be free to do whatever he wanted instead of babysitting a bunch of coyotes who hated him.

"How deep is the forest?" Luther asked.

Josiah gestured around them. "It's not the biggest territory in the forest, if that's what you're asking, but it's big enough. Certainly bigger than rodent territory."

Luther was aware of how much people distrusted the rodents, and from the stories he'd heard, he understood. He didn't like the thought of dumping all of them in one bag, but Josiah and the other shifters would know better.

"Bobcat territory is probably the biggest, although now that Thomas and Morris are allied, theirs is."

"That's not just one territory, though."

"It might as well be. Their families are linked, and they always will be from now on. It's not just an alliance, either. Levi and Dimitri truly love each other, which is the best part of this. And of course, there are Eddie and Joel, too."

Luther knew Joel was one of Thomas's sons, and he'd seen him around with a tall guy, but he didn't know Eddie. "Is Eddie a bear?"

"He's Dimitri's best friend. He's not part of Morris's family, but they're close. It's one more bond between the badgers and the bears."

Luther nodded. He was fascinated by the relationships between the different kinds of shifters. "While Alex is married to . . ." Luther knew Seamus—and he doubted he would ever forget him since he was the reason Luther had found out about carriers—but he didn't know much about him.

Josiah smiled. "Alex is married to Seamus. Seamus is a rodent, a beaver."

"He's part of the most hated group in the forest?" Luther was surprised.

Josiah's smile vanished. "He is, but he's like me."

"A carrier."

"It's more than that. He's a rodent, but he was abused. His family was related to an old rodent alpha, and his parents were killed while he was chained in the basement so he wouldn't step into that role."

Every time Luther heard about what the carriers had gone through, he wanted to kill someone. Instead of showing Josiah how angry he was, he tried to focus on their conversation. "I know about the Bishop house, but I don't know how many carriers lived there."

"Quite a few of us. Maybe all of us at one point. Thomas and the badgers were good to us, and they protected us. They cared about us. They made sure we were safe, and I'll never be able to repay that."

"I don't think he wants you to repay him."

"That's what makes him a good person." Josiah stopped walking and turned to Luther. "Are you done interrogating me?"

Luther spluttered. "I'm not interrogating you. I'm just curious about the people here."

"You're not gathering information for your boss?"

Luther shook his head. "None of what you just said is going to him. The less he knows about you guys, the better it will be. My boss isn't a good person, Josiah. I didn't want to accept the job, but I knew that if I didn't, he would have found someone else. And that someone might be worse. I'm doing what I can to protect the forest and you, but I don't know how much success I'll have. Eventually, Hawley is going to have enough of me pulling him around."

Josiah reached up and cupped Luther's face with both hands. "There's a lot weighing on your shoulders, isn't there?"

Luther nodded. "Much more than I'm comfortable with, but I'll bear the weight if it means you and your people are safe." And they were, at least for now.

Hawley had to be busy, because he hadn't called Luther again. That wouldn't last long, but Luther was trying to ignore that and focus on Josiah.

Josiah kissed Luther. Luther closed his eyes instinctively, tilting his head up toward the man he was starting to fall in love with. Or maybe he was already in love with Josiah. It was hard to understand, because of how much he'd always liked Josiah. He even liked that Josiah was taller than he was.

"We should head back," Josiah whispered.

There was promise in his voice, and Luther nodded. "We should. Are you expecting anyone this afternoon?"

"Nope. We have the entire afternoon to ourselves." He grinned. "I wonder what we can do."

"I'm sure we'll find something." They'd limited themselves to kissing for now, but Luther wanted more, and he thought Josiah did, too. They would take their time getting there, for Josiah's sake, but the problem was that Luther didn't know how much time he had.

Once again, he pushed those thoughts away. He would have time to worry when he headed back to his team.

Josiah stepped away and retook Luther's hand. Together, they walked back toward his house. Luther found himself staring several times, and when Josiah noticed, he smiled at him. Luther had a hard time believing this kind and beautiful man wanted him. Josiah could have anyone he wanted, yet he'd chosen Luther.

They were almost on Josiah's porch when someone noticed them. They probably shouldn't have been holding hands for everyone to see, but Luther didn't care who knew, and he didn't think Josiah did, either. The problem was that Josiah had to deal with the band and with how angry they were.

"It's not bad enough that we have to accept you as our alpha. Now you want to have a human alpha mate?" a woman snapped.

Luther looked around until he saw her. She was standing on the porch of a house in front of Josiah's.

Josiah groaned. "She's one of the ladies who saw me bare-chested the other day," he murmured. He straightened and faced her. "Good afternoon."

"Don't *good afternoon* me," the woman said, pointing a finger at Josiah. "This is too much. You can't have a human alpha mate. You need to find a nice girl and marry her. It's the only way you can fix this."

What she meant was that Josiah needed to marry a woman and forget he was a carrier. Luther was angry for Josiah's sake, but he knew better than to step in. Josiah was the alpha, and he needed to deal with this on his own, no matter how much Luther disliked it. He was a guest, and Josiah was in charge. If the woman had to be punished, *he* would be the one doing that.

Josiah wasn't surprised at Betty's reaction to seeing him with Luther. What he *was* surprised at was that she and the others hadn't realized how important Luther was to Josiah sooner. That was a good thing. He might not have had the strength to face them before, but now that he knew Luther wanted him, he did.

Josiah didn't like feeling like his strength depended on something or someone else, but he wasn't an idiot. He saw how much stronger Luther felt when his team backed him. Josiah couldn't deny that he felt better when he knew Thomas was there. Everyone needed someone to be there for them and support them, and right now, that someone was Luther.

Josiah wasn't ashamed of who he was, being a carrier, or being with Luther. He wasn't going to hide, never again. That was why he faced Betty, never letting go of Luther's hand.

"I don't think you'll be the one to decide that," he told her.

She huffed and crossed her arms over her chest. She hadn't been one of his father's friends, but she was married to one. Her husband had died during the battle with the badgers, which probably explained why Josiah hadn't seen much of her until recently.

"You'll ruin the band," she said.

"Some people think I'm ruining it just by being the alpha. I doubt that who I'm with is going to change that."

"What will happen if you get pregnant? You can't be the alpha and carry a child." She spat out the words.

Even though Josiah was used to this, it hurt. He wished he didn't care and could face these people without feeling like he wasn't enough.

Luther's hand squeezed around his, and Josiah realized it didn't matter. Who cared what Betty thought about him? Who cared what she thought about Luther? Josiah was the alpha, and as long as he was, he would do whatever he could to keep the band safe. That didn't mean he was going to stop living the way he wanted. Being with Luther didn't influence the way he led the band.

"I suppose that if I get pregnant, I'll have the baby. The band needs an heir, after all."

Betty's eyes widened. "Your wife needs to give you an heir. You can't do that yourself." She sounded outraged.

"Why not? I can do it myself, so why shouldn't I?"

Betty opened her mouth, then closed it. "Because it's not done. Alphas don't carry children. They need to be strong for the band. You're already weak as it is. Do you really want to make things worse?"

Josiah wasn't even offended. Betty was saying what everyone in the band thought, and it was a relief that someone was being honest to his face for once. "Being able to carry a child doesn't make me weak." Betty opened her mouth, but Josiah had enough of listening to her. "You have children. Did carrying them make *you* weak?"

Josiah didn't wait for an answer. He turned around and pulled Luther toward the house, not wanting to know what she would say. He had enough of having that kind of conversation, and he wanted to focus on Luther while he had the chance.

He couldn't stop thinking about what Betty had said. Luther couldn't stay in the forest, but would he want to be alpha mate if he could? Was that possible since he was human?

Would he even want to marry Josiah?

Josiah pushed those thoughts away. He and Luther had just gotten together, and neither of them was thinking about marriage. It was hard enough to think about a future without Luther once he had to go home. Josiah didn't know what the future would be like for them, but he wasn't ready to face it yet. Whatever happened, he deserved whatever he wanted in life.

After what his father and his brother had done, after what the band was still doing to him, he deserved to have the kind of life he wanted. If that was with Luther, he didn't see why anyone should have anything to say about it. Whatever Luther might do by being an alpha mate couldn't be worse than what Josiah's father had done. He'd been a horrible alpha who'd used cruelty and fear to guide the coyotes. Luther would never do something like that, even if no one respected him.

Besides, Josiah was the alpha. Luther never would be, so it was pointless to think about what he would do for the band. Being an alpha mate might give Luther some power over the band, but Josiah would still be the one in charge.

Unless someone volunteered to take his place as the alpha, he was going to guide the band the way he saw fit. He wasn't hiding and scurrying around trying to make people happy. They never would be, no matter what he did. He had to focus on the people he could help, like Bennett, and ignore the naysayers. That was the only way he would make things work and he could be proud of himself.

"That was something," Luther said once they were inside the house.

"I'm sorry. I'm not surprised she had something to say about us being together. I expected it."

Luther dragged Josiah closer and wrapped his arms around him. Like every time he did it, Josiah instantly relaxed. He was safe here, in Luther's arms, and he was able to forget about what had just happened in the world outside the door. It was only for a moment, but it was enough.

"I'm not surprised, either. Does she really think I want to be the alpha mate?"

"Even if she doesn't, she knows we're together. I guess she wanted us to know what she thought about it." And the rest of the band probably shared her opinion.

"You think that's possible?" Luther asked.

"What? You becoming my alpha mate?"

"Yes. Not that I'm aiming for that, but as far as I know, I'm the first human who's even been considered for that role."

Josiah leaned away. "You're not being considered for the role. Besides, I'm pretty sure our relationship is the first shifter-human one in the forest in decades, if not longer. That's why a human has never been alpha mate. There are no humans here." And there wouldn't be any more once Luther and his team left.

"What if there could be?" Luther asked.

Josiah wasn't sure whether to feel excited or terrified of his words. "Honestly? I don't care what Betty or any other band member thinks. If they have something against the way I lead the band, they can come to talk to me. I'll be more than happy to step down if someone worthy decides to be the alpha and take my place. I doubt that's going to happen, unfortunately. That means the band is stuck with me, and while I'll do everything I can to be a good leader, I won't sacrifice my personal life for that."

"You shouldn't," Luther said.

"Damn right, I shouldn't. My brother and my father hurt me more than enough. They took a lot away from me, and the band stood aside and watched them. A few of them even joined in and abused me. I think that when it comes to the person I want to be with, I should be free to choose."

And right now, he was choosing Luther.

Josiah didn't know how long things would last with Luther, but hopefully at least until Luther had to leave the forest. Josiah wanted to make the most out of what little time they still had. He didn't know how long it would be, but eventually, Luther would go. Josiah would be left behind with his love and pain, and he would have to deal with it. Betty would feel smug about the fact that he'd been dumped, and he would have to stand up in front of her and act as if nothing had happened, as if he wasn't hurt.

All of that was in the future. He didn't have to think about that right now. The only thing he had to think about was Luther and being happy, or at least as happy as he could.

Luther was impressed and proud of Josiah's words to that woman. It would have been easy for him to ignore her or go along with what she was saying so she wouldn't get angrier. Instead, Josiah had stood up for himself, and Luther had faith that he would continue doing so even in the future.

The future Luther wasn't sure he would be part of.

A noise outside made him peek through the window. His eyes widened when he saw that Betty wasn't alone on her porch anymore. They were another two people there, and if Luther wasn't mistaken, that guy who had been beating up Bennett was one of them. He could also see other people gathering, which could mean trouble.

"I think we should head out," he said slowly.

Josiah frowned and looked out the window, too. "Dammit! What do they think they're doing?"

"I'm pretty sure Betty is telling everyone about the conversation you two just had. I think it would be safer for both of us to be away from this place for a bit until they calm down."

Josiah looked worried. "What do you think they'll do?"

"I don't know, and that's what scares me." Because these people weren't human. Even against a group of humans, Luther would have had a hard time because he and Josiah were alone. Against a pack of coyote shifters, though? They could tear both Luther and Josiah apart before either of them could do anything.

"We can leave through the back. We won't be able to take the cars, but we can hide in the forest for a bit."

"Won't they try to follow us?"

"I don't know. I hope not."

Luther prayed that once they saw they couldn't get to Josiah, these people would calm down and go back home. In the meantime, he needed to get Josiah out of here and in a safe place.

He followed Josiah to the back door. He peeked outside, but thankfully, no one seemed to be there. That wasn't going to last long, given the sounds that came from the front of the house, though, so Luther hurried out, dragging Josiah with him. They made sure to lock the door, although if these people wanted to get in, they would be able to without too much of a problem.

That wasn't something they could focus on now. If the house was trashed when they came back, they'd deal with it then. In the meantime, Luther would make sure Josiah was safe.

They rushed into the forest. Luther had no idea where they were going, so he let Josiah take the lead. He'd been born here, and while he hadn't been allowed to roam the forest until recently, he seemed to know what he was doing.

"Should I call my team?" he asked as they walked.

Josiah hesitated. "Would you have to report this if you did?"

"I wouldn't write it in my report, but one of them might, if anything, because they'll be angry at my being in danger."

"Then no, please. I know you should and that this kind of situation is what you were sent here to solve, but nothing has really happened. They're angry, and they might try to get to me, but I'm not home. I don't want the band to be in trouble because of a few idiots."

To Luther, it had sounded like more than a few people were gathering, and he doubted they were idiots. Even if they were, it didn't make them less dangerous. Josiah might be the alpha, but the band didn't fear him like they had his father, and they might hurt him.

After a while, it started raining. Josiah swore and glared at the sky, then back toward his house. "I think we can stop here and try to stay dry under a tree."

"Won't they be able to scent you?"

"Not if it rains heavily, but even if it doesn't, I don't think they'll want to get wet. We should be okay to go back in a bit. I just want to make sure they're gone before we do."

They huddled under the biggest tree they could find. Luther wrapped his arms around Josiah, but there was no keeping him dry, especially when the rain started coming down harder. Josiah was taller, and he hunched over Luther as if trying to shield him. The tree helped, but after a while, they were both soaked.

"I'm going to kill them," Josiah muttered.

This was nothing like the romantic walk they'd taken just an hour earlier, and Luther was worried, but he didn't mind being pressed against a wet Josiah. It gave him ideas he wasn't sure Josiah was ready for, so he didn't say anything, not even as a tease.

"Is there someone you can call to know what's going on?" he asked, trying to distract himself.

"I don't know if anyone will answer, but I saved everyone's phone number on my phone, just in case." Josiah took it out and huddled over it. "Maybe Bennett? He didn't seem to hate me as much as the others."

It broke Luther's heart to hear Josiah say that so casually, but he wasn't wrong. A lot of band members hated him.

It took three tries before Bennett answered. Luther couldn't hear the other side of the conversation, but Josiah asked him if the crowd was still gathered in front of his house. Bennett answered, and Josiah said, "Are you sure? Because I'd rather not walk in on them right now."

Luther waited. He was cold, and he couldn't wait to get out of his wet clothes. Driving back to Northwood wasn't going to be fun, but he'd been through worse.

Josiah finally hung up. "Bennett said they left once it started raining hard. There might be a few people still around, like Betty, but that's because she lives close by. We should be fine going back."

"What did they do? Did they try to break into your house?"

"No. They were just yelling at each other, although Bennett doesn't know about what. He could hear the sounds, but he didn't go."

"Because he hates you less than the others?"

Josiah shrugged. "Maybe. Or maybe because he's still in pain from what Gordon did to him. I'll try talking to him tomorrow, but for now, I think we should head home."

But this wasn't Luther's home. He didn't bring that up as he and Josiah trudged back toward the house, though. Their feet made squelching sounds as they walked in the mud, and it made him want a shower almost desperately. It was going to be a while before he could grab one, but he was glad he'd been here with Josiah when this happened.

Josiah shouldn't be doing this on his own. The council had promised they would support him, but he was alone, and if Luther hadn't been here, he might have gotten hurt. That thought was enough to make Luther break out in a cold sweat. He needed to help, but he didn't know how or even whether he could.

They slowed down when they reached the house. They peeked out of the woods, trying to figure out if people were still around, but Luther couldn't see or hear anything. From Josiah's expression, he couldn't, either, and when he moved toward the house, Luther followed him.

They walked in through the back door and locked it again as soon as they were inside. Josiah made a beeline for the front of the house, looking out the windows, and Luther followed him.

There was no one there. The rain was coming down harder than ever, and everyone had gone home. They were safe, at least for now.

Luther sighed in relief. "I'm not looking forward to that drive back to Northwood." Both he and Josiah looked like drenched rats.

"Why don't you stay, then?"

Luther was stunned at the offer, although it might not mean what he thought it meant. "For how long? Until it stops raining?"

"For however long you want to stay. To begin with, you should take a shower. I only have my clothes around, but I think I can find you something big enough you can fit in. We can have dinner, and you can decide if you want to go back once we're done."

It wasn't the first time they had dinner together, and Luther hoped it wouldn't be the last. He enjoyed those quiet, mundane moments when he and Josiah were together. It gave him a hint of what his future could be like if he stayed, and it made him want it even more.

As if he needed that. He already wanted it enough to try to find a way to stay. Whether or not he would find one, it was still to be seen, but he'd never been stopped by hard work or even by something that seemed impossible.

Josiah kept peeking at Luther. He looked good in Josiah's clothes, and Josiah wanted him more than ever. He wanted Luther to stay the night and to wake up in his arms.

Maybe it was just a reaction to what he and Luther had just gone through. Josiah had tried to be brave as they fled, but he'd been terrified. It hadn't been hard for him to imagine what the band would do to him and Luther if they wished to hurt them, and he never wanted to think about that again.

The problem was that he couldn't ignore it.

He was the alpha. He could wait the rest of the day, but tomorrow, he would have to face this. If he didn't, he would lose what little respect the band had for him — if they had any. He couldn't afford for them to think they could do this without consequences, but he was going to need some help, which meant he'd have to call the council, or at the very least, Thomas.

That was a problem for tomorrow. Right now, Josiah wanted to forget the fear and anger and focus on Luther. It might not be enough for him to ignore what the band had almost done, but he would try.

Once they were at the table with food in front of them, he took a deep breath. "Do you have to go back to town tonight?"

Luther froze with his fork halfway to his mouth. "I'm not sure what you're asking."

Now that Josiah had started, he had to finish it. "If you could stay here. I don't want to be alone." There was more to it, but Josiah wasn't sure if he should be that open. He didn't want to be hurt, and while he trusted Luther, he couldn't be a hundred percent sure of what would happen.

Luther's expression softened, and he put his fork down. "I can stay if you need me to, of course. You're shaken because of what happened."

Josiah wanted to say he wasn't, but it would be a lie. "A little." He bit his lower lip. He wanted to say more, but he couldn't bring himself to, so instead, he turned his attention to his plate.

He listened as Luther called one of his team members and told them he wouldn't be coming back that night. Josiah did what he could not to hear, but he was curious about Luther's team. He didn't think Luther had told them where he was spending so much time when he was with Josiah, and Josiah wondered what they would think if they knew. Would they criticize Luther for fraternizing with the enemy? Were he and Josiah even enemies?

"All done," Luther said as he put down his phone. "They know not to expect me."

"What did you tell them?"

Luther's smile was disarming. "That my car broke down. Dean offered to pick me up, but I said I was taking care of it and not to worry."

"And he didn't push?"

"I suspect he wanted to, but no, he didn't. He might ask tomorrow, but for tonight, everything is settled."

It was hard to get through the rest of dinner without staring. Luther didn't seem to mind, and every time he caught Josiah staring, he smiled softly.

Josiah always smiled back.

Things got even more awkward once they were done and the kitchen was cleaned up. There was nothing else for them to do, but it was too early to go to bed, at least to sleep. Josiah wouldn't mind dragging Luther to his bedroom for other reasons, and he suspected Luther would be agreeable, but he wasn't sure he had the guts to do anything.

They each sat on one side of the couch, and he turned on the TV, looking for something they could watch. He eventually settled on a movie, even though he had no idea what it was about or even if he'd already seen it.

Time passed. Josiah couldn't tell how long, but it was almost painful. He hated how he and Luther were together right now. Ever since they'd started spending time together, they'd been natural. Becoming friends had felt like the easiest thing in the world, and Josiah wanted to go back to that.

He wanted so much more, too.

He was pretty sure Luther wouldn't say no, and maybe it

was time to face it, even if he did. Josiah wouldn't know one way or another if he didn't try, and Luther wouldn't be around forever. If Josiah wanted to find out, he was going to have to take this step and get over his fear. He wasn't used to doing anything like that, but maybe it could be part of the new Josiah.

He was an alpha. He was a man, a carrier.

He was in love with Luther, and he wanted more than just sitting on the same couch while watching a movie.

He twisted on himself and reached for Luther, startled to see Luther doing the same. They both stopped moving, and this time, Josiah was the first to move again. He scrambled onto his knees and toward Luther, and when he got there, Luther welcomed him with open arms, wrapping them around him and pulling him into his lap.

They kissed without saying anything, without talking about it. Josiah was relieved. There would be time to talk later, but for now, he wanted to feel Luther and just think about him and what they were doing.

Josiah's lips collide with Luther's. It was painful but also easy to ignore as they kissed.

Luther gentled the kiss, but the passion was still there. There was no need to rush. Luther wasn't going anywhere, not tonight.

But soon he would, and remembering that made Josiah go faster. He reached between their bodies and grabbed the bottom of the borrowed t-shirt Luther was wearing to pull it up. Luther didn't try to stop him, so Josiah dumped his own shirt to the floor once it was off.

The first touch of their naked chests made him groan in surprise and pleasure. He'd often imagined this moment, but he hadn't thought it would be this perfect.

And it wasn't. He knew he was using too much teeth as he kissed Luther, and the position wasn't the most comfortable, but it was perfectly imperfect, just like them.

Josiah couldn't have chosen a worse man to fall in love with, but he didn't regret it, and he didn't want his feelings to change. He just wanted Luther, for however long he could have him.

Josiah thrust his hand between their bodies, trying to reach into Luther's pants. He would have succeeded if Luther hadn't caught his wrist. When Luther did, Josiah tried to pull away, but Luther shook his head and kissed him again. Then, he kissed Josiah's cheek, his jaw, his neck. "There's no rush," he murmured.

Josiah thought he knew what was going on. "There's no need to keep this slow just because I'm a virgin."

Luther leaned back, arching a brow. "Maybe I want to take things slow because I want to savor this."

"Can we savor it later? Or can you do this only once per night?" Josiah was teasing, and he was happy to see the amusement on Luther's face.

"It's true that I'm not as young as you."

This time, when Josiah reached down, Luther didn't try to stop him. Josiah leaned down and kissed him again, marveling at how different, yet similar, Luther's hard cock felt in his hand. "Don't worry. I'll make sure we can do this again once we go to bed." He had every intention of keeping that promise.

Luther's pants made it hard to do what Josiah wanted, so he pushed them down, hooking them under his balls. Luther hissed but stayed still, giving Josiah free access to his body.

Josiah took advantage of that. He explored Luther's cock, torn between looking down at it and looking at Luther's face. He alternated, needing to know if he was doing something wrong but not wanting to stop.

Luther's cock was bigger than Josiah's, and the tip leaked much more than Josiah's usually did.

Luther gave Josiah all the time he wanted to explore what he could of his body.

Josiah knew it wouldn't be enough, but that was what the rest of the night would be for. For now, Josiah was ready to come and to do it with Luther.

He let go of Luther's cock and grabbed his own, pulling it out. Then, he hesitated, unsure how to make this work. Should they both jack themselves off? Or should they do it to each other? Josiah didn't want to ask, even though Luther already knew how inexperienced he was.

Thankfully, Luther took it in hand — literally. He straightened from his slouch and wrapped one arm around Josiah while taking both their cocks with the other. Josiah's almost slipped out, so he added his own hand while he clung to Luther's shoulder with the other.

They kissed again. All of this was overwhelming, but in the best of ways, and Josiah never wanted it to stop.

The problem was that it would, and very soon. Josiah would have been embarrassed, and maybe he was a bit, but he knew Luther wouldn't care, and for once, Josiah wanted to let go.

He wanted to be free.

Josiah screwed his eyes shut and wrenched his lips away from Luther's. He threw his head back as his body trembled and he came on their stomachs and their hands, waves of pleasure pushing him almost to tears.

Luther let go of Josiah's cock and took only his. He pulled on it, and Josiah watched, fascinated. Luther's expression twisted as he came. Josiah cupped his cheek, marveling at the fact that he'd done that.

He realized anyone could do it. It was sex, nothing more. But it made him feel powerful and, at the same time, like he wanted to burrow under Luther's skin.

Instead, he leaned against him, needing to be supported.

He'd never felt so vulnerable, but for once, he wasn't afraid of it. Luther would catch him if he fell, so he closed his eyes and breathed.

CHAPTER EIGHT

Josiah was nervous. He wanted to do this, but it was the first time for him, and Luther's touch made him want to wiggle.

Luther continued kissing his way down Josiah's naked back. He stopped as he reached Josiah's ass, gently squeezing it and opening the cheeks. Josiah swallowed.

"We don't have to do this if you don't want to or if you're not ready," Luther murmured against Josiah's skin.

"I want to. I'm just nervous."

"Remember that you just have to say the word, and I'll stop."

"I know." That was one of the reasons Josiah wanted to do this with Luther.

Since they'd first kissed the other day, they'd been spending as much time together as possible. It meant a lot of kissing and sex, but this was the first time Josiah was going to let Luther fuck him. He wanted it, more than anything he could think of, but that didn't mean he wasn't nervous. He would be nervous with anyone. It was his first time, and he realized that wanting it to be perfect was stupid. That wasn't what he expected. He just wasn't sure *what* to expect, which made him anxious.

Luther kissed one of Josiah's ass cheeks, then the other. He'd already stretched him, driving him crazy as he did so, and Josiah had been able to forget what was about to happen until now. It had been easy to allow Luther to play with his body, to drive him wild with need. The need was still there, under his skin, making him want to be filled. It was a strange sensation he wasn't used to, and he couldn't help but wonder if things would be different if he was with someone else.

He was falling in love with Luther. He couldn't deny that, and he didn't want to. He also didn't want to think about it right now. He wanted to lose himself in Luther's body, so he wiggled his ass, hoping it was enticing.

Luther smiled against it. Josiah could feel it. Then Luther straightened, and Josiah swallowed.

"Are you sure you want to do it in this position?" Luther asked. He was still stroking Josiah's skin.

"I'm sure." On all fours maybe wasn't the perfect first time when you were in love with the person you were with, but Josiah was afraid of what Luther would see in his expression if they were face to face. He wanted to be able to hide it, whatever happened. Besides, he didn't mind feeling like Luther was in power. He wasn't enjoying being in charge, at least not in the bedroom—not all the time. He had enough of that in his role as alpha.

"All right." Luther kissed the middle of Josiah's back.

He didn't ask Josiah if he was sure again. Instead, Josiah felt him move, then something hard pushed against his entrance. He sucked in a breath, but Luther didn't push in like Josiah expected him to. Instead, he continued stroking Josiah's body, softly talking to him until Josiah relaxed. Only then did Luther push in, and even though it hurt, Josiah was happy.

Luther was the perfect person to do this with. Josiah would never regret his first time, and hopefully, once the pain of Luther leaving softened, he would remember it fondly.

Josiah forced himself to relax. It was the strangest feeling ever, having something in his ass, and he had to resist the urge to push out. Once Luther started moving, that disappeared, too. Luther was gentle but firm, and like always, his main focus was Josiah. He reached under Josiah, grabbing his cock and jacking him off as he fucked him. It was overwhelming, a sensation Josiah wasn't sure he could ever get used to. He didn't want to, not unless he was with Luther.

He pushed those thoughts away for now. Luther was here. Today, he wasn't going anywhere, and neither would he tomorrow. That had to be enough.

But no matter how many times Josiah told himself that, he knew it wasn't. He wanted Luther to be with him, and he was, but it wouldn't be forever.

Josiah pushed those thoughts away and focused on what was happening to his body. He hadn't thought this could possibly be pleasurable, but he'd been wrong. Luther had already found his prostate, and he was pegging it almost every time he pushed inside of him. The onslaught of pleasure was driving Josiah crazy, and he screwed his eyes shut, focusing only on that. It was a push and pull on his body, and the next time Luther thrust inside him, he came.

Everything was easy after that. He was pretty sure Luther had come, too, but he was still inside of him, and when Josiah slipped down to the mattress, Luther followed him. He laid on top of Josiah like a blanket as if trying to protect him, and Josiah didn't want him to move.

Luther kissed the side of Josiah's neck. "Are you okay?" Luther murmured.

"I'm not sure. Ask me once my legs stop shaking."

Luther chuckled. "As long as you're not in pain."

"I'm not."

Now that they'd both come, the sensation of still having Luther inside of him was even stranger, but Josiah didn't hate it. He couldn't help but imagine what might happen if they stayed this way until they were both ready for round two. He knew that wasn't possible, not since Luther was wearing a condom, but he yearned for it.

A knock on the front door made both of them jerk. Josiah

screwed his eyes shut and sighed heavily. "Do I really have to answer?"

Luther moved behind him, and he finally slipped out. "Dammit."

Josiah rolled to his back and looked up at Luther. "What's wrong?"

"I didn't hold the condom well when I pulled out. It spilled."

"We can change the sheets. It won't be a problem." Josiah set up. There was another knock, and he huffed. "I have to take care of this."

Luther looked worried, but he nodded. "Of course. Get dressed. I'll be right with you."

Because as long as Luther was here, he wouldn't let Josiah face any band member on his own. After what had happened, he wasn't ready for that, and neither was Josiah.

A few days after the band had scared Josiah enough to send him and Luther running into the forest, Josiah had called for a band meeting. Only two people had come, which meant that Josiah had needed to go knock on doors to talk to everyone. Most band members hadn't opened, and he wasn't sure how to deal with that. Right now, he didn't want to, but someone was knocking on his door, which was probably important. Hopefully, it wasn't just someone wanting to insult him.

He quickly dressed and went downstairs before Luther was ready. He wasn't far behind, though, and Josiah waited for him at the front door. Once Luther was there, he nodded, and Josiah threw open the door.

A man was standing on his porch. Josiah didn't think he'd ever met him, and he cocked his head, frowning. He couldn't even tell if this guy was a coyote, which was a problem since he was the coyote alpha. "Yes?" he asked.

To his surprise, the man smiled. "You look like your mother."

That wasn't something Josiah heard every day, or ever. "You know my mother?"

"I knew her once. It's been a long time since I last talked to her."

"Well, she doesn't live here if you're looking for her."

"I'm not. I was looking for you, Josiah. Or should I call you Alpha?"

Josiah sighed. "I've stopped hoping anyone would call me that, so no. You don't have to." He hesitated. "Are you a coyote?" He sounded too nice to be one, but Josiah could hope.

"I am. I heard you were looking for me. My name is Stephen Wright."

Josiah's eyes widened. "Stephen Wright?"

"You can call me Stephen."

"I was looking for you, yes. I didn't think I would ever find you. I was starting to think you were a ghost or that you'd never existed."

"Well, I'm here, and I'm ready to help."

That was the best thing Josiah had heard today. That, and Luther's laughter, but the circumstances had been very different. Josiah stepped to the side and waved Stephen in. "Come in. We probably shouldn't be talking about this on the porch."

Luther didn't belong in this conversation, but he wasn't going anywhere. He didn't want to leave Josiah on his own, especially with someone neither of them knew. It was odd not to be in charge, though. He was used to that with his team, but this was Josiah's game. The only thing Luther could do was be by his side if he needed him, so he followed Josiah and Stephen to the kitchen.

He didn't miss the way Stephen kept peeking at him, but thankfully, Stephen didn't ask who he was. He probably already knew. He also didn't have to ask what Luther was doing here. It was kind of obvious to anyone who had eyes.

Luther was wearing sweatpants and a t-shirt, and his feet were bare. He'd washed his face, but he doubted there was much he could do for his hair. Josiah's was even worse. Luther's hair was short enough that the fact that Josiah had been running his fingers through it until five minutes ago might not be obvious, but Josiah's hair was longer. It stuck out all over the place, which Luther had tried telling him before he went downstairs. But Josiah had been in a rush, and Luther hadn't managed. He wasn't sure if he was pleased about it or not. He doubted Josiah would enjoy Stephen knowing what he and Luther had been up to until a few minutes ago.

"Do you want something to drink?" Josiah asked.

"Coffee, if you have it. Water if you don't. Don't bother making a pot just for me."

"There's one ready, although I'm not sure how warm it is."

"Let's see."

Josiah filled a mug and placed it in front of Stephen, who sat at the table. When Josiah looked at Luther, Luther shook his head. He didn't want coffee. He wanted to know what Stephen was doing here.

Josiah didn't take anything to drink, either, and sat in front of Stephen. Luther moved until he was behind Josiah, close enough but not too close.

"I'm listening," Josiah said.

Stephen took a sip of his coffee and nodded. "Like I said, I heard you were looking for me."

"I've been looking for you for a while. Where were you?"

"I live deeper in the forest. It's pretty isolated, and I don't come back often, especially after the mess that happened with your brother. I didn't want to know what was going on with the band, not yet. I expected the council to tear us apart, to be honest. I was surprised when someone told me that you were the alpha."

"Because I'm a carrier."

"In part, yes."

"And the other part is?"

"I know your father and your brother were abusing you. I didn't expect you to want to be the alpha."

"I never did. I just couldn't say no to the council." Josiah snorted softly. "Although maybe I should have. I'm pretty sure anyone else would have done a better job."

"I talked to a few people, and I know things aren't easy for you. You still don't have a beta?"

"I don't, and that's why I was looking for you. I remember you talking to my mother. You wanted her to take me and run away from my father."

Stephen grimaced. "I did. I was in love with her at the time, and I hated how your father treated her and you. I wanted to help, but she refused. I don't blame her, not knowing what your father would have done if he found out. That's when I retreated. I didn't want to have to watch him abuse you and your mother the way he was. It was a coward's way out, and I regret it, but I'm ready to do anything I can to atone."

"Does that include becoming my beta?"

Stephen hesitated. "I've never thought about doing anything like that."

"And I never thought about becoming the alpha until I was asked. I can't force you to say yes, but I would like you to. I don't trust anyone in the band. Things are getting out of control, and I need someone the band will listen to. Unfortunately, that's not me. If things continue this way, the council will have to step in. Either they will assign us a beta who's not a coyote, or they'll use force. No one wants that, yet no one wants me as the alpha, either."

Stephen slowly nodded. "I see." He looked at Luther again, but he didn't ask about him. "I can't promise the band will listen to me, either. I kept myself isolated for a long time.

Some of them might not even remember me."

"But you're a coyote, and you're not a carrier. I'm pretty sure that's the only thing they need to allow you to take charge."

"It won't solve the problem they have with you."

"I don't expect it to. I just need for something to happen before this becomes a disaster. I can deal with the band disrespecting me and hating me as long as the council doesn't have to step in. I can work on that later."

Stephen stared at Josiah for a moment.

Luther almost expected him to insult Josiah or say that it wasn't surprising that Josiah couldn't do this since he was a carrier. Since he'd arrived in the forest, he'd been told several times that carriers weren't men the way they should be. For a lot of people, they were nothing more than incubators, and it made Luther angry. He was ready to hit anyone, including Stephen, if they even mentioned something like that to Josiah.

"I think it can be done," Stephen said slowly. "It's good that as the alpha, you have good relationships with other alphas and the council. You can take care of that while I'll take care of the band. It won't work forever, but for a start, it could have been worse."

"I don't see how," Josiah said.

"I'm sorry I wasn't here for you when you needed me."

Josiah shook his head. "I never expected you to be. I don't know you, and you don't know me. As long as you're ready to help me now, you don't have to apologize for anything."

"That's why I'm here. To help you and get to know you."

Josiah leaned back in his chair. "You said you've been living isolated in the forest. Where? What do you know about the situation in the band and the forest in general?"

"Quite a lot. My cabin is close to bat and weasel territories. I have several friends in both groups, and they've been keeping me up to date with what was happening. They didn't know you were looking for me, though. Only a coyote would have, and I haven't talked to any of them in a long time. I was getting everything I needed from the bats and weasels."

Josiah slowly nodded. He looked stunned, which wasn't a surprise considering everything that was happening.

He'd been looking for a beta, and it looked like he'd finally found one. Hopefully, that would mean he was safer than he'd been until now. Luther had been doing his best to stick close by in case Josiah needed him, but he had a job to do, and he still hadn't found a way to stay in the forest, not a legal one anyway. He wouldn't be allowed to be here for Josiah forever, and he would rest better if he knew Josiah was safe and had someone on his side.

Luther wasn't sure he fully trusted Stephen yet, but there was no other option. Stephen looked like a nice enough man—in his early forties, maybe—with dark hair that was starting to turn white at the temples. His eyes were a startling blue, and for someone who had lived alone for years, he appeared rational enough. He was talking like he truly wanted to help Josiah, and Luther hoped that was the case. Josiah couldn't afford to say no to Stephen's offer, and Stephen had to know it.

"You have to move back if you want to be my beta," Josiah said.

"I realize that," Stephen answered. "I can't say I'm looking forward to it, but I'll do it if I have to. I should have been here for you a long time ago, Josiah. I might be late, but I'm here now."

Josiah didn't know if he could trust Stephen, but he wanted to, desperately. It wasn't even that he needed a beta. He wanted someone in the band that he knew he could trust with his life, and hopefully, that someone would be Stephen.

Josiah needed help, and he hoped that with Stephen by his side, he would have more time with Luther. The time they had together was short, and every day they saw each other, Josiah expected Luther to tell him he was going home. Josiah wanted to be with him more than anything, but he had to dedicate a lot of his time to the band, even though they didn't deserve it. But Josiah had agreed to do this, and he wanted to do it the right way, even if it took him away from the man he loved.

Now he wouldn't have to think about the band anymore. He would let Stephen take care of it, and while he would have to be the one who made the decisions and to talk with Stephen every day, knowing he wasn't alone anymore was a relief. Knowing he wouldn't have to obsess over the band and what was going to happen to them was, too.

He realized that spending more time with Luther probably wasn't the best idea. He was already falling in love with him, and he would only fall harder as time passed. It was something he would have to deal with when Luther went home, though. He wasn't ready to take time away from them now because of that.

"What do you think the band's reaction to you working with me will be?" he asked Stephen.

Josiah had been looking for Stephen, hoping that since he'd been his mother's friend, he would agree to help, but he hadn't expected Stephen to be so isolated from the band. Would they follow his lead and obey his orders? Would they even recognize him? Josiah supposed that for the band, anyone would be better than him as the alpha, especially if it was a normal man.

Stephen wrapped his fingers around his mug. "I had good relationships with most of the band before I left. I'm not sure what they'll think of me now, but I have hope. Several people noticed me as I walked here, and your neighbor even stopped to talk to me. She seemed happy to see me."

"Betty would be happy to see anyone but me," Josiah grumbled.

"I understand she's the reason you were almost attacked a few days ago?"

Josiah sucked in a breath. He didn't want to talk about that, but if Stephen was going to be his beta, he had to know everything. "I don't know if Luther and I were almost attacked, but it was a possibility. Betty noticed us together, and she made sure we knew what she thought about our relationship. Others started gathering around the house, and we were afraid they would do something stupid."

Stephen slowly nodded. He hadn't asked about Josiah's relationship with Luther yet, or even who Luther was. Josiah was surprised, although maybe Betty had told Stephen about Luther.

"Whether or not they were planning on attacking you, it was irresponsible and unacceptable."

"I agree. I've been trying to talk to the band, but they refuse to obey my orders or even to come to a band meeting. I'm not sure how to deal with it, to be honest."

Stephen straightened in his chair. "I'll take care of it."

Josiah was so relieved he could have cried. He'd carried the weight of the band on his shoulders, even though the band didn't want him to. It was good to know he wasn't shouldering it alone anymore. "But I'm the alpha. I should be the one to do that," he said.

"I can't say I have experience in being a beta. I watched your father for long enough, though. He was the alpha, but he didn't do it on his own. That's what a beta is for. We take care of the everyday problems and of making sure the band runs as smoothly as possible. Your father didn't have good relationships with other alphas and an even worse one with the council, but you're different. I think that's what you should focus on. It will be important for the band and for the forest in general. I'll come to you with any big problems I have with the band, of course, and they should always be your priority, but it doesn't mean you have to deal with every small trouble."

Josiah felt he hadn't been dealing with anything, let alone small problems. This was what he'd wanted, though. He knew he couldn't do this on his own and that the band wasn't going to love him because he had Stephen by his side suddenly. What Stephen was offering was the best solution, and Josiah couldn't say he was sorry. He couldn't wait to be able to stop dealing with coyotes who looked at him like he was disgusting and who would rather have a cruel alpha than a carrier who cared.

Josiah twisted around to look at Luther. Luther wasn't the alpha mate, but Josiah trusted him. If Luther agreed that Stephen was the best person for this job, Josiah would give it to him. He trusted Luther's opinion since, after all, he was a team leader. It might be for the humans, and it might be nothing like being an alpha, but it was still more experience than Josiah had.

Luther moved closer and put a hand on Josiah's shoulder. Josiah pressed his own on top of it, and even though he hadn't told Luther he could ask questions, he didn't stop him when he did.

"How can you know the band will listen to you?"

"I can't," Stephen answered. He still didn't ask who Luther was and why he was asking questions. "I'll be honest. Most of them probably will be wary. Before I isolated myself, I didn't make it a secret that I didn't like your father or how he was guiding this band. But I spent many years away. Even if they don't like me, they probably don't hate me."

"You mean they won't hate you as much as they hate me," Josiah said.

Stephen grimaced. "We need to give them time to realize that even though you're a carrier, it doesn't make you less of a person. Once they see you're good at leading the band, they'll accept you."

"It would be easier for you to become the alpha," Luther pointed out.

"It would," Stephen agreed. "But it's not something I want to do. If I could, I'd go back to my house and stay there. I've heard enough about how the band has been behaving not to want anything to do with them. I want to do this for Josiah. He needs me, and he has my help. I'll do everything I can to respect his position as the alpha and not infringe on it. I suspect it's going to take a little time for us to find our place with each other, but it can be done. I'm sure of that."

"But you don't owe me anything. Why would you want to do this when you clearly don't wish to?" Josiah asked.

"Like I said, I was a friend of your mother's. I was in love with her, and I wanted nothing more than to protect her and you."

"I don't think she's ready for another relationship." Not after how abusive the first one had been.

"I don't expect her to be. I don't expect anything from her or you. I just want to help as much as I can."

Josiah looked at Luther again. They both knew there was only one answer to this, and Josiah was ready to give it. Still, he waited until Luther nodded at him to turn back to Stephen. "All right. Stephen, I'd like you to be my beta."

Stephen smiled. He still looked nervous, but Josiah thought that everything would be okay.

It had to be.

"And I'm happy to accept the charge. We'll make it work."

Josiah hoped Stephen was right.

CHAPTER NINE

Things were finally starting to look up. Josiah was afraid to hope more than he already was, but he couldn't deny that having Stephen in his life made it easier.

He hadn't had to deal with a rude band member since Stephen had agreed to become his beta. He didn't know if it was because the band members were avoiding him since they didn't need him, or if Stephen had talked to them and made it clear they would be punished if they stepped out of line, but he didn't care. Whatever Stephen had done, it had worked, and Josiah was finally free of the hatred.

He was still the alpha. He wouldn't be able to step down, even though some days, it was still tempting. There just wasn't anyone who could take his place. When he'd mentioned it to Stephen, the man had laughed in his face. Then he'd repeated that he'd never even wanted to be a beta, let alone an alpha. He was doing this only because Josiah needed help, and Josiah was grateful. It would have been easy for Stephen to stay in his cabin and ignore the band, but he hadn't. He'd stepped forward and was doing something he'd never wanted to do.

Pretty much like Josiah had.

Both of them were stuck because of duty, but it was starting to get easier, and Josiah could go along with that.

It hurt, though. He'd wanted the band to respect him, and they hadn't. They'd barely even looked him in the face. Yet here Stephen was, having been away from the band for years, and they respected him more than they'd ever respected

Josiah. He shouldn't have cared, but he did. The coyotes were his, and he couldn't help but wonder if they ever would get used to him being the alpha.

Josiah had years to show them that being a carrier didn't make him a bad alpha. He had years to show them that his father had been a cruel man and that he wouldn't make the same mistakes. He would never use fear to guide the band, which didn't make him weak. Hopefully, the coyotes would realize that Josiah truly only had the best for the band in mind. He didn't know what he would do if they didn't.

But that was a problem for the future. Josiah had more than enough problems right now that he couldn't afford to focus on what would come next. Stephen had the coyotes in hand. That meant that Josiah had more free time — time he could spend with Luther while Luther was still here, and that helped, too.

A knock on the door made Josiah smile. He got up from his desk and went to open it, finding Stephen there. They had a meeting planned, and he gestured at Stephen to come in. "You're the one person who doesn't have to knock, you know."

Stephen grinned. "I'm pretty sure I'm not the only one, and I don't want to walk in on something I'd rather not see."

Josiah and Stephen hadn't talked about Luther and his presence in Josiah's life. Stephen hadn't asked, and Josiah hadn't volunteered any information. Who Luther was didn't matter.

They went back to Josiah's office and sat at the desk. Josiah hoped Stephen had good news for him, but if he didn't, Josiah felt like he could face it for the first time. He wasn't alone anymore. Stephen's presence wasn't working miracles, but it was helping much more than Josiah could ever have expected.

Stephen took out his phone and unlocked it. "I have a list

of coyotes I managed to convince to work on the houses and community buildings that need it," he started.

Josiah breathed out. He'd told Stephen how much of a problem those buildings were and that he hadn't been able to convince anyone to work on them, even though it would be for the band's benefit. Stephen hadn't been happy, and Josiah understood. It was something the band members should have been eager to do since it was for them, but they'd rather go against Josiah's orders.

"That can't have been easy," Josiah commented.

"It wasn't, and believe me—I had some choice words for them. I doubt you're going to have any problem with them anymore, but if you do, come to me."

"I don't like feeling like you're my guard dog and that you have to fight my battles for me."

Stephen lowered his phone. "I think you have to choose the battles you want and can fight. You've already tried this one with the band, and you didn't win. No one is going to unless something happens. That's why I'm here."

"I know." But Josiah was sorry about all of this.

"What about the council member? Have you thought of someone?" Stephen asked.

That was Josiah's main business, but it was as hard as finding a beta had been. "The only person I can think of is my mother, but I doubt she'd want that."

To Josiah's surprise, Stephen didn't laugh in his face. "Have you talked to her about it?"

"I haven't." Josiah hadn't even talked to her about Stephen. He'd promised himself he would, and it had been important, but he hadn't been able to face her.

"Will you? Because I don't think it's such a bad idea. Unless, of course, you don't trust her."

"I'm not sure who to trust at this point." If Josiah had a choice, he would pick Luther for the role. Unfortunately, he couldn't do that, since Luther was human—and of course, since he was leaving.

Stephen leaned back in his chair. "You don't have to choose her if you're not comfortable with that, of course, but I still think you should talk to her."

"I'm aware. Everyone thinks I should talk to her."

"But you're not ready. That's entirely understandable."

Josiah closed his eyes. "I'm not angry at her. I understand that she was just as abused as I was and that she couldn't do anything for me. Trying to intervene would have made everything worse for both of us. I don't blame her, but I'm afraid that if I see her, I won't be able to stop thinking about what my father and my brother did. I don't want her to be associated with only those bad thoughts, but I can't help it."

"I doubt anyone would blame you for that."

"Not even her?" Josiah asked, looking at Stephen again.

"I don't think so. I don't know her anymore, and I haven't seen her since I came back, but if she's still the woman she was when I left, she only wants the best for you."

"Why didn't she agree with you, then?" Josiah asked before he could think about it. "When you told her that she needed to take me and run. She said no, and we stayed."

Stephen sighed. "It took me a long time to understand why she did. Try to put yourself in her shoes. What would have happened if she'd run? Who would you have run to?"

"The badgers. The bears."

"Which we both know are allies *now*. Then, though, they weren't. They're good people, but we coyotes didn't know that. Your father was the only person who had any contact with their alphas. He could tell us whatever he wanted, and we believed him. Your mother didn't have anyone to run to, and she knew what would happen if your father got the two of you back. He would have taken it out on you, and she didn't want to risk that."

Josiah had never thought about it that way. Stephen wasn't wrong. His mother hadn't had any way to know that Thomas and Morris would have helped her. She and Josiah hadn't been allowed out of coyote territory. Some days, they hadn't been allowed out of the house. It had to have been awful to have to make the decision to stay rather than run. Besides, Josiah was a carrier. If the wrong person had found them while they were on the run, it could have been a disaster.

Unfortunately, Josiah's mother had to choose two equally awful options, and she'd decided to stay. Josiah had never really blamed her, and now he did so even less. Through Stephen, he felt like he understood his mother better. He didn't know if knowing about it would help, but he wanted it to.

His mother was the only family he still had. He didn't want to lose her.

Luther didn't have much time left. He and his team had visited all the territories in the forest, and they'd talked to every alpha and the council. Everything was under control, even though Luther wasn't exactly happy at how some of the alphas behaved. That wasn't his business, unfortunately. As long as shifters weren't going to start a war between themselves or with humans, his job was done.

Hawley wasn't happy about that. He'd wanted Luther to find something that would allow him to be harsh on the forest, but Luther wasn't playing that game. He expected to get his orders to leave the forest at any moment, so he wasn't surprised when his phone rang while he was with the team. Everyone stopped talking, and he answered.

"Sir."

"I read your last report."

Hawley sounded angry. Luther didn't give a shit.

"It's not what I expected," Hawley continued.

"It's what's happening, though, sir. The forest is peaceful, and shifters are getting along, even with their differences. They're not a danger to humans. I don't think they're even a danger to each other." That wasn't quite the truth, but Hawley didn't need to know that. He would use every excuse to attack, and Luther wouldn't give him one.

"I want you to stay there."

Luther blinked. He hadn't expected that, and he wasn't sure what to think of it. "Sir?"

"Stay a bit longer, just to be sure the shifters aren't behaving because you're there. Maybe try not to be seen too much so they forget about you."

Luther was pretty sure the shifters wouldn't forget about him. Everyone in the forest was aware of his presence and his team's, and while most shifters didn't seem to mind, others were easy to anger. So far, Luther had managed to avoid a fight with those, and he hoped that would continue.

"So our orders are to stay in the forest and wait to see if anything happens?" he asked to be sure.

"I'll email you so you have it in writing, but yes. They're shifters. That means they're up to something, and you have to find out what."

Luther didn't mind staying, so he didn't argue. It would give him more time with Josiah, which was what he wanted. It would also give him more time to try to find a way to stay.

Anyone else would have gone to their superior, but he couldn't afford to go to Hawley. The man wouldn't hesitate to hold it over his head if he tried, and he wouldn't help find a solution anyway. He probably would be outraged that Luther wanted to stay. He couldn't understand that shifters were as human as he was or that anyone would want to spend time with them. His head would probably explode if he found out what Luther and Josiah were up to.

"All right, sir," Luther said. "We'll stay, then."

"And work harder. I expect results from you. You won't like it if I don't get them."

So it was time for outright threats, then. Luther wasn't surprised, but he *was* surprised that Hawley had waited for so long to make them.

The asshole hung up before Luther could add anything, but that was perfectly fine with Luther. He put his phone down and looked at the rest of his team.

They were gathered around the table. Their job was done, since they'd visited all the territories and had talked to everyone they needed to talk to, and they were at a loss. He supposed they should treat this as a vacation. They weren't going to find anything Hawley would want to hear, and Luther wasn't about to fabricate evidence that the shifters were plotting something. That meant that they were free to do what they wanted in the forest until Hawley called them home.

Hawley wouldn't like that, but that was a problem Luther would have to deal with once they were home. His team didn't have anything to do with it, and he wasn't going to burden them.

"Why does he want us to stay?" Suzanne asked.

Luther sighed. He wasn't surprised that not all his team members were happy to stay. "He doesn't believe that the shifters aren't up to something, and he wants us to find proof. He thinks that if we stay, they'll forget we're here, and they'll say or do something."

She rolled her eyes. "He's an idiot."

Normally, Luther would have said something against that, but his team was his family. Besides, he agreed. "Be that as it may, we have orders, and we'll follow them."

"What are we supposed to do, though?" Marlow asked.

"Whatever you want. I doubt you'll ever have the chance to spend time with shifters again, so maybe take advantage of that. Make friends."

Marlow snorted, but he didn't seem to hate the suggestion. "Hawley wouldn't be happy if he could hear you."

"I don't care. He wants us to fabricate evidence that the shifters are doing something they shouldn't be doing. I don't condone that, and I know none of you do, either. I'm not sure how things are going to play out, but I might have to contact someone higher up."

Luther was ready to do just that, but he wasn't looking forward to it. It was never seen in a positive light to go over your superior, even when that superior was a problem. It might also mean he would never be allowed to move into the forest, but at this point, he doubted he would anyway. He had a conscience, and he would do what it told him to do. He wouldn't be able to live with himself otherwise.

The team scattered. Luther stayed where he was, wondering if talking to Hawley's superior might help him stay in the forest. He wasn't even sure who was supposed to make that kind of decision. As far as he knew, no human had ever requested to be allowed to stay with shifters, so there probably wasn't anyone in charge of that.

"Tell me what's going on in your head," Dean asked.

Luther hadn't heard him come back. He'd disappeared, and Luther had thought he'd left. Instead, he held out a bottle of water to Luther, who took it with a smile.

"Nothing is going on," Luther tried.

"Bullshit. Don't try to lie to me, Luther. It's obvious to everyone that you've been distracted, and you're spending less time than ever with us. I understand, since we don't have work to do, but still. It's weird."

Luther sighed and leaned back in his chair. "It's not something I should talk about to you or anyone else." Hell, he hadn't even talked to Josiah about it, and he was concerned.

Luther had been afraid to mention it to Josiah because he didn't want Josiah to be hurt, but he was going to have to. He couldn't decide to stay if Josiah didn't want him. Maybe for Josiah, this was just a summer fling. Maybe he didn't love Luther the way Luther loved him.

And that would be okay. Luther realized that Josiah had never had a chance at a normal life, and he was humbled that Josiah had trusted him enough to want to be with him. He was going to have to ask, though. Luther didn't want to make a mistake just because he hadn't opened his mouth. No matter how much he might hurt, he should know what Josiah wanted, and Josiah should know what he wanted.

"How bad is it?" Dean asked, leaning closer. "Does it have to do with the shifters? Are they plotting something you haven't told Hawley about?"

"They're not plotting anything." Luther hesitated, but in the end, he wanted to talk about this. "It's Josiah. Things have become more serious than I expected."

Dean nodded. "I hoped it would be something like that."

"You hoped it would?"

"I want you to be happy. We all do. I can't say I expected you to find that with a shifter, but I don't care."

"But you understand why I've been distant. I love him, and I want to stay, but I'm not sure it's going to be possible. It's never been done, and I can't mention it to Hawley. Who am I supposed to talk to about it? And will I be allowed to stay?"

Dean's expression was enough to make Luther feel bad. "I'm afraid I don't have an answer. I wish I did. The way I see it, you might have to quit your job and sneak back in."

That was what Luther had been afraid of. If it came to that, he was ready to do it, but first he needed to be sure it was what Josiah wanted, too.

The only way to be sure was to talk to him, and the time had come to do just that.

When Josiah heard a car park in front of his house, he wasn't as nervous as usual. Things were going pretty well, and Stephen had promised he was taking care of the band. He'd kept that promise, which meant that so far, Josiah had managed to avoid having to talk to any of the band members who hated him. He wouldn't be able to hide forever, but it was a welcome reprieve.

He peeked out the window since he wasn't expecting anyone, then grinned when he saw Luther climb out of his truck. They hadn't agreed to see each other today, but Josiah was always happy to see Luther.

He couldn't help but wonder what would happen once Luther had to leave. It would hurt, that was for sure. But Josiah would deal with that when it happened and not one second sooner. He didn't want to ruin the time he and Luther still had together by thinking about the future.

He rushed to the front door, pulling it open just as Luther raised his hand to knock. Luther was startled, then he smiled when he saw him.

"Eager?" he asked.

"You know it." Josiah grabbed the collar of Luther's t-shirt and pulled him in, not caring one bit about who might see them. The entire band knew they were together. They didn't have anything to hide, and Josiah didn't want to. He never wanted to again, not after what he'd gone through with his father.

Josiah was who he was. He was an alpha, a carrier, and in love with Luther. If anyone didn't like that, they could go fuck themselves.

Josiah slammed the door shut behind Luther and kissed him. Luther made a surprised sound, but his hands flew to Josiah's waist, and he pulled him closer. They kissed, frantically at first, then more slowly. It was always like this. Josiah missed Luther when Luther wasn't with him, and he was at his happiest when Luther was. That was going to be a problem, but not now.

When they stopped kissing, Luther looked pleased. "I didn't expect this kind of welcome."

"I didn't know you were going to come around today."

Luther smiled gently and kissed Josiah's nose. "How could I resist seeing you? I miss you when you're not with me."

Josiah was surprised that Luther was admitting it. Luther wasn't one of those guys who didn't want to talk about feelings, but he also wasn't exactly open with them. They hadn't told each other they were in love or anything like that, but Luther knew how Josiah felt, and he suspected he knew how Luther felt, too.

Not that their feelings would change anything when it was time for Luther to go home.

Josiah shook himself and smiled. "I miss you, too."

Now that they'd said hello, Josiah looked closer at Luther. There was no ignoring the tense set of Luther's jaw or the way he was looking at Josiah in the eyes. Something had happened, and Josiah could think of only one thing.

His mouth went dry. He was afraid to ask, afraid that if he did and Luther answered, it would become a reality. He'd promised himself he wouldn't back down at hardships, though, and this situation wasn't any different.

"You had a call with your superior?" he asked. He tried to step away, but he couldn't make his feet move.

Luther grimaced. "I did. He ordered us to stick around for a bit longer."

Josiah blinked. That wasn't what he'd expected to hear. "Why? Your work is done, isn't it?" They hadn't talked about that, either, but Josiah knew enough people in the forest to be aware that Luther and his team had talked to every alpha and visited every territory. That was why they were here, so having them stay for longer didn't make sense.

"He's convinced you guys are doing something, and he wants me and my team to catch you at it. That way, he'll have a reason to punish the forest or to imprison you. I'm not sure what his plans are, to be honest. I just know they're bad. I'm going to have to talk to the council about it. They should know something is going on."

Luther frowned.

Josiah gestured toward the kitchen, and Luther followed him there. "Why would your boss want to punish us? What did we do to him?"

"As far as I can see, you exist, and that's enough for him to be angry. He's one of those bigots who think shifters are no more than animals."

Josiah grimaced. He didn't know anyone like that. He'd never left the forest, and everyone here was a shifter. He'd visited the Internet enough times to know that those people were definitely out there, though. He wasn't even entirely surprised that Luther's boss was one of them. "What did you tell him?"

"That we'll stay, of course. I can't go against a direct order."

"Not even if he asks you to create proof that we're bad people?"

Luther stood up straighter. "I would never do anything like that."

That wasn't what Josiah had intended to imply. "I know you wouldn't. But what would your alternatives be? You just said you can't go against a direct order. What will you do if he gives it to you?"

Luther sighed and sat on one of the chairs. "I'm not sure. I've been thinking about it. And the only way I can see out of this is talking to his superior. That's not going to be easy, and people aren't going to like it."

"And you care about what people think." Josiah could

understand that.

Luther rubbed his face. "Some people, sure. I don't care about Hawley, and I wouldn't hate seeing his ass in jail for attempting to do whatever he's doing. But a lot of people would have a problem with me going over his head to talk to his boss. It could mean I'd have to quit my job."

Josiah sucked in a breath. He sat in front of Luther, his mind going nuts.

Luther had been the one to tell him he didn't have a lot in his life except for his job. He had his family, but he wasn't close to any of them. What would happen if he quit his job? He wouldn't have a reason to stay in the city anymore, although, of course, he also didn't have a reason to move to the forest. Josiah hadn't allowed himself to think about that, but now, he did.

He wanted Luther to stay.

He didn't know if what they had could be permanent, but he knew himself. He was falling in love with Luther, and if Luther had a way to stay, they could be together. Neither of them had mentioned it, and maybe it was time to. Josiah didn't think it was his place, but since Luther wasn't saying anything, he was going to have to be the one to take that step. "What would you do if you had to quit your job?" he asked softly.

"I don't know. I've never thought about quitting my job, because it's not something I could see myself doing."

"Even now?"

Luther stared at Josiah for what felt like an eternity. "I've been thinking about it recently," he said slowly.

Josiah told himself not to hope, not yet. "Have you reached a conclusion?"

Luther swallowed loudly. "Maybe. I realized that while I love my job, it's not what it used to be. I don't enjoy being sent around the way I have been, especially for this kind of job. It's not right, and it shouldn't be allowed."

"You could try changing things from the inside."

"I could, but it's not my job. Other people should realize what's going on and take the needed steps to fix it."

"You would be good at it, though." And whoever his boss's boss was, they would be fools not to ask him to stay.

Luther was a good man. He was nothing like Josiah had expected from a human, and Josiah would be destroyed when Luther went home. He had no idea if there was a way for Luther to stay, but he knew that he wanted to find it if there was. He wanted Luther to want it as much as he did.

Josiah licked his lips. "I want you to stay," he said.

Those were the words Luther had been yearning to hear, but he was still cautious. "And I *am* staying, at least for now," he said.

Josiah shook his head. "That's not what I meant. I want you to stay here permanently, with me, in the forest."

Luther felt like he was having a heart attack. His heart felt like it was about to beat out of his chest, possibly right into Josiah's, where it belonged. Because Josiah had his heart, and Luther didn't think that would ever change, even if he had to leave.

But Josiah was telling him he didn't want him to. He was telling him that if Luther wanted to stay, Josiah would welcome him.

Luther swallowed. "That's what I want, too."

Josiah opened his mouth, then snapped it shut. A moment later, he scrambled out of his chair and threw himself against Luther, who caught him. Luther cradled Josiah, even though Josiah was taller, and they kissed.

It felt like coming home. It felt like a promise, like one of those warm summer days in which you knew everything would be okay. Luther had no idea if that would be the case, but Josiah wanted him to stay, and for now, it was all he needed.

When they stopped kissing, Josiah leaned back. "I wasn't sure you'd want the same thing," he whispered.

"I've been forcing myself not to mention anything in case you weren't ready. I'm your first relationship, and I didn't want to put all of this on your shoulders too soon."

Josiah swatted at Luther's chest. "Well, next time, put it on my shoulders. I don't mind, and if we're going to be together, we have to act like it."

Luther was properly chastised. "I promise I won't keep anything important from you again."

Josiah nodded. "See that you don't." He paused. "You think it's at all possible?"

This was the part of the conversation Luther hadn't been looking forward to. "I don't think it will be if I want to keep my job. I've been trying to find a solution and a way around Hawley, but I haven't been able to think of anything. I'm not even sure who I'd have to talk to in order to be allowed to stay."

Josiah's shoulders slumped. "I should have known it was too good to be true."

Luther never wanted Josiah to be in pain. "That doesn't mean there isn't another way," he started.

"How?" Josiah interrupted. "I'm not trying to be an asshole here. I just don't want to hope if there is no reason to."

"I haven't gone through all the details yet, but one of my team members mentioned it earlier, and I've been giving it some thought." Luther's mouth was dry. He might not have stopped thinking about this since he and Josiah got together, but it didn't mean it was easy to say out loud. It felt like it was becoming too real, and it was scary. "I think the best way to do this would be for me to quit my job, then sneak back into the forest. I don't think anyone would think about trying to find me here. Besides, no one would have a reason to once I quit."

"What about your family? You wouldn't be able to visit them if you were stuck here with us."

Luther sighed. "I love them. They're my family, and I'll miss them. But I don't think I see them enough to need to consider them in this case. Besides, I could still call them."

"I don't want to separate you from them."

"You're not. I'm the one who'll have to decide, and I've thought about this enough. I know what I'm doing, even though I'm still not sure how I'm doing it yet."

That made Josiah chuckle. "You really want to find a way."

"I do. It's a relief to know that you want me to stay, too."

"How could I not? I'm not giving up what we have, and I'll have to if you leave."

Luther swallowed. "What would I do if I stayed? I'm not a shifter. I don't belong anywhere in the forest." Although he supposed he could stay in Northwood, where a lot of shifters lived. Them being there meant they weren't part of any shifter group, not even the one they'd been born in. It would probably be the easiest place for Luther stay.

"You could stay in Northwood, at least in the beginning." Josiah sounded hesitant. "Although I have to admit I don't like having you out of my sight for long."

"Afraid I'll sneak out and you'll never see me?"

"No. You wouldn't do something like that, and I'm relieved that Northwood is so close to coyote territory."

In fact, Northwood bordered with coyote territory, which was how Luther had been spending so much time with Josiah. The town was right smack in the middle of coyote, bear, badger, and bobcat territory. There was another, smaller town further away, and while Luther had gone through it a few times on his way to porcupine and skunk territory, he hadn't stayed there for any length of time.

Josiah sighed and pressed his cheek against Luther's shoulder. "I want you to stay here, with me. I know it's probably too soon and that it would be too complicated."

Luther wanted to deny it, but he couldn't. It would be a lie, and they would both be aware of it.

He ran a hand down Josiah's back. "I think that the best way to do this would be for me to stay in Northwood in the beginning. It would give us time to be together, and hopefully, for the band to get used to the idea of having me around. And of course, you have to decide how to do things with them. I can't be your alpha mate, which might be a problem."

Josiah straightened. "Why would it be a problem? And why couldn't you be an alpha mate?"

"Because I'm not a shifter."

"So? Until now, a carrier couldn't be an alpha. Things are changing. Even though some days, I think it's too slow."

"So if the two of us stay together, you'd want me to become your alpha mate?" Luther hadn't been able to avoid thinking about that, but he hadn't given it much thought. It was too strange, like it couldn't fit in his life.

Josiah nodded. "Not anytime soon. I don't think the band is ready for that, and I'm not sure the other shifters in the forest are, either. But one day, I would like that. If you're okay with it, of course."

"I wouldn't know where to start."

"And I didn't know where to start when I had to become the alpha. It's not something you have to figure out now or on your own. We're in this together."

Luther couldn't stop himself from smiling. "We are." And it felt good.

Luther had no idea what would happen to them, but he knew what he wanted. Apparently, Josiah felt the same, which gave Luther hope. It also felt good to have a plan. It was still nebulous, and he had no idea if it could work, but he would find out soon enough.

And he would find out with Josiah.

Because this was real. Luther loved Josiah, and he was pretty sure Josiah loved him. That was a conversation they needed to have before he quit his job and moved, but for now, this was perfect. Luther had never felt happy the way he was now, cradling Josiah in his arms, finally at peace.

He was still worried. Hawley wouldn't stop at anything to get what he wanted, and while Luther wasn't sure what that was, it had to do with the shifters in the forest. If he couldn't get it through Luther, he would find another way, and Luther had no doubt he would manage eventually. If Luther wanted to be sure Josiah and the others were safe, he would have to take Hawley down before he quit.

He could think about that later. For now, he wanted to focus on Josiah. This could be what his future would be like every day, and suddenly, he couldn't wait to see what happened next. He wasn't afraid anymore, not as long as Josiah was with him."

CHAPTER TEN

Josiah retched into the toilet, his stomach feeling like it was turning itself inside out. He was surprised there was so much for him to throw up, since this was already the third time this morning. Apparently, he *really* didn't like the smell of coffee these days.

Once he was done, he sat on the floor and leaned against the cupboard under the sink. He closed his eyes and tried to take a deep breath, but he couldn't, and it had nothing to do with him being ill.

It could be something he'd eaten. Although he couldn't think of anything that could have been bad enough to have these consequences, it would make sense.

The only other explanation terrified him, and he didn't want to think about it.

He took a deep breath. He was done hiding from what he feared, and that included this situation. The reason he was throwing up could be something he'd eaten, but he could also be pregnant.

It was something he'd always had to live with. Carriers could get pregnant, and there was no way to avoid that if he was having sex. And he was—a lot. He and Luther had been careful, though. Luther always wore a condom, and Josiah hadn't thought this would be an issue.

He bit his lower lip and opened his eyes. He needed to use some mouthwash, and then to find an answer. He didn't have a pregnancy test, and while he could go buy one in Northwood, with his luck, he would stumble on someone he knew, and he would have to give them an explanation. There was nothing worse he could think about right now.

Josiah got to his feet, his knees weak. He might not be pregnant. Maybe he should keep this to himself for a bit and see what happened. Ignoring the problem wouldn't make it go away unless he was sick. Maybe that was how he should do this — wait a week or two and see what happened. If he didn't get better, he would take a pregnancy test. If he did, it would have been nothing, and he would be relieved.

The thought made him pause. He looked down at his stomach, trying to imagine how it would be and feel if it were stretched with a child. Part of him would be delighted. He'd known he could get pregnant for years, but until now, it hadn't really hit him that he could have *children* with Luther. There was no one more perfect to have kids with, and if that was what had happened, Josiah would be happy.

But it would also bring so many complications that he wouldn't know how to deal with.

He was still the coyote alpha. Having Stephen by his side made things easier, but that didn't mean they were easy. The band still didn't like him being in control, and while they'd calmed down a lot and had stopped insulting him to his face, he wasn't stupid. He knew they trusted Stephen more than they trusted him, and that wasn't going to change anytime soon. Maybe they would be able to get over the fact that he was a carrier eventually, but not if he was pregnant.

If he was pregnant, the proof that he was a carrier would be there for everyone to see. The coyotes would use it as a reason not to obey his orders, and he didn't want to deal with that.

He would have to, eventually. Even if he waited ten years to have a child, even if the coyotes respected him by then, some of them would have a problem with him having a baby. It might be easier in the future, but it also might not. There was no way for Josiah to know the future, and frankly, he didn't want to. It scared him too much.

But if he was pregnant, he wasn't giving up his baby, not for anyone, and especially not for the band. He'd done everything he could to help them, even when they'd rejected him. He wouldn't give this up, too. For once, he was going to be selfish.

That was what he was doing with Luther. Josiah realized that not being with a human would probably have made things easier with the band, but he hadn't been willing to give that up. He was in love with Luther, and after what his father and his brother had done to him, he deserved a bit of happiness.

The same went for this baby, if there was one. Josiah couldn't say he'd been planning on this happening or that he'd expected it, but life was unexpected. It had dumped Luther into Josiah's lap when Josiah hadn't thought his life could change, and maybe this baby was the same.

If Josiah was pregnant, of course.

There was only one way to be sure of that, but he'd already decided he would wait. If he was pregnant, he wasn't far along, and there was time. Not seeing a healer right away wouldn't hurt him or the baby.

He sighed and washed his face, drinking some water and spitting it out before reaching for the mouthwash.

Being pregnant would complicate everything, and not just when it came to the band. They wouldn't accept it, so Josiah wouldn't hold his breath for that. But what about Luther?

He and Josiah hadn't been together long, but Josiah loved him. They'd never talked about having a family, even though Luther knew it was a possibility. What would he think about Josiah being pregnant? Would he accept it, or would he run away screaming?

This was too much for Josiah to deal with right now. He

couldn't make any decision until he knew for sure what was happening, and he wasn't going to anytime soon. Maybe the best thing he could do for now was to forget about it and focus on his work and on his relationship.

Besides, Luther wasn't even sure he'd be able to stay. They'd talked about him quitting his job, but he hadn't done it yet, and even though Josiah understood why, he was starting to doubt.

Luther wanted to try to neutralize his superior before he quit, but Josiah wasn't sure he could. He was taking on a lot, including things he shouldn't be the one to deal with. He was only one human, and it wasn't his job to protect the forest and its shifters.

Josiah wasn't sure anyone else could, though.

He sighed again. All of this was confusing and made him want to go to his bedroom and hide under the blankets. He didn't want to have to deal with any of it, but it was part of life. It was part of being an alpha. He couldn't ignore problems just because he wanted to, which meant he had to face them head-on.

Even though it scared him.

But not today. Today, he would go back to his office—and leave his coffee behind in the kitchen—and go to work. He still had to meet his mother to talk to her about the council member thing, and that thought was enough to distract him from a possible pregnancy.

They'd been talking over texts, and they'd even called each other once. It had been awkward and tense, but it was a first step Josiah was happy he'd taken. That didn't mean he could fix things with his mother or even that she would agree to become the band's council member, but that was what Josiah had to focus on for now.

Everything else would still be here later anyway. That was what problems did—they never went away, no matter how many times or how hard he wished they would.

"What do you not understand when I say that I need you to find proof they're planning something?" Hawley snapped.

Luther took a deep breath, then another because he still felt like telling the guy to fuck off or maybe throwing his phone at the wall. He would if he didn't need it. "I can't find proof if there's nothing here," he said through gritted teeth.

"I'm sure you can come up with something."

Luther sucked in a breath. "Are you telling me to *make up* a reason for the government to tighten their hold on the shifters in the forest?"

Hawley was silent for a moment. Luther was recording this conversation, and he'd recorded every conversation they'd had recently. He wasn't sure if Hawley would say something compromising, but he wasn't willing to take the chance.

It would be easy for Hawley to find a way to get Luther fired. Hell, it would be easy for him to find a way to get Luther *killed*. That was why Luther was careful, and he knew he was right to be. He wasn't willing to compromise on this, whatever Hawley might have thought about him. The idiot should have known better.

"You have to see that we need better control over them," Hawley said instead of answering Luther's question.

"I don't. The shifters are still locked in the forest. They're not going anywhere, and they're not planning on trying. They're more than happy to stay here without any contact with humans."

"Why would they want to stay there when they could have the entire world?"

Was that what Hawley thought shifters wanted? "They don't want the entire world. They want to be able to live their life as peacefully as they have until now. I won't deny that some of them would be more than happy to kill a few humans, but most of the shifters here have been accommodating and, frankly, nice. They don't have anything against humans, and they're not planning on going anywhere. I doubt they would leave even if they could."

That was how important the forest was to shifters. Luther was starting to understand it. He hadn't in the beginning, but the forest felt like home now. He was hoping he would be able to stay, although he knew hoping was pointless. Even if he decided to quit his job, he needed to do this first. He had to neutralize Hawley and make sure he would never be able to hurt the people Luther was starting to love.

He wasn't just thinking about Josiah. Josiah was the main reason Luther wanted this, of course, but there was also Nico, Josiah's best friend. There were Chris and Jacob, who had found their way back to each other and were finally happy. There was Thomas, who was one of the best men Luther had ever known.

Luther didn't want any of them to get hurt, which was what would happen if Hawley had his way.

"What about that alpha who was shot?"

Luther blinked. As far as he knew, no one had been able to find anything about the shooter. The council was still investigating, but he doubted they would tell him anything about it. "He's fine. He's already back at work as the bobcat alpha."

"That's not what I was asking." Hawley sounded angry. "Who shot him? Why? That's why I think shifters are starting a war. There's no way someone could shoot an alpha and not be punished for it."

Luther didn't know why Hawley had suddenly brought this up. He hadn't mentioned anything about it until now, and Luther was even surprised he knew about it. Luther had included it in his report, but he was pretty sure Hawley wasn't reading any of them. "It could have been personal."

"It wasn't," Hawley spat out.

"How do you know that?"

"There's no way it was. I want you to investigate that. I want you to give me a name. I don't care what name, as long as we have someone to blame for this."

"But it's none of our business."

"I'm making it your business. Find me a reason to intervene. I'm sure there are more than enough."

Hawley hung up without adding anything, leaving Luther to blink at his cell phone. He couldn't believe this had just happened, and he didn't know what to think of it.

Something was going on. He'd thought Hawley was just looking for a reason to take control of the shifters, but maybe he'd decided to fabricate one. Luther wouldn't put it past him, not after he'd outright asked Luther to do it.

What if that reason was a war between alphas?

Luther was still thinking about it when he went back to the living room he shared with his team. Miriam was typing on her phone, and she smiled when she saw him. He sat down next to Dean, ignoring Marlow, who was playing a video game on the TV.

His thoughts were on Hawley and the conversation they'd just had.

"I'm surprised you didn't tell him to fuck off," Dean said.

"I almost did," Luther told him. "But I was trying to get him to admit something."

Dean looked surprised. "Admit what?"

Luther hesitated, but if what he thought was true and Hawley was involved, the team deserved to know. He didn't know where Suzanne was, but he had no doubt that whatever was about to be said would be referred to her. He would do it himself if he had to.

"Hawley has been trying hard to get me to understand that he wants me to fabricate a reason for him to intervene. We all know that the shifters aren't planning on trying to escape the forest anytime soon."

Marlow snorted. "Why would they? This place is perfect. Hell, *I* want to live here, and I'm not even a shifter."

Luther agreed. "They're not doing anything they shouldn't be doing, but Hawley won't accept that. He wants more."

"And you think he wants *you* to give him that more?"

"I think that he realized a while ago I wouldn't, even though he hasn't stopped trying. You all remember when the bobcat alpha was shot, right?"

Everyone nodded. Marlow even put down the controller, which was enough to tell Luther he was taking this seriously.

"No one knows what happened or who did it," he continued. "The council has been investigating, but it doesn't make sense. The only people who would have benefited from the alpha dying are his two sons, and I don't think Nico and Chris had anything to do with it. But what if it was another alpha? What if one of them hated Chris's father enough to kill him?"

"They wouldn't have benefited from it, though," Dean pointed out.

"Exactly. The only thing that would have happened if another alpha had tried to kill him is a war between two shifter groups." And war would be enough for the government to step in, even if it was only to make sure it was restricted to the forest.

Understanding dawned in Dean's gaze. "You think Hawley was behind that?"

"I think it's possible. I don't know how he did it, but I don't think he managed to get another human in the forest, not without someone noticing. He has to be in league with at least one shifter, but I have no idea who."

"We have to find out." Dean sounded a bit panicky.

Once again, Luther wondered what was going on with him. He wanted to ask but now wasn't the right moment or place. "I agree. If this is the truth and Hawley truly is behind an attempted assassination against an alpha, it's bad." And not only for shifters.

If Hawley had done this, Luther would have to find a way to report him. He also had to make sure the shifters were safe and that no alpha was killed. The bobcat alpha was okay, but the next one might not be. If Hawley decided to take a drastic step, any of the alphas in the forest could be in danger.

And that included Josiah.

Josiah was puking again—he'd thought he would have tuna salad for lunch, but his stomach hadn't approved—when he heard the front door. There was nothing he could do, so he stayed on his knees and prayed it was Stephen. He'd have questions, but Josiah could get around them. It would be harder to do with Luther or Nico.

So, of course, when he walked out of the bathroom, Nico was waiting for him in the hallway. He took one look at Josiah's face and grimaced. "I thought I heard you throwing up in there. Are you okay?"

"I wouldn't be throwing up if I were okay."

"What happened?"

Josiah shrugged. He was still hoping he was sick, but every time he threw up because of a strong scent, he was one inch closer to believing he was pregnant. Maybe he shouldn't wait a week before taking a test, but he didn't want to admit he'd been so stupid.

No matter how many times he thought about it, he still didn't understand how this was possible. Luther would have told him if the condom had broken so it couldn't be that. It wasn't like Luther's swimmers had superpowers, either. They couldn't teleport out of the condom.

Josiah walked past Nico, headed back to the kitchen. He

regretted it when he stepped inside and saw what should have been his lunch still on the counter. His stomach lurched, and he took a step back.

Nick's eyebrows shot up as he looked from Josiah to the counter. "What's going on?" he asked slowly.

"Can you clean that up?" Josiah asked instead of answering.

Nico stared at him for a moment. "Only if you tell me what's happening."

Josiah wanted to say no, but he also wanted someone to talk to, and Nico was better than Stephen in this situation. Luther would be the best, but Josiah wasn't sure how he would feel about having a child, especially with a carrier, so he wasn't ready to bring it up. "I'll tell you as soon as I can walk into the kitchen without feeling like my stomach is flipping around."

Nico nodded and walked into the kitchen. Josiah watched him from the hallway, and he smiled when Nico opened the window after cleaning up. It wouldn't work miracles, but it was better than nothing, and when Josiah finally stepped into the kitchen, the smell of tuna was faint enough that it didn't send him running to the bathroom again.

He flopped into one of the chairs and buried his face in his hands. "I've been sick a few times in the past couple of days," he admitted.

He heard the sound of a chair moving, and when he looked up, Nico was sitting next to him. He looked worried, and he reached for Josiah's forehead. Josiah allowed him to touch it, even though he knew he didn't have a fever.

"Have you seen a healer?" Nico asked.

Josiah grimaced. "I don't want to see her. I don't trust her."

"I don't think I would trust her, either, if I was in your place. You can't do *nothing*, though."

"But I can't talk to her."

"How about a healer in Northwood? Or maybe the badgers'? I don't think Thomas would have a problem with you asking."

"I don't need a healer." Not yet anyway. He would have to see someone later in the pregnancy. He couldn't even think about talking to the coyote healer, and the next best thing as far as he was concerned was the badgers'. Arlene had been there when Seamus had given birth to Scarlett recently, and she would be there for Kari, too. That was who she had to focus on, not Josiah. Every day, Kari looked more like his stomach was about to explode, and Josiah didn't want to take Arlene's attention away from him.

"You just said you've been throwing up for several days. To me, it sounds like you need to see someone. Arlene wouldn't mind, but if you'd rather, I can talk to my father and ask our healer to talk to you."

Josiah shook his head. He trusted Arlene, but he'd never met the bobcat healer. "You know Arlene is busy with Kari. I can't take her away from him."

"It's not like the baby is going to pop out of his stomach at any second. Even if he goes into labor, she has more than enough time to take care of him. Come on, Josiah. I won't be able to stop thinking about you if I don't know you're okay."

He wouldn't let it go, and Josiah both loved and hated him for that. It was strange to have someone who cared so much about him, but it would be easier to hide what was going on if Nico didn't.

Josiah swallowed. "I think I'm pregnant," he managed to say.

Nico stared at him.

Josiah waited, sure that Nico would have something to ask. When he didn't, Josiah bit his lower lip. "Did you hear me? I think I'm pregnant."

"I heard you," Nico finally said. He was still staring. "Is

Luther the father?"

Josiah barked out a laugh. "I'm not sure if I should smack you. Of course Luther is the father. Do you think I've had sex with a lot of guys?"

Nico shook his head. "I didn't want to assume. Does he know?"

"I'm not even sure about it. I haven't taken a test or anything like that. I've just been throwing up, and I don't think it's because I'm ill."

"So you might not be pregnant."

"What are the odds, though?" Josiah looked down and put a hand on his stomach. "I'm pretty sure there's a baby in here."

"What do you think about it?" Nico sounded cautious.

"I'm happy. Terrified. Wondering what that means for the band and for Luther. He's been trying to find a way to stay with me, but we don't know if it's going to work, and if it does, how long it's going to take. He wants to stay, or at least, that's what he says."

Nico leaned back in his chair. "You think he was lying?"

"No." Luther wasn't the lying kind. "I think he truly wants to stay, for now. He might not be in love with me forever, though. What's going to happen then? Besides, we don't even know if he'll be able to stay."

"But he's trying. That has to count for something. And don't talk like he's going to realize he doesn't want you suddenly. You're a catch, and he's lucky to have you."

"Not every relationship goes well, though."

"That would be the case even if you were with a shifter. I saw the two of you together. You're in love, whatever you're trying to convince yourself of." Nico hesitated. "I realize it feels easier to keep this to yourself and wait for Luther to leave. He deserves to know, though. He's already decided to stay, so it's not like knowing you're pregnant would push him toward that. But he's the other father, and he should know that. It's the right thing to do, even if you don't want to be with him."

But Josiah wanted to be with Luther. He'd never wanted anything more, and he couldn't imagine his life without Luther, especially now that he was probably carrying Luther's baby.

But the fear froze him. When he thought about telling Luther about it, he freaked out, because even though Luther was accepting of carriers, even though he'd known that Josiah might get pregnant when he had sex with him, he probably wasn't ready for this. He might not be ready for a baby at all, but especially not with someone he barely knew.

Nico was right. Luther deserved to know about this baby, but what would telling him mean? Would he get himself in trouble trying to stay even more than he already was? For now, it would be hard if he couldn't find a way, but they would both survive it. They might try the long-distance thing for a while, then, Josiah supposed, they would drift apart. If there was a baby involved, though, Luther would do everything he could to be there for his child, even if it put him in danger.

That was the last thing Josiah wanted.

CHAPTER ELEVEN

L uther hung up the phone, trying to wrap his mind around what he'd just learned.

It paid to have friends in his job, and he was glad he had them. It meant hearing all the gossip about Hawley and what was going on, and while there was no way to know what was the truth and what might be embellished, Luther was starting to have a pretty good idea of what Hawley was plotting.

No one knew why Hawley hated shifters, but they knew he did. Luther had heard more than one account of what Hawley had said or done to shifters, so there was no denying that. It gave him a reason to want to mess with the forest and the shifters who lived here, which was what he'd been doing.

Luther rubbed his face and leaned back in his chair. He was alone in the apartment kitchen because he'd waited for his team to leave to make his calls. Since they didn't have a job to do, they'd been spending a lot of time out, hopefully making friends, or at the very least, showing shifters they weren't a danger. Northwood was the best place to do that, since the shifters there tended to be more open and welcoming.

But Luther had stayed home. He couldn't even remember how many phone calls he'd made, but it was a lot, and the beginning of a headache pounded between his eyes. He couldn't stop working. He didn't have proof of what Hawley was doing, but he knew he was right, which meant the time had come to talk to someone.

He could contact the council directly, but he wasn't sure he trusted all its members. Besides, they might not believe him.

That was why he decided to call Thomas instead.

He quickly dialed the number and waited for Thomas to answer. As he did so, he wondered if Thomas and the other shifters in the forest would want him to stay. Unfortunately, his quest to find a way to do that had gone on the back burner since he was busy with Hawley. He hadn't changed his mind, though. Now more than ever, he wanted to stay with Josiah, keep him safe and happy. Unfortunately, it would be impossible to keep him safe as long as Hawley was still around. Even right now, he was probably plotting to send his assassin to shoot at another alpha, or maybe a council member. Luther hadn't given him any of what he'd wanted, and he'd made it clear that was what would happen in this case.

"Hello?" Thomas answered.

"Hi. It's Luther."

"I know." There was humor in Thomas's voice. "I can read the screen."

"Right. I apologize."

"You don't have to. To what do I owe this pleasure?"

"I'd like to talk to you."

There was a pause before Thomas said, "That sounds serious."

"Because it is. I don't want to talk about it on the phone." Even though it would be easier, this was something to tell an alpha to his face. After all, Thomas might be in danger, and if not him, one of his sons or his friends.

Luther disliked being the bearer of bad news, but he wouldn't shy away from it.

"You can come over. It would be faster if you could explain now, but I understand you might not want that."

"I'll be there soon as I can."

It was tempting to stop in coyote territory and see Josiah, but Luther knew that he would have the hardest time leaving him if he did. Maybe once he was ready to go back to

Northwood, he would stop and visit. He and Josiah hadn't seen each other in a few days, which wasn't like them, but it also made sense. Josiah was busy with Stephen and the band, while Luther had to focus on Hawley and what he was planning.

He went over everything once again as he drove toward Thomas's house. The problem was that he only had a puzzle of information and a few guesses that could be good or bad. More information was coming, but while he waited to get it, he had to do *something*.

Thomas was waiting for him when he got there. Alex was there, too, and both of them looked worried. There were no signs of Seamus and the baby, which made Luther sad. Even though it had taken him a while to wrap his mind around the fact that Seamus had been pregnant and had given birth, there was no denying how happy both he and Alex were.

Maybe once he moved to the forest, Luther would have the occasion to visit them more often. They were starting to feel more like friends than people he needed to keep an eye on, although he wasn't sure they'd ever felt that way, to begin with. Hawley had thought Luther was the best man for the job, but Luther was starting to realize that had never been the case.

"We're listening," Thomas said once they were in his office, the door closed behind them.

Luther swallowed. "I'm going to start with what you already know. I think we need to go over everything so I'm sure you have all the information."

Thomas nodded.

"We all know that my team and I were sent to investigate the attack against the badgers. We were supposed to find out if there was a war brewing in the forest, and if it could impact the humans who live outside. If that was the case, we needed to make sure it didn't happen."

"Which, if you ask me, is a lot to ask from one team," Alex pointed out.

"I agree. I suspect that my superior didn't think about the kind of reaction we would get once we got here. He's never said it in those words, but he thinks shifters are little more than animals. If that's the case, he probably believed it would be easy for me to control you."

"That's not the case," Thomas said pointedly.

"I've always known shifters weren't animals."

"Good. It's one of the reasons I like you."

That was good to know. Luther would need all the help he could get if he wanted to stay. First, though, he had to take care of this. "So my team and I started visiting the various territories, including yours and the coyotes. As we did so, one of my team members worked with one of your council members to sabotage the mission. We took care of that and continued with our work. That's when the bobcat alpha was shot."

Thomas looked surprised. "I'm not sure what Dan has to do with this story."

"I'll get to that. The council still doesn't know what happened there, though, right?"

"Not as far as I know. They investigated both of Dan's sons, but of course, neither Nico nor Chris had anything to do with it. They cleared everyone from the clowder, but they can't investigate everyone in the forest. There are just too many people."

Luther nodded. "What would have happened if Dan had died?"

"Chris would have taken his place. Well, or Nico."

"And I suspect the clowder would have been vulnerable."

"Obviously, but they're not alone. The badgers would have helped, along with the bears. Things aren't the way they were before."

That wasn't what Luther had been going for. "And what

would have happened if another alpha had been behind the shooting?"

Thomas frowned and leaned back in his chair. "Well, depending on who the alpha was, it could have created a war."

"Exactly. I think that's what my superior is aiming for. He wanted me to find a reason to tighten his hold on the forest, or maybe to eradicate all shifters. Honestly, I'm not sure, and I don't want to find out what his final goal was. When he last called me, he told me to make up a reason for him to do that. I refused, and he started asking about the shooting. That's what made me wonder about it. I'd only ever mentioned it in my reports and maybe once on the phone, but he never showed interest in it."

"That sounds strange, if what he really wants is peace in the forest."

Luther nodded. "So I started making phone calls. I thought he had something to do with the shooting, and I'm pretty sure I'm right. I haven't been able to verify any of this yet, but I think he gave the order to have Alpha Wiley shot. I think he wanted to create a war in the forest so he'd be able to step in and intervene. His main goal is to get rid of as many shifters as possible or to control them, and he was trying to use my team and me to do that."

And that wasn't something Luther was going to tolerate.

Josiah was still queasy. He felt like he always was these days, and it wasn't a nice sensation. Every time he threw up, he wondered how long it was going to last. Hopefully, it would only be a few more weeks and not the entire length of the pregnancy like Nico had mentioned was possible. The thought was enough to terrify Josiah and make him rethink the pregnancy.

Or maybe not. He might hate throwing up with a passion,

but if it meant he would have a healthy baby, he was ready to do pretty much anything.

The problem was that the pregnancy and thoughts of Luther kept distracting him.

He was supposed to be working, but instead, he was thinking about Luther. They'd only seen each other once since Josiah had realized he was pregnant, and he missed Luther. Luther called him every day, several times a day if he found the time, and he'd told Josiah he was working on something big. Josiah understood, but that didn't make him miss Luther less.

If thoughts of a man were enough to distract him from his job, it wasn't good. Josiah was supposed to be the alpha, to think about the band instead of Luther. His father had been able to do it. His brother had, too, even though he'd gone about it the wrong way. He'd thought he would keep the band safe by attacking the badgers, and he'd failed. Or maybe he'd just wanted to kill Thomas and get rid of the badgers. Josiah wasn't sure, and he would never find out. He'd known his brother well enough to suspect what the correct answer to that question was, though.

So he was nothing like his father and his brother when it came to being the alpha. He didn't usually think that was a bad thing, but maybe, in this case, it was. How was he supposed to work if he couldn't focus?

He raked his hand through his hair and pulled at it. It stung, but it helped a bit to give him clarity.

He was never supposed to be the alpha. He was never supposed to become important to anyone, let alone the band. He didn't know how to deal with any of it, or even if there was anything he could do. He'd been doing his best, but he hadn't even managed to see his mother face to face yet. Stephen was taking care of the band, leaving the council member problem to Josiah, and he hadn't solved it.

He'd tried to talk to his mother once. He'd gotten as far as her front porch. Then he'd panicked, and he'd left. He couldn't face her, not when he didn't know if the sight of her would bring back bad memories. Thinking of her was enough to make that happen, and he could only imagine how much worse it would be if he saw her.

But he couldn't stop thinking about asking her if she wanted to be a council member. It might be good for her, too. Even though they hadn't seen each other, they'd talked several times on the phone, and he knew how much she disliked living with the band. They hated Josiah, but not just him. She'd tried to be a good wife to Josiah's father all her life, even though she'd been forced to marry him and bear his children. She hadn't wanted to give him any reason to hurt her, but the problem was that Josiah's father didn't need a reason to hurt anyone.

She'd done everything she could, but it wasn't enough for the band.

After Josiah, she was probably the most hated person here. Josiah wanted to help her, and having her as a council member would help both of them. Besides, Josiah wanted to talk to someone about his pregnancy. Nico was great, but he wasn't Josiah's mother. He and his mom might never have been as close as Josiah wished they had been, but there was a reason for that. Now that the reason was dead, maybe they could fix their relationship.

He got to his feet, wincing when the back of his chair hit the wall behind him. His main job right now was to find a council member, and he was going to. Hopefully, he would also be able to talk to his mother about his pregnancy. He was still worried he would lose what little respect he was earning as an alpha, although he wasn't sure how much of it there was. The band had calmed down, but that might only be because of Stephen, not because they were coming around to liking Josiah.

And, of course, there was Luther. There was no way for Josiah to be sure Luther would be able to stay or would actually want to once he found out that Josiah was pregnant with his child. From what Josiah knew, Luther wasn't that kind of man, but they hadn't known each other long. Maybe Josiah didn't know Luther as well as he thought. Maybe Luther had been hiding his real self from Josiah to get what he wanted.

Josiah shook his head as he walked out of the house. That was wrong, and Josiah should stop thinking about it. Luther hadn't lied to him. He was a good man, and their situation was complicated. It didn't mean either of them was a bad person.

Josiah tried to keep all of that in mind as he walked to his mother's house. That was easier than thinking that he would face her in mere seconds, and it helped him not to panic and run away. Still, by the time he was at her front door, his legs trembled and he felt like he was going to throw up. He forced himself to raise a hand to knock on the door, then, to stay where he was instead of running away.

He could hear his mother walking inside the house, her footsteps coming closer. He sucked in a breath when the door started to open, and then they were facing each other.

She looked older. Her face had more wrinkles than he remembered, and her hair had more white strands. She was still beautiful, and she looked at peace, which heightened her beauty.

Her eyes widened when she saw him, and she reached for him, only to freeze as if she expected him not to want that. He wasn't sure he did, but he still took her hand and squeezed. "Mom."

She opened her mouth, then closed it. She swallowed heavily. "Josiah. I didn't expect to see you today."

Josiah chuckled nervously. "Or ever, I'm sure. I'm sorry I treated you badly."

She shook her head. "Don't be. You had every reason to." She looked around. "Why don't you come in? I don't think either of us wants to do this on the porch."

Because someone would hear, and they would repeat it to the rest of the band. If Josiah and his mother were going to make peace, he wanted it to be private.

He followed her inside. He was relieved that seeing her hadn't made him freak out the way he'd expected, but it still wasn't easy. Like he'd thought, it brought back memories he wished he never had to think about again. The fact that she didn't live in their old house anymore helped. This place was clearly all hers, and it was different enough that Josiah found himself relaxing.

"Do you want something to drink?"

Josiah shook his head. "I have so many things to tell you that I think I should get to the point."

She sat down. "And I'm sure you have a lot of work to do."

Josiah shrugged. "Stephen has the band in hand, mostly."

"I'm sorry you had to become alpha. I know you never wanted anything like that."

"I didn't, but I'm getting used to it, at least in part. Stephen's presence has helped a lot."

She nodded. "He came to talk to me. He told me that you'd heard that conversation between us, the one where he pushed me to leave with you."

"I know why you did it. We don't have to talk about the past." Because Josiah wasn't sure that he was ready to face it.

His mother stared at him for a moment, then nodded again. "I understand. Just know that I'm here if you ever want to talk about the past. I'll answer all your questions as well as I can."

"I'm not sure I'll ever want to talk about it. It's the past, and the less I think about *them*, the better I feel." He didn't have to say who *them* was. His mother would know.

"You're not wrong there." She smiled. "Now, what did you

169

want to talk about?"

Josiah opened his mouth, and everything came tumbling out.

CHAPTER TWELVE

Something was wrong with Josiah. Luther had no idea what it was, and while he wanted to ask, he was also hesitant to do it.

If anything had happened, it probably had to do with the band, and knowing about it wasn't his business. He was only a human, while Josiah was the alpha. Luther had to respect that, and he did, but it was hard to see the man he loved so worried.

It had gotten to the point that Josiah had started to withdraw even from their relationship. He was always lost in his thoughts, but when Luther asked, Josiah brushed him off. Luther couldn't help if he didn't know what was happening, although maybe he wouldn't have been able to help even if he did. He wasn't a shifter or a coyote, and besides, he had to admit that he'd been distracted himself.

After his conversation with Thomas, he knew he had the support of the council. He wasn't quite sure what he would need that support for, but he was starting to come up with a plan.

He had to get rid of Hawley for the safety of the forest and the shifters who lived here. At the same time, he wanted to help those shifters. The best way to do that was for him to reach out to one of the people campaigning for the shifters to be free. They might not be able to force the government to do it, but it could be enough to neutralize Hawley, which was the most important thing right now.

He could admit he'd been lost in his thoughts for most of

the evening, even though he'd spent it with Josiah. It had made Josiah snappish, although Luther couldn't help but wonder if maybe that had to do with how inadequate he was. Like Josiah repeated often, he was the alpha, and he needed an alpha mate. No matter what Josiah had said about Luther becoming one, Luther doubted that would ever happen. The coyotes wouldn't accept him, but more importantly, Josiah needed someone who could truly stand by his side and support him. Luther didn't think he could do that, no matter how much he tried.

He watched Josiah, who was at the sink rinsing plates. His back was tense and his movements jerky. It wasn't like him, but then, maybe it was. It wasn't like Luther knew him that well. They were friends, and they'd been together for a few weeks now, but it wasn't enough. Luther needed more time with Josiah, and he didn't know if he would get it.

He was still planning on quitting his job and moving to the forest once all of this was over. The problem was that he didn't know when it would be or if that would ever happen. He was trying to find a way to contact Hawley's superior without Hawley finding out, and it wasn't the easiest thing to do. That was where the contacts he had with people campaigning for shifter freedom were coming in handy.

But Luther didn't want to continue thinking about that, not tonight. He got to his feet and walked closer to Josiah, wrapping his arms around him and pressing his chest against Josiah's back. Normally, Josiah would have relaxed in his hold, but this time, he tensed even more, to the point that Luther wondered if he might snap.

Luther took a step back. "Do you want help?"

Josiah turned around. "Do I look like I need help? Do you think I can't even rinse dishes on my own?"

This wasn't like Josiah, so something *had* happened. "That's not what I said," Luther said, trying to keep his calm.

Nothing would come out of fighting with Josiah, especially if they yelled at each other.

Josiah glared. "Then why did you ask if I needed help?"

"I didn't. I asked you if you *wanted* help, because I know you can do this on your own, but it doesn't mean you should have to."

"You cooked. It's only right I take care of the dishes."

It was a rule they'd come up with when they'd started eating meals together, but Luther had never intended it to be rigid. "If you're especially tired, though, I can—"

Josiah threw the sponge in the sink and turned to face Luther. "What are we doing?"

Luther frowned. "I thought it was obvious. Bickering over who should be washing the dishes."

"That's not what I'm talking about. I'm talking about us as a couple. What are we doing?"

"We're together." Luther wasn't sure what Josiah was talking about, and he was afraid to ask.

Josiah sighed and pinched the bridge of his nose. "*Should* we be? Because no matter how many times you promise that you'll move here, I don't know if it's doable. I don't know if we really can make it work."

Luther's heart ached. He wanted to be able to make promises, but he couldn't. "I want us to make it work. If things come to that, I'll quit my job."

"And what will happen if you move here? Do you think the band will accept you?"

Probably not, which would be a problem for Josiah.

Luther wanted to ask if Josiah was breaking up with him, but he didn't have the courage. He didn't want to hear those words, so instead, he said, "I don't know. It's something we both have to think about before I do anything, but there's time." He gestured at the door. "I should probably head out. It's obvious you need rest, and for some reason, my presence is irritating you."

Josiah's shoulders slumped. "I don't want you to go."

"It's okay." Luther moved closer, reaching for Josiah and breathing easier when Josiah allowed him to touch him. He kissed Josiah's forehead, then his cheek. "I can feel how tense you are, and me being here isn't helping. Go to bed. Hopefully, you'll feel better tomorrow, and we can talk then."

Because they needed to talk. Maybe giving each other space would help, or maybe it wouldn't. Luther didn't have a way to know, but he was sure of one thing.

The next time he and Josiah saw each other, something was going to happen, and Luther wasn't going to like it.

Josiah stayed still until he heard the front door close behind Luther. Then he dropped into a chair and buried his face in his hands as he tried to fight the tears prickling at his eyes.

Gosh, he was an asshole.

He didn't even know why he'd snapped at Luther the way he had. Luther had only been trying to help, but for some reason, Josiah's brain had taken that as him insinuating that Josiah was weak and couldn't even wash dishes on his own. How stupid was that? How stupid was *Josiah*?

And now Luther was gone, and Josiah would have to spend the night alone. He was getting used to it, since both he and Luther were busy, but he'd been looking forward to not having to tonight. He'd been planning on spending as much time as he could snuggled against Luther, just in case Luther eventually decided to leave permanently.

He wanted to go after Luther, but instead he stayed where he was and listened to Luther's truck driving away. Once the sound had disappeared and the forest was silent around him, Josiah allowed the tears to come out.

What was he doing? This wasn't fair to Luther. No part of

this was. Luther was human, and even though he wasn't close to his family, he shouldn't be moving to the forest. Like every other human, he had a life outside the forest, and he shouldn't give it up to end up stuck in the forest with Josiah. What would happen if something happened to his family and he wasn't able to get out of the forest?

It was too easy to imagine Luther growing resentful toward Josiah over the years –and also toward their baby. That was what scared Josiah the most. He'd been through so much hardship even as a child, and he didn't want his baby to have to go through the same thing.

Josiah tried to take a deep breath, but the only thing he managed was a strangled sound as the tears continued rolling down his cheeks. He could see one solution out of this mess, and he wished he didn't have to do it.

It was the only way out. The coyotes would never accept Luther, and Josiah couldn't ask him to have to deal with the hatred and insults, especially since Luther would have no way out. Even if Luther later decided to break up with Josiah and step away, he'd be stuck in the forest and having given up his entire life. If he knew about the baby, he would decide to stay, so Josiah wouldn't tell him he would be a father, even though Nico was right and it wouldn't be fair.

But life *wasn't* fair. Josiah had learned that a long time ago, and it continued to show him that he was right.

He didn't want to give up Luther. He didn't want to give up what they had. But it was the only thing that made sense, and he was going to have to break up with the man he loved.

Josiah would get over it. Luther was his first love, and he couldn't imagine himself being with anyone else, but he was only twenty-three. He supposed that not a lot of men would want to be with a single father, especially one who came with an entire coyote band, but that was a problem for later.

For now, Josiah had to act like an alpha, even though it was breaking his heart. Luther might not be part of his band, but Josiah wanted the best for him anyway, and that best would be for Luther to stay away from the forest and never come back. Luther would refuse to do that unless Josiah broke up with him, so that was what Josiah would do.

Not today, though. Today, Luther had left, and Josiah had no intention of doing anything on the phone. That meant he would have to wait until he and Luther saw each other again, and even though it was selfish, he was going to give himself that. He hoped he would have a last kiss, a last hug, a memory to cherish during the nights that he would feel alone.

He got up from the chair and tried to dry his eyes, but the tears kept coming down. He found himself reaching for his phone before he could think better of it, and when his mother answered, he started sobbing again.

He could hear her on the other side of the phone. "What's going on? Josiah?"

"I'm going to break up with him," Josiah said. His mother knew what he was talking about. He'd told her he was thinking about it, and while she hadn't been happy about it, she hadn't tried to stop him.

"You haven't already?" she asked.

"I couldn't, not tonight."

"Would it be okay if I came over? I don't want you to be alone."

"Please. Come." Now more than ever, Josiah needed his mother.

She'd never had been the perfect mom, but he didn't care about that. She was *his* mom, and after the conversation that they'd had, the first conversation in which they'd been honest with each other, he understood her better.

She'd been trying to protect him and herself, and they'd both been stuck. It hadn't been her fault, just like it hadn't been Josiah's. It might take some time for them to get the point where they were truly comfortable with each other, but they were working on it, and Josiah would need all the help he could find to do this.

It didn't matter that neither his mother nor Nico approved. It didn't matter that deep inside Josiah couldn't help but wonder if he was doing the right thing. His only intention was to protect Luther and their baby, and he understood better what his mother had gone through.

There hadn't been a good choice she could make. She'd had to go with the less horrible option, which had been to stay with his father. In Josiah's case, the less horrible choice was to let Luther go, and that was what he was planning on doing.

CHAPTER THIRTEEN

Luther looked around the room. He hadn't meant to do it, but he'd managed to assemble a perfect team.

There were the humans, of course. Luther's team had wanted to be involved, and Luther was proud of them. A few might not be happy to be stuck in the forest for now, but they still wanted the shifters to be safe.

Then there were the shifters. Thomas had suggested Luther talk to some of them because he might need help, and he'd agreed. Chris, Jacob, and Jacob's friend Raven had decided to work with Luther. Luther wasn't sure how he would use them, but he and his team had succeeded in keeping the forest peaceful for now. That had everything to do with Chris and Jacob, who had managed to soothe the alphas angry at having Luther and his people sticking their noses in their territories. It gave Luther hope that maybe they *could* do this, but he was always careful with his hope. It had been dashed too often, and this time wasn't any different.

"Have you heard from Hawley?" Raven asked.

Every time he mentioned Luther's superior, Raven looked like he wanted to kill someone—probably Hawley himself.

"He's been emailing, and he's running out of patience. I think that if we don't act, he's going to do something, and no one is going to like it."

"You still think he'll try killing another alpha?" Chris asked. He was understandably worried. His father had survived the shooting, and he was back at work and healthy, but seeing him in the hospital couldn't have been easy for Chris, especially after what he'd already been going through. Besides, his brother was training to be an alpha, and he wanted to protect Nico.

"I think it would be the easiest way to get a war started in the forest," Luther answered. "I could be wrong, of course, since I'm not one of you, but it would be fairly easy for him to get an alpha killed and to blame it on another alpha. Even if the proof was fake, who would check?"

"Either that, or they would accuse you guys, and that would create an entirely different problem," Jacob said. "Because if someone accused you of killing an alpha, the forest would rebel. You wouldn't make it out alive, and it would give your boss the perfect excuse to barge in and get revenge and to get everyone to believe we should be kept under lock and key."

Luther's stomach dropped. He liked Jacob's thought even less than the one about a dead alpha. If Hawley did that and tried to get Luther accused of being the killer, if he pushed the shifters to kill Luther, he would use that not only to get revenge on the forest but also as proof that shifters were animals and that they shouldn't be free to mingle with humans. If that was what he was aiming for, it would be perfect.

"What about those people who want us to be free? Have you talked to them?" Raven asked.

"I did. They've been getting me to talk to more and more people in the government, and I'm pretty sure I'll have a phone number by the end of the week. Once I do, I'll call Hawley's superior and tell him what's happening. Hopefully, he'll believe me."

"You have enough proof for him to believe you," Dean said. "You've been recording all the conversations you've had with Hawley since you started to suspect something was wrong, and I heard them. He's a nasty piece of work, and he shouldn't be in charge of any kind of shifter, not when he hates all of them as much as he does."

Luther wanted to believe Dean was right, but the problem was that he didn't know Hawley's superior. He'd never had to deal with the man, since the only person he answered to was Hawley.

That hadn't always been the case. Hawley was fairly new at this, and before him, there'd been someone else. Luther had liked his old superior, but the man had retired, and now Luther was left to deal with Hawley.

He wasn't usually one to hate people, but Hawley definitely belonged to that category. Luther would be happy if he never had to deal with him again, and he hoped that eventually, he would get to that.

"I don't understand how you guys work," Raven grumbled.

"Think of it in these terms. If you found out that someone was planning to kill an alpha, who would you contact?"

"That alpha."

"Would you be able to find their phone number, though? And if you did, would they believe you without proof?"

Raven grimaced. "You probably have a point. It doesn't mean I have to like it."

"I don't think anyone here likes any of this. I don't want the guy to brush me off when I tell him about Hawley, though, which means I need support from the right people and all the proof I can get. That's what I've been working on, and I'm pretty sure I have everything I need now." He was still surprised, although maybe he shouldn't be.

He'd always believed the people in the government thought about themselves before anyone else, and that might be the case often, but not always. Now that he'd talked to some of the people campaigning to free the shifters, he realized they truly cared. For some, it was because they had family members locked up in forests, and they wanted to see them before they died of old age. Others were just trying to do the right thing. Luther was humbled at the thought that they were including him in that. He'd never thought he would want to fight for shifter freedom, but meeting these people had changed him.

He'd always believed it wasn't right for shifters to be locked up in their forests, but he'd never realized just how wrong it was. Now, he did, and he was planning on doing everything he could to help.

He was also planning on quitting his job as soon as he was done. He didn't want to have to leave Josiah behind, and he'd already been neglecting him more than enough. Once this was over, he was moving to the forest, whatever happened. His parents wouldn't be happy, but they would learn to deal with it.

A lot of people would have to learn to deal with it.

Because if Luther truly did this, he would have to become an alpha mate. He didn't know where to start when it came to that, and he wasn't sure he wanted to find out, but he would. If he was going to be with Josiah, he would be all in. Josiah had been let down by enough people. He didn't need Luther to do it, too.

Raven pushed away from the wall. "All right. Well, let me know if anything happens. I thought this would be more exciting when I agreed to be part of this group."

Jacob barked out a laugh. "Of course you did. Not everything is about punching people, though."

"Maybe not, but if you ask me, things would be much easier if we could just get rid of Hawley and his people that way."

He wasn't wrong, and sometimes, Luther wished it was that easy, but they had to do this right. It was the only way to make it work, and even though he wasn't sure he'd be allowed to stay once it was over, he didn't want to leave destruction in his path if he could help it. The people who would come after him would need to continue the good relationships, and they would need all the help they could get. Unfortunately, that meant Luther couldn't afford to burn all his bridges.

Josiah had hoped that having a beta would help, and it did, but it hadn't worked miracles. The band still disliked him, and they made it known every time they could. Stephen was running himself ragged trying to keep them under control, and Josiah supposed he should be relieved they were mostly leaving him alone. He knew that once they found out he was pregnant, they would turn on him, and they might hurt Luther.

That was one of the reasons he needed to keep Luther away from the band. It was the reason he needed to break up with him.

Josiah rubbed his face. He wanted to hide in his office and forget about everything out there so he could focus on Luther and their baby. He hadn't told Luther about it, and he wasn't planning to do so anytime soon. It was hard to imagine raising his child on his own, but it was even harder to imagine Luther being hurt by the band or coming to resent Josiah because of the choice he'd made to stay in the forest.

"Josiah?"

Josiah jerked, his heart racing until he realized the voice belonged to Stephen and not Luther. He'd been the one to tell Stephen he could come into the house without knocking, and he didn't regret it, but he would have liked a warning.

"In the office," Josiah called out.

He listened to Stephen's footsteps coming closer. Stephen's face appeared at the door, then the rest of his body as he stepped into the office. "Am I disturbing you?"

"Not at all. Come in."

Stephen closed the door and sat on the other side of the desk. "How are you?" he asked.

Josiah wondered if he knew about the baby. Josiah had only told Nico and his mother, and while he realized he had to see a healer now that he was sure he was pregnant, he didn't feel ready to do it, not until he knew how things would go with Luther.

"I'm fine," he told Stephen even though it was far from the truth.

Stephen's frown stayed where it was. "Are you sure? Because it's obvious you've been dealing with something, and I'd like to help if I can."

"It's nothing you can help with." Or at least, Josiah didn't think so. "You could take my place," he added because he had to try.

Stephen blinked. "You mean as the alpha? We already had this conversation. We both agreed it would be best if you stayed."

"We didn't agree. You said you never wanted to be the alpha, and I didn't push. I never wanted to be the alpha, either. Why am I being forced to do it?"

"That doesn't sound like you." Stephen's voice was soft. "What's going on?"

"I'm pregnant." The words were out before Josiah could stop them, but he didn't regret them. He would have to tell Stephen eventually anyway, and the sooner he knew, the better he would prepare for the band's reaction.

"I want to congratulate you, but from your expression, I'm not sure that would be the best thing to say."

Josiah snorted. "I'm not even sure how I feel about it. I'm happy, angry, sad, and a whole lot of other emotions I don't know how to deal with. I can't stop thinking about how the band will react when they realize, though. They're going to kill Luther, and I can't afford for that to happen."

"So the human is the father."

"Of course he is. Have you seen anyone else spending time with me?" And what was it with everyone asking him that?

Stephen raised his hands. "I didn't mean to offend you. You know I never asked what kind of relationship you had with him. I just wanted to be sure before I said something stupid."

"Nothing you do or say could be stupider than what I did. I got myself pregnant, and I don't know how to deal with it."

Stephen hesitated. "I can't be the alpha in your place. Not only don't I want to, but I think you're doing a good job."

"In what world? The only thing I managed to do was convince my mother to become our council member. That's it."

"And you found me. We got the buildings that needed it repaired. The band is settling down again. That's thanks to you."

"It's thanks to *you*. You're doing all the hard work, and I'm sitting here wondering what I'm supposed to do."

Stephen's expression turned sharp. "You're not thinking about giving up the baby, are you?"

"I'm not going to ask the healer for an abortion, if that's what you're asking. I realize I'm young and that the situation is far from ideal, but I'm not giving them up. I just don't know how the band will take it except that they'll think it's a sign of my weakness. I don't think they'll allow me to stick around once they find out."

"Or maybe they will. You have nine months to convince them that you're a strong alpha, even with a child. Besides, you're not doing this alone. I don't know Luther, but I've seen the two of you together. He loves you, and I doubt that anything can push him away from you."

Josiah swallowed. "The band already thinks I'm not a good alpha. Being pregnant isn't going to change anything."

"Or maybe it will show them that you can do this even while pregnant, which is kind of the point of having a carrier alpha. You and all the other carriers have a lot to deal with, and you shouldn't also have to show everyone that you're as good at this as anyone else. You have to, though, and I'm sorry about that. It's a step forward for the band and the forest. Some people will be more ready to accept it, while others, like the band, will take more time. You can't show them that you're giving up, though."

"How can I not give up?" Josiah could hear the trembling of his voice, and he knew Stephen could, too. "I'm breaking up with Luther, so I won't even have him by my side. How am I supposed to do all of this on my own?"

Stephen looked shocked for a second. Then he smoothed out his expression. "Why are you breaking up with him?"

"Because it's for the best. We both know the band isn't going to accept my pregnancy, and I don't want them to turn on Luther. Besides, he's human. He doesn't belong in the forest with us."

"He might be able to find a way to stay."

"And what would happen if he did? He wouldn't be able to leave this place, just like we're not. He would be stuck, and it would be my fault."

"I doubt he would make the decision only because of you."

But Stephen didn't know Luther the way Josiah did. Josiah wasn't even sure he knew Luther that well. "I've already made my decision. I'll break up with him, and hopefully, he'll leave the forest soon and never come back."

Stephen hesitated. "Will you tell him about his child?"

"I want to, but I can't. It would give him one more reason to try to stay." And maybe, one more reason to resent Josiah in the end.

Neither of them had wanted this. Josiah didn't want Luther to go, but he was acting the way he should, the way an *alpha* should. Even though Luther wasn't one of his band members, Josiah would take care of him, and he would make sure Luther was happy.

In the beginning, Luther would be angry. He wouldn't understand. Once he left, though, he would soon forget about Josiah and the forest, and he would be able to continue living his life the way he'd always been supposed to.

Luther was human. No matter what he thought or how he felt, he didn't belong in the forest.

He didn't belong with Josiah.

CHAPTER FOURTEEN

Luther had hoped that when he saw Josiah again, Josiah would feel better, but Luther didn't think that was the case. If anything, Josiah looked even worse.

There were dark shadows under his eyes, and he was pale, so pale that Luther wondered if he'd been eating. He looked almost sick. Luther wanted to fret, but he didn't think Josiah would accept it. He was worried, though, and he needed to do something and to make sure Josiah was fine.

"Do the coyotes have a healer?" he asked. He'd never thought about it, but he guessed they did.

Josiah was once again rinsing the dishes, and his back went ramrod straight at Luther's question. "Why do you ask?"

Even his voice was feeble, as if he were feeling weak. "Because you're not okay. Are you sick?"

"I'm fine."

"If you don't want to talk to the coyote healer, I can take you to Northwood to the hospital. That way, no one here will know you're sick."

Luther understood why Josiah wouldn't want the coyotes to know about this. They didn't respect him as the alpha, although from what Luther had seen, things were getting better. His not wanting them to know he was ill didn't mean he shouldn't get help.

"Drop it," Josiah said slowly. He turned off the water in the sink and dried his hands. "I'm fine."

"You're obviously not. What's going on, Josiah? You wouldn't have hesitated to confide in me not too long ago.

What happened that you're keeping me at arm's length now?"

Luther was pretty sure this was the moment he'd been fearing was going to happen, but he couldn't back down. He wanted to know that Josiah was okay, and if things ended badly, he didn't care. It would hurt, but he would deal with it. What he couldn't deal with was seeing Josiah in pain.

"You shouldn't care so much," Josiah said.

Luther desperately wanted to put Josiah back together, but he didn't think there was anything he could do. Josiah was making all of the decisions here. "How can I not care? I love you. I want you to be happy and healthy."

Josiah finally looked at Luther. Unless Luther was wrong, Josiah had lost weight, and he hadn't had a lot of it to lose to begin with. Luther wanted to help, but what could he do when Josiah clearly didn't want him to?

"You shouldn't be saying that," Josiah said.

"What? That I want you happy?"

Josiah shook his head. "That you love me."

Luther sucked in a breath. "But I do."

"For now. That's going to fade, though. I'm sure that in a few years, you'll barely remember me."

That didn't sound good. "How can I not remember you if I'll be here by your side?"

"I don't think you will be," Josiah whispered. He wasn't looking at Luther anymore but rather at something beyond him. "I know you said you would try to find a way to move to the forest, but I don't think you should. Go back to your life, Luther. You're human, and you don't belong here."

Luther's heart was breaking, but he was used to not showing emotion. He would break down later. Now, he needed to focus on what Josiah was saying and to counteract his words. If there was even one chance that Josiah would stop doing this, Luther wanted to find it.

"You thought I belonged here until recently. What changed?"

Josiah opened his arms. His t-shirt hung over his body, making him look like a child wearing his father's clothes — not that Josiah would wear anything that had belonged to his father. "How can you not see it? I wanted everything to be okay, but it's not going to be. The band is still a mess. They don't accept me, and they won't accept you. If you decide to stay, things will be even worse, and I don't want you to saddle yourself with the band and me and lose everything else. Besides, I can't allow myself to rely on you."

"Why not? You relied on me until now."

Josiah's eyes narrowed. "Exactly. Maybe that's part of the reason the band hasn't accepted me."

"Because I'm human."

"Because of that, and because as the alpha, I should stand on my own two feet. Having you by my side means I can't, and they can't accept that."

"Your father was married to your mother. They never thought he was weak."

"But he wasn't a carrier. That's enough for them to think I am, and I have to show them otherwise. Being with a human isn't going to help in that regard, and I can't afford it."

"So this is it?" Luther didn't want to believe it, but he'd heard the words coming out of Josiah's lips.

Josiah was breaking up with him. He didn't want him to stay, even though they'd talked about it many times. He didn't want Luther anymore, and Luther didn't know what to do with that.

He wouldn't be one of those guys who insisted when someone broke up with him. He had no doubt that Josiah had thought about this long enough to be sure of his decision. This was what he wanted, and Luther wouldn't force him into anything. Josiah had already had enough of that in his life. He was old enough to make this decision, and Luther loved him enough to respect it, no matter how much it hurt.

He wanted to tell Josiah everything he'd been working on in the past few weeks, but he didn't have anything concrete yet. His contacts still had to get him a phone number he could use to reach Hawley's superior, and there was no way for Luther to know how the man would react once Luther talked to him. Luther might be able to save the forest and maybe even to do more. He might also not be able to do anything, though, which was why he didn't bring it up.

He didn't want to give Josiah false hope the way Josiah had with him.

Luther swallowed, but there was something stuck in his throat, and it wouldn't budge. "Are you sure?" he asked around it.

Josiah hesitated, then nodded. "I think this will be best for both of us. I know it hurts. It's painful for me, too. I truly think we wouldn't have worked in the long run, though. We're too different, and you don't belong in the forest. I never understood why you'd want to give up your freedom to be with me, and I can't risk it. I can't risk you resenting me in the future, and you can't promise me you won't."

He was right. Luther couldn't make any promises about how he'd feel in the future, and it was obvious Josiah wouldn't want to hear them even if he could.

So instead of insisting the way he wanted to, he nodded and moved toward the door. "The team and I aren't leaving yet. I'll be in Northwood for a while if you want to talk to me, and you still have my number. You can use it anytime you want, even after I'm gone. If you need anything, let me know."

"I will."

But they both knew that was a lie. Why would Josiah want to call Luther when he'd broken up with him? Luther walked through the house with his focus on getting to the front door. Then it struck him. He wasn't sure how he was supposed to drive back to Northwood when his heart was breaking in his chest, but he would find a way. He couldn't impose on Josiah, not when Josiah didn't want him anymore.

He managed to reach his truck without stumbling and falling on his face. Once inside, he took a deep breath, then another. He pushed away the feeling that a piece was missing from his heart and locked it in a small box in the back of his mind. He had to get back to Northwood and the apartment he shared with the team. Once he was in his room there, alone, he could unlock that box and let the pain take over.

But not one second sooner.

Josiah wasn't sure what happened after Luther left the kitchen. He felt lost, like nothing around him was real. He jerked when he heard the sound of Luther's truck driving away, and he finally unfroze. He ran to the door, wanting to stop Luther from leaving him.

But Luther was already gone. Josiah stood there, his front door open in front of him, staring at the patch of grass where Luther usually parked. Josiah could still see the truck in the distance, but it was quickly disappearing, and Luther wouldn't see him even if he looked at the house.

Why would he anyway?

Josiah had broken his heart.

Josiah took a step forward anyway, wanting to be with Luther, but he forced himself to stop. He'd said everything he'd meant to say, and Luther had accepted it better than Josiah had thought he would. He'd asked if Josiah was sure, but that was all. He trusted Josiah to know what he was doing when not even Josiah did, and as the first tear fell from Josiah's eyes, he wondered if he'd done the right thing or if he'd ruined his life for nothing.

He'd thought about it so many times. He wanted to do what was best for Luther, and that hadn't changed. When would it be time to do the best thing for himself, though?

He screamed. He didn't care who heard him and ran to see what had happened. He didn't care if the band thought he was weak. His entire body was breaking, and he couldn't keep the pain inside.

He stumbled back inside the house and closed the door. He could hear people in the distance asking what was going on and who had screamed, but he ignored everyone. He pressed his back against his front door and slid to the floor, hugging his knees and letting the tears go.

Yes, he'd done the best thing he could for Luther, but the worst he could do for himself. Now he was left alone, having to raise a baby and guide the band. The band still hated him, and there was a chance they would try to hurt him when they found out he was pregnant. He wouldn't have Luther there to protect him anymore. He was alone, and he was the one who had done that.

And he felt guilty. He hadn't thought he would, and he'd decided that not telling Luther about the baby was the best thing for Luther, but he knew he was the only one to think that way. If Luther ever found out, he would be angry. Nico and Josiah's mother already were, although Nico was more vocal about it.

Telling Luther about the baby would have shackled them together, and he wouldn't have been so willing to leave. He wouldn't have allowed Josiah to push him away the way Josiah had, so Josiah knew this was the only way he could do this.

But it hurt. He'd known it would, but it felt as if someone had reached inside his body and torn his heart out. He didn't think it would ever be back, and if it was, it wouldn't be in one piece.

But he'd done it. He couldn't allow Luther to be torn between two worlds, which was what would have happened if he'd stayed. This way, he wouldn't have to choose between his life and his family and Josiah.

And Josiah was alone once more.

He supposed he should get used to it. He didn't know if he ever would, but he hoped that in time, the pain would fade. Right now, it didn't feel like it, and he continued crying for what felt like an eternity.

"Oh, baby," a gentle voice said after a while.

Josiah startled at the feeling of hands on his back, and when he looked up, he saw his mother crouching next to him. She opened her arms, and he dove between them, even though he hadn't done that since he was a child.

"I hope you're not making the biggest mistake of your life," his mother said, stroking his hair.

He wished she hadn't said it, because he felt the same way. He'd never wanted to hurt Luther, but he'd had to. It was the only way to show Luther they shouldn't be together and that Luther would be happier if he went back to his life outside the forest. It didn't feel right to be the one making the decision, but Luther would never have backed down after promising he'd find a way to stay. Besides, he loved Josiah.

Josiah had known Luther did, even though they hadn't told each other. He was glad he'd heard it at least once. He would cherish the memory of those words, but they wouldn't keep him warm at night. They wouldn't be there to comfort him when he needed it. They wouldn't wrap around him the way Luther had. They wouldn't love him.

Josiah was once against alone, the way he'd been all his life, but this time, it was by his own hands.

CHAPTER FIFTEEN

Luther wasn't giving up. It had taken him a few days and a chat with Nico to realize why Josiah had pushed him away. It was everything Josiah had said, but also a lot of what he hadn't. He wanted to keep Luther safe, and he was doing it by pushing him away.

But Luther wasn't going anywhere. He didn't know if Josiah would ever want him in his life again, and that wasn't his goal. But just like Josiah wanted to keep him safe, he wanted Josiah to be safe, and he wouldn't stop until Josiah was.

So now he was working even harder. After talking to his team and Thomas, Luther had decided to attend a council meeting. They ought to know what was going on with Hawley so that if Luther didn't manage to neutralize the man, they would be on their guard. He also wanted them to know that he had nothing to do with what Hawley was doing.

No matter what happened, Luther was quitting his job once this was over.

He hadn't told anyone yet, and he still hoped he would be able to move to the forest. He wanted to show Josiah that he wasn't doing it just for him, although he wasn't sure he would manage. He hadn't seen or talked to Josiah since they'd broken up, even though he'd been dying to. Josiah had made his choice. If he wanted to reach out, he knew where to find Luther. If he didn't, like it seemed, Luther would have to get used to it.

His outside life had been empty. He had his family, but they didn't see each other often enough for them to be part of his life. He had his team, but that was work. Luther had spent most of his life working before he'd arrived in the forest, and he didn't want to go back to that. He hadn't had friends. He hadn't had anyone outside of the job.

The forest was giving him the opportunity to change that. He didn't know who he should talk to, but maybe the council was the best place to start. He should probably have mentioned something to Thomas, but he was learning to go along with the flow, so he'd see how things went.

"They're ready for you," a woman said.

Luther blinked. He'd been lost in his thoughts so much that he hadn't seen her come up to him. "Thank you."

He got to his feet and moved toward the door she'd left open. The council was meeting behind it, and while Luther had met them more than once, he was still nervous. These were the people who made all the big decisions in the forest and who could allow or deny his request to stay. They were also the people who could keep the alphas safe, and he needed to talk to them and convince them he was a good person.

He walked in. He recognized several council members, including Calder, the badgers' representative. The man smiled at him, and that gave Luther hope. He smiled back and came to stand in front of the long table the council was sitting around. It was U-shaped, so once he was standing in the middle of it, all the council members could see him.

There was a new one. Luther couldn't see her name on the tag in front of her from his position. He wanted to ask, but it wasn't his place. She reminded him of someone, but now wasn't the time to think about that.

"Welcome," one of the council members said. Her name — Marjory — was on a metal tag on the table in front of her, along with the shifter group she belonged to. She was an ally, since she was the bear council member.

"Thank you for seeing me," Luther answered.

"You said it could be a question of life or death, so we thought it was important."

"It is."

"We're listening."

Luther took a deep breath and began. He'd already gone over his story about Hawley several times. His team knew, of course, and so did Thomas. He'd repeated it in front of Morris, the bear alpha, so Marjory probably knew about it already. She didn't interrupt him as he explained how he'd found himself accepting this job and what Hawley had been asking of him since he and his team had arrived.

"I've been trying to contact his superior," Luther explained. "I'm hoping that I can show him how dangerous Hawley is. He needs to be removed from his job, but it's not something I can do personally. I don't have enough power."

"What if you can't convince his superior?" a man asked.

Luther squinted at the man's tag. It said that his name was Drake and that he belonged to the bobcats. He had a special interest in this, since his alpha had been shot recently. "Then I'll continue going higher up until someone does something," Luther told him. "I'm not willing to compromise on that. I won't say it'll be easy, because it won't. I'm not alone in this, though."

"Who's helping you?" the woman Luther hadn't recognized asked.

Now that he was in a good position to do it, he looked at her tag. He almost gasped when he saw that she was the coyote council member. Her name was Juliet. Josiah had to have chosen her, and Luther remembered he'd been talking about asking his mother to take this job. Was that her?

Once again, Luther wanted to ask. Instead, he told her, "I'm sure you're aware of the shifter freedom groups."

She nodded. "They want us to be free of the forests."

"They think it's not fair for you to be locked up. They think that no one should have a say in how you live your life, and no one should have so much power over you. I agree."

"And you think you can make this work?" She sounded skeptical.

"Not right away, and maybe not ever. I'm not a politician, and I'm sure those people are better suited to get new laws in place for your sake. Right now, I'm only focused on Hawley and making sure he doesn't cause more trouble. Once he's removed, we can think about the rest."

"Why would we want to leave the forest?" another woman asked.

"I don't know if you do," Luther told her. "But you should have the choice. That's what most shifter freedoms groups are saying, and once again, I agree. You should be treated like every other human being in the country. It happens in other countries, so I don't see why it can't here."

"I don't think this is a topic we should face right now," Abel, the deer council member, said softly. "I'm grateful you told us about this. We need to be prepared, since you suspect your superior will try to start a war between alphas. We can't hide all the alphas, though. This won't be easy."

"I realize that. But at least now, you can all tell your alphas that they might be in danger. It's a start. I'll continue working on getting Hawley fired and possibly arrested while you focus on keeping your people safe."

Luther wasn't involved in the conversation that followed, but he thought that the council members believed him. They were taking this seriously, like he'd hoped, and he was relieved.

"Is there something else?" Calder asked. He looked like he knew something, which he probably did considering how close he was to Thomas.

"I have a request, if I may," Luther said.

"We're listening."

And they were. Everyone turned their attention to Luther again, which made him nervous. Still, this was his best chance to be allowed to stay in the forest, and he wasn't going to waste it. "As I'm sure some of you know, I've become close to several shifters since my team and I arrived. They're friends, and I find myself unwilling to part from them, even when my job is done. I'd like to request to be allowed to stay in the forest."

"Permanently?" Juliet asked.

Luther couldn't read her expression, and he didn't try. He just hoped she would tell Josiah about this. If Josiah had pushed him away because he thought he was doing the best for Luther, Luther wanted him to know that he was staying anyway. "If I'm allowed, yes. I don't have much to go back to in my life. I found more people here than I ever did outside of the forest. I realize it has never been done before, but maybe it could be the first step to showing the world that humans and shifters truly can live together."

Luther was convinced of it, and he hoped the council would agree.

Josiah was in his bedroom when Nico found him. His best friend had walked into the house without knocking, which was the only reason he'd found Josiah. Josiah had been trying to hide from him because he already knew what Nico had to tell him, and he didn't want to hear it.

Yes, he'd ruined his own life. No, knowing that wouldn't change anything. No, he wasn't going back on what he'd done. He was keeping Luther safe and as happy as possible, and that was all that mattered. Luther and everyone else would understand how right Josiah had been in the future.

The problem was that it didn't stop them from bothering

him right now.

"You're an idiot," Nico said when he walked into the bedroom.

"I love you too. If this is the kind of compliments you want to give me, you know where the door is."

Nico rolled his eyes and stretched onto the mattress next to Josiah. He knocked their shoulders together, a sign he wasn't angry.

Josiah hoped so, because he didn't want to be yelled at.

"Why did you break up with him?" Nico asked.

"Because it was the right thing to do."

"Or because you're as much of an idiot as my brother was. You know he did this exact same thing."

"He did what he thought was right, and I did, too."

"And he was wrong. So are you, by the way. I don't understand how the two of you thought you could make a decision that wasn't yours to make."

"I don't have to be with Luther if I don't want to."

Nico snorted. "But you *do* want to. And don't say no, because I know it's a lie. I'm your best friend. I know you better than anyone, except maybe Luther. Honestly, I don't understand how he didn't see right through you when you broke up with him."

"What do you want?" Luther was gone, and Josiah didn't want to talk about this. He didn't even want to talk to Nico unless Nico stopped mentioning Luther.

Nico sat up and crossed his legs under himself. "You had everything you wanted, but instead of letting Luther decide like the adult he is, you made the decision for him, and it was stupid. Did you even tell him he was going to be a father?"

Josiah didn't want to be the only one on his back, so he sat up, too. Besides, this position made it less obvious that he was pregnant. His stomach was starting to show, just a tiny bit, but enough for him to notice. He had a hard time not touching his belly all the time and marveling at the life that was growing inside it. Then he remembered that he would be alone to raise this child, and he turned sad again.

"I didn't tell him," he murmured.

He expected Nico to be angry, and he probably was. He seemed sadder and disappointed, though, which was painful for Josiah.

"He doesn't deserve this," Nico said. "He's always treated you right. You're not doing the same for him, and it's not fair."

"Nothing's fair in this situation."

"It's not, but you're the one who made it that way. Luther was ready to stand by your side and give you everything you needed and wanted. I'm sure he would have tried to be an alpha mate if you'd asked, and he would have stepped back from the band entirely if you didn't. He respects you, which he's showing once again by not bothering you now that you broke up with him. I understand why you did. You're trying to keep him safe, and you don't think he will be if he stays in the forest. The problem is that you didn't think this through."

Josiah blinked. "What are you talking about?"

Nico ignored his question. "You made a decision you didn't have the right to make, and you have to talk to him and explain what happened. Let *him* decide what he wants to do. But you have to tell him everything this time."

Josiah glared. "Tell me what you meant when you said I didn't think this through."

Nico grinned. "I talked with Drake."

He was the bobcat council member. Josiah wasn't sure what he had to do with this conversation. "And I care because?"

"You care because the council just talked to Luther. Drake said your mother was great."

"I'll talk to her about that myself. What did Luther want

from the council?"

"He told them about the situation he's dealing with concerning his superior. The man sounds like a dick, by the way."

"He is." Josiah had been witness to a few phone calls between the man and Luther, and he wouldn't spit on him if he were on fire and that was the only way to put it out.

"So Luther told them what he's been doing to help. It's impressive. He truly cares about the forest."

"He's a good man," Josiah murmured. He'd always known that, and this was one more thing that proved he was right.

"He is. He also asked the council if he would be allowed to stay in the forest once this is over."

Josiah gaped. He tried to wrap his mind around Nico's words, but it was impossible. "He asked to be allowed to stay?"

"Yep. Apparently, he doesn't have a lot outside of the forest. He said he's met a lot of people here and that he made friends, and he wants to stay. He also thinks it might be a way to show the world that shifters and humans can live together, although I'm not sure how well that's going to work."

"It does in other countries."

"But it doesn't here. I mean, everyone in this place can see what happens in other places. Why should this situation be any different? If they don't want to see, they won't."

Josiah shook his head. He didn't want to talk about this, but rather, about Luther. "Why does he want to stay? We broke up."

Nico took one of Josiah's hands and squeezed. "Did you ever think that maybe he wanted to stay because that's what he wants, period? It might not have anything to do with you."

Josiah arched a brow. Nico snorted.

"Okay, so maybe it *had* something to do with you," Nico continued. "But not everything. I wasn't there for the conversation, so I don't know what was said. But Drake explained what I already told you about why Luther wants to stay. He never mentioned you. Instead, he talked about how he became friends with Thomas and other shifters."

Josiah's head was spinning. He couldn't believe Luther truly was going through with this even though they weren't together.

In the beginning, it had been only sex between them. It was why Josiah had been able to ignore the fact that Luther would have left eventually and why it had felt safer because if that was all there was between them, people wouldn't care.

But lust had turned to love quickly. Now, here Josiah was, in love and pregnant, and he didn't know what to do. He'd tried to protect Luther, but apparently, Luther didn't care about that and was doing what he wanted. It made sense. Like Nico had said, Luther was an adult, and he could make his own decisions. Josiah shouldn't be the one making them for him.

But he had. He still didn't know what to do about it. He wanted to get back with Luther, but would Luther even talk to him? And, of course, there was the baby. Luther should know about it, and he would be angry when he found out.

"I see you're finally getting it," Nico crowed.

Josiah glared at him. "Don't sound so happy. And I'm still thinking about this. I haven't decided to do anything yet, and I might not. I still think that the best thing for Luther would be for him to leave. Staying is too dangerous."

Nico huffed. "Fine. I'll stop talking about him now that you know what's going on." His gaze drifted down to Josiah's stomach. "Have you seen a healer?"

Josiah groaned. "Can we talk about Luther again?"

"I take it that the answer is no. Okay, we're going to the badgers, and we're going now. I'm sure Arlene can find some time for you."

Josiah wanted to say no, but Nico was right. It was time for him to see a healer, and he trusted Arlene more than he trusted any other healer in the forest.

"Where did you get that number?" Luther asked, looking at Dean. They were in Thomas's house in badger territory, where they'd arrived after Luther had talked to the council. Calder had dragged him here, and Dean had followed. Luther hadn't minded. He considered Thomas a friend, and he needed reassurance that the council truly would think about allowing him to stay. Thomas was on the phone, so Dean and Luther were waiting for him in the living room.

Dean shrugged. "Does it matter?"

"Did you do anything illegal to get it?"

"I promise I didn't. I just know people who know people, all right?"

Luther nodded. He didn't tell Dean that he already had the number. Dean was trying to help, and no matter how he'd done it, he'd managed to get his hands on the number Luther needed to contact Hawley's superior.

It was time to do this.

Luther grabbed the piece of paper Dean was offering him, took his phone out, and dialed. The phone rang several times before a gruff voice answered. "Yes?"

The number belonged to a private phone, which was no doubt why the man hadn't answered with his title and name. Luther wasn't quite sure how to respond. He wasn't used to dealing with superiors unofficially. "Sir? My name is Luther Mallory."

There was a pause before the man answered. "I've seen that name on reports."

"It's because I work for Hawley."

"Yet you're calling my private number."

"I apologize, sir."

"Stop that and call me Gerald."

Luther swallowed. That, he *definitely* wasn't used to. "Gerald. And you can call me Luther."

Gerald snorted. "I have to say that I didn't expect your phone call, although I suspect I know why you're calling. And I don't want to know how you got my private number. Someone talked too much, and they shouldn't have."

"But I'm relieved they did. Since you already know why I'm calling, you know something has to be done."

"I agree. Hawley has proved not to be the right man for this kind of job."

"So you'll have to remove him?"

"I'm trying. I'm sure you realize that's not as easy as saying it, though. I can't make any promises, but I'm doing everything I can."

Luther had learned that Gerald—as he was now allowed to call the man—supported the shifter freedom movement, albeit not publicly. That was a surprise, but he supposed that a lot of people from different walks of life agreed with it. He understood that Gerald couldn't be open about it considering his job, but it was a relief to know they were allies in this. "The situation is going to escalate soon if we don't do something. Hawley has been getting impatient about me not finding a reason for him to attack the shifters here, and he's going to step in."

"What are you talking about?"

Luther quickly explained how he suspected Hawley to be behind the shooting that wounded the bobcat alpha. "I'm afraid he's going to do something similar if you don't stop him," he added.

"Dammit. I should never have allowed him to be promoted to this position. All right, I see things have become urgent. Leave it to me. Focus on doing everything you can to keep the people in the forest safe. That's our main objective. You're working directly for me now, not for Hawley. The same goes for your team."

Luther was relieved. He hadn't liked sneaking around without anyone knowing what he was doing, but it had been necessary. Now, he had the approval of someone higher up in the command chain, which made him feel better. "Sir? There's something else."

"Only if you call me Gerald," Gerald said pointedly.

"I apologize."

"Just tell me what you need."

"I'd like permission to stay in the forest even after this is over."

"Explain." Gerald didn't sound angry but confused.

"I met a lot of people here. I feel like I have more friends in the forest than outside of it. I also fell in love with someone, and I don't want to leave them. I'm planning on quitting my job, and I'd like the authorization to move to the forest with the shifters." Even if he couldn't move in with Josiah the way he'd thought he would eventually, he could find a place in Northwood.

"This isn't a request I expected," Gerald said slowly.

"It isn't a request I expected to ask. But I truly am happier here than I've ever been outside of the forest, and I don't want to lose it." And maybe Luther hoped that showing how much he wanted to stay would get Josiah to take him back. He wasn't counting on it, but he had hope.

"I can't make any promises when it comes to that, either. But I'll see what I can do. I'll let you know what's happening as soon as I can. Stay safe, and keep the forest safe."

Luther was out of breath when they hung up. Gerald hadn't denied his request right away, which gave him hope. Now that he'd dealt with that and knew someone was working to remove Hawley, he turned his attention to Dean. "Okay. Tell me how you got his number."

Dean stared at Luther for a moment. Luther expected him to decline to answer. It hadn't been an order, and Luther wouldn't push. He trusted Dean and the rest of his team enough that he would allow Dean to keep his secret.

"I'm part shifter," Dean finally said.

Luther cocked his head. "What do you mean by part shifter? I know you have shifters in your family tree."

"That's what I mean. I can't shift or anything, but it doesn't make me fully human." He hesitated. "I've been working with the shifters freedom people."

That, Luther hadn't expected. He sat on the couch, gesturing at Dean to do the same. "Tell me."

"There's nothing much to say, really. We want shifters to have the same rights as humans and to be able to leave their forest if they want to. I want to visit my family. I'd never met most of them because they've been locked up in here and other forests for as long as I've been alive. It's not fair, to them or to me, not to be able to be with them. Besides, other countries have shown that shifters and humans can live without killing each other. Me and the shifters freedom movement want shifters to be free. That's all. A lot of humans agree, and some of them are in the government and military. That's how I got that number."

Luther was surprised, yet at the same time, he wasn't. He'd always known about Dean being part shifter, but he hadn't realized how important that was to Dean. Maybe he should have, especially after he'd met Josiah and the others and he'd started to understand shifters better.

They were human beings, no matter what some people thought. They deserved happiness and freedom, and if the shifters freedom movement was able to give them that, Luther wanted to support them, too.

The front door slammed so hard the sound made Luther and Dean both jump. They looked at each other before rushing toward the entrance. From the sound, they could tell something had happened, and Luther was terrified.

Calder and Kari were there when Luther and Dean arrived. Thomas wasn't far behind them, his wife with him, her eyes wide.

Calder was supporting Kari, who looked like he wanted to strangle someone—possibly Calder himself. "He's in labor," Calder said.

He looked terrified, much more than Kari. That didn't surprise Luther or anyone in the room. It was Kari, after all.

"I'll call Arlene," Thomas's wife said.

"We could have done this at home," Kari said. "Why do I have to give birth in Thomas's house?" He looked at Thomas. "No offense, but I don't live here."

"Allow Arlene to visit you. You're here anyway. If she says you can be moved back to your house, we'll do it," Thomas told him.

The sound of a car stopping in front of the house had all of them turning toward the front door, which was still open. Luther moved toward it, wanting to know what was going on, and froze when he saw Nico's car. Nico was driving, and there, in the passenger seat, was Josiah.

Josiah groaned when he saw Luther. "Did you know about this?" he asked Nico. He wouldn't put it past his best friend to try to fix things between him and Luther.

"I swear I didn't. I have no idea why he's here."

Josiah stared for a moment before deciding he believed Nico. Nico looked too shocked to have had a hidden reason to want Josiah to visit the badgers.

"I can drive you home if you want," Nico offered.

Josiah sighed. "We might as well do this."

"He could find out about the baby if you talk to Arlene

while he's here."

Josiah arched a brow. "Isn't that what you want? For him to find out about the baby, to sweep me off my feet so we can live happily ever after?"

"I do want that to happen, but I can't force you to face him. It wouldn't be right."

"You wouldn't be forcing me. Do you think I don't want to talk to him? I've been yearning to since I broke up with him."

"Are you ready to explain what happened, though? Because he'll ask. When he realizes you're here to see Arlene, he's going to think you're sick. And knowing him, he won't let it go until you tell him what's happening."

Josiah knew that, but he was ready to face it. He'd thought about this enough to realize he'd made the wrong decision. He should have told Luther about his doubts and let Luther decide what he wanted to do. Besides, Luther was doing what he wanted anyway. If he was allowed, he would stay in the forest, whether Josiah wanted him to or not. Josiah might as well face him now.

"Let's go," he said, hoping he sounded less hesitant than he felt. He didn't know how Luther would deal with this, but Josiah was pretty sure he wouldn't take it well.

He swallowed and got out of the car. Luther was still by the front door, but he took a step forward as if he wanted to come to Josiah. Then he froze, leaving the decision in Josiah's hands.

Josiah could go to Luther and ask for his forgiveness. Luther would give it to him eventually, and they could go back to what they had before. Or he could go back to the car and ask Nico to drive him home, and he would lose Luther forever.

No matter his doubts, it was an easy decision to make.

Josiah moved forward. He could hear someone talking loudly in the house, but he didn't care about anyone but

Luther. He was almost at the bottom of the porch steps when a loud sound made him jump. Pain seared through his shoulder, knocking the breath out of him while at the same time something heavy barreled against him. He crumbled to the ground.

It hurt. That was the only thing Josiah could think of, and he didn't even realize when he hit the ground. There was pain there, too, but it was nothing next to the pain rushing through his shoulder and arm.

Someone screamed. Josiah tried to keep his eyes open as the weight on top of him moved away, but he had no idea what was happening. Air rushed into his lungs, and he felt better, but also so much worse. The pain felt like it had multiplied, to the point that Josiah wanted to die.

"Josiah? Answer me!"

Josiah blinked to see Luther kneeling next to him. His hands were hovering over Josiah's body as if he was afraid to touch him. Josiah opened his mouth to tell him he was fine, but only a croak came out.

Now he could hear more things happening around him. People were screaming and yelling at each other, and it was overwhelming.

"I'm going to carry you inside," Luther said. "I'm sorry if I hurt you, but I can't leave you out here."

Josiah nodded. He screamed when Luther hauled him into his arms, and he clung to him with his good arm. The other felt like it had fallen off because he couldn't move it, but it hurt too much for that to have happened.

Luther almost ran inside. Josiah was stunned to see Kari and Calder were in the entrance and even more so to find that Calder was trying to keep Kari inside.

"I'm going to find those fuckers and shoot them," Kari snarled.

"You can't go out there. You're in labor." Calder's voice

sounded calm, but his expression was anything but.

"I'll finish giving birth to this baby after I'm done shooting them."

"Kari."

"They shot at Josiah. He's wounded. How do you expect me to stay here?"

It would have been funny in any other circumstance. Josiah hadn't known Kari was in labor, and he didn't want his friend to go out there. He hadn't even realized someone had shot at him, although that explained why he was in so much pain.

"I'm fine," he told Kari.

Kari's expression said he didn't believe him. "You're bleeding on the carpet."

"But I'll survive. It's my shoulder. It's not deadly, right?"

Luther gently put Josiah on one of the chairs in the entrance. He pulled away Josiah's t-shirt from the wound, and Josiah had to stifle another scream. "It's a shoulder wound, so it should be okay. Arlene is here, though, and she can help you."

Josiah shook his head. "She needs to take care of Kari."

"I can take care of both of you," Arlene snapped as she walked into the room.

She'd obviously come in through the back door, and she looked pissed. She pointed a finger at Kari and Calder. "The two of you. Go into one of the guest bedrooms. When I come in, I want to find you on the bed, Kari. You're not going out there, and I don't care how much you protest."

"Someone shot at Josiah," Kari repeated.

Arlene crossed her arms over his chest. "I'm aware of that, thank you. You can't do anything about it, not while you're in labor. Don't worry, though. Raven is already hunting the fucker who did it."

"Raven?" Josiah asked.

"He's the one who saved you," Luther said. "He realized

what was happening and pushed you away, but he wasn't fast enough."

To Josiah, it sounded like he'd been plenty fast. If he hadn't been there, Josiah would be dead.

"The two of you," Arlene said, turning her attention to Josiah. "Find another guest room. I'm quickly going to visit Kari to see how far along he is. It shouldn't be a problem to leave him on his own for a bit. First-time labors usually aren't quick."

"Don't say that," Kari said with a groan.

Luther leaned down to take Josiah into his arms again, but Josiah shook his head. "I can walk."

Luther moved back. He looked sad and hurt, so Josiah caught his wrist. "But you should stay with me. I'm afraid I'll fall on my face if I try to walk on my own."

That seemed to make things better, and Luther helped him back to his feet. Josiah looked around for Nico. He found him just inside the house, pale and trembling.

When Nico caught him looking, he waved at him. "I'm just shaken. You should listen to what Arlene is saying. She'll take care of you."

Josiah didn't have a choice, because Luther guided him into the hallway. They quickly found a guest bedroom, and by the time Josiah had settled in a sitting position on the bed, Arlene was with them.

"Kari will be fine. He's in labor, all right, but it's going to take at least a few hours for him to be ready to push. I have plenty of time to take care of you until it happens."

Her arms were full of medical supplies. She put them onto the dresser and turned back to Josiah. "Now, I'm going to need some help, and since Luther is here, he can be my helper. Is that a problem with you?"

Josiah shook his head. He had a question to ask, but that would out him in front of Luther. He couldn't *not* ask, though, not when he was terrified that the wound would put his baby in danger. "How dangerous is the wound?"

"Well, I haven't seen it yet, but you should be fine since it's a shoulder wound. It's going to hurt like hell for a while, and you're probably going to have to do physical therapy, but you'll be okay."

"What if I were pregnant?" Josiah was afraid to look at Luther. He didn't know what he would see Luther's eyes, but he expected anything—fear, of course, but also hate, disgust, anger.

He wasn't ready to face any of those.

CHAPTER SIXTEEN

For a moment, Luther thought he'd heard wrong. Why was Josiah asking what would happen if he were pregnant? Then Luther realized what those words meant, and he had to reach out and grab the edge of the dresser to avoid falling on his face.

"Is that an actual question?" Arlene asked. Her tone was brisk but gentle.

"I'm pregnant," Josiah said. "I'm not far along, so I can't feel the baby yet, and I'm kind of freaking out."

"All right. I can't make any promises, but the wound shouldn't be dangerous for the baby as long as I take care of it right away. I'll ask Patrick to head back to my house to get the portable ultrasound scan. I'm pretty sure we're going to need it anyway. You should have come to see me sooner."

Luther's brain was still stuck on the fact that Josiah was pregnant. He had so many questions to ask, but Arlene was already working on Josiah's wound, so instead he helped her as much as he could. As soon as she was done, he stepped away, needing to call his team. He called Dean, since he'd been present when Josiah had been shot, and thankfully, Dean answered right away.

"Where are you?" Luther asked.

"Hunting the bastard who shot your man. Did you need anything?"

"No. I was going to give you the order to do just that."

"Well, don't worry about us, and focus on Josiah. We'll be fine."

Luther hoped that would be the case. He couldn't lose Josiah, but he also didn't want to lose any of his team members.

He hung up to find out that Arlene had disappeared from the bedroom, leaving him and Josiah alone.

He wasn't sure what to say or even how he felt. He was stunned, angry, terrified, all at the same time. It was going to take him a few hours to wrap his mind around everything, but the most important thing was that Josiah was okay. "What did Arlene say?"

Josiah was still on the bed, but now his chest was bare.

That made it easy for Luther's gaze to slide down to his stomach. There was no way for him to hide the slight bulge there, and Luther had to resist the urge to reach for it.

"She went to see where Patrick is and to check in on Kari again. She'll be back soon," Josiah whispered.

Luther didn't want Josiah to be uncomfortable or force himself on him, but he had to know. "Did you know you were pregnant when you broke up with me?"

Josiah hesitated, and it was enough for Luther to know he had. "I knew that telling you would make sure you'd find a way to stay with us," Josiah admitted.

"Of course I would have. Do you hate me so much that you don't want me to be in our baby's life?"

Josiah finally looked at Luther. He was obviously in pain, his expression tight, his face pale. "I don't hate you. It's the opposite. I did this because I love you, and I wanted you to be free."

Luther took a chance and went to crouch in front of Josiah. He took one of Josiah's hands, relieved when Josiah didn't pull it away. "What makes you think I'm not free?"

"I thought you wanted to stay here in the forest because of me. I didn't want you to come to resent me in a few years because you lost your freedom. It's not right to ask that from you."

"So you took my freedom of decision away from me?"

"I didn't mean to. I didn't even realize that's what I was doing. I'm sorry. I didn't want you to get hurt, and I know the band won't accept you, especially when they find out I'm pregnant. They'll be pissed, and I didn't want them to take it out on you."

"You should have told me."

"I wanted to. I never imagined I would raise a baby on my own, and I didn't want to. I want this child to have both parents, and I think you'd be a great father."

"I want to be one."

"Nico told me you decided to stay in the forest even though we weren't together."

Luther was going to have to buy something for that man, maybe erect him a statue or something. "I asked permission from the council, and I finally managed to call Hawley's superior. I asked him about it, too. He might not find a way, but as long as the council agrees I can stay, I will."

"Even if you're not with me?"

"Even if I'm not with you, although I want to be," Luther confessed. There was nothing he wanted more, and now that he knew Josiah was pregnant, it was too easy to imagine them living together and being a family. "But I'll understand if you don't. I'd just like to have a place in my child's life."

Luther got to his feet. He'd said what he needed to say, and he wanted to check in on his team and see what was happening outside this bedroom. Besides, if Arlene was coming back, Josiah would need some time alone with her.

But Josiah caught Luther's wrist again. "Where are you going?" he asked.

"Outside. I know you need time to think about this, and I don't want to force you into anything. I'm just happy you're okay."

"Stay. Please."

"Are you sure?"

"I am. I was going to talk to you anyway. I didn't know it would happen this way, but maybe it was supposed to."

Luther frowned. "You think you were supposed to get shot at?"

"Not that. It forced me to talk to you. It forced me to admit that I was pregnant, and I should have told you a long time ago."

"That's why you were sick?" Luther suddenly remembered when Josiah had been so pale and withdrawn. He'd known he was pregnant then, but he hadn't asked for support, probably because he'd already been thinking about breaking up with Luther.

"I kept hoping it was something I ate, but I knew better," Josiah said.

"I wish I could have been there for you."

"You weren't because I didn't want you to be. I tried to act like an alpha even when it came to you, but I shouldn't have. I have no right to tell you what to do or not do, and I shouldn't have pushed you away, especially when I didn't want to. I love you, and I don't think I'll ever stop loving you, no matter how stupid it sounds."

Luther didn't want to hope, but he couldn't help it. Josiah was saying all the right things—all the things Luther wanted to hear. Luther would need more, though. He needed Josiah to be precise and tell him exactly what he wanted and what he expected. Luther didn't think his heart could take it if Josiah pushed him away a second time.

Josiah stared at Luther and prayed that Luther felt the same way he did. He'd just opened his heart to Luther, and he hoped it wasn't about to get squashed.

"I love you, too," Luther said.

Josiah's heart raced. That was good, but did it mean Luther wanted to be with him again? "Is it—what do you want?"

Luther frowned. "I already told you. I want to be able to be in my child's life. If you allow it, I want to be in yours, too."

"That's what I want," Josiah murmured. "I know you were planning to stay even if I continued pushing you away, but what does this change?"

"I'm not sure what you're asking."

Josiah didn't want to sound like Luther owed him something, because he didn't. He had to know, though. He'd just been shot at, and he was pregnant. Was Luther going to be with him to get through this, or would Josiah have to do it on his own? He knew that Luther would help him if he asked, but he wanted Luther to want it as much as he did. He wanted Luther to *want* to be with him, but Luther wasn't saying anything about that, and it was making Josiah nervous.

Josiah was going to have to say the words, wasn't he? He had to be as open as possible with Luther because otherwise, they would ruin this, and now that he had Luther back, he didn't want that to happen.

He swallowed. His mouth was dry, but he could do this. He knew Luther loved him, and he loved Luther. "I want you to stay in the forest. I want us to date and to be parents together. We're in love. I want us to be a couple, and maybe for you to move in with me."

"What about the band?"

Josiah grimaced. "That'll be the hardest part. They're going to be angry when they find out I'm pregnant, and since you're the other father, they'll take it out on you, too. I'm afraid they'll hurt you."

"So far, the only person they've hurt is you."

"You don't think they were behind the shooting, do you?" Josiah didn't know what he would do if that was the case. He was aware of the hatred the coyotes felt for him, but was it strong enough to try to kill him? That sounded too much even for them, although he wouldn't put it past Gordon.

Luther shook his head. "I'm pretty sure they're not, but that's not what I was talking about. They hurt you with their words and with their refusal to even talk to you."

Josiah felt better, albeit only a bit. "It's been getting better with Stephen there."

"You shouldn't have needed him to get the band to listen to you. I know you're worried, but I promise I'm more than able to take care of myself."

"Yes, but they're shifters, and there are a lot of them. You can't take on the entire band, not by yourself."

"I doubt I'll have to take on the entire band. A few members might have a problem with me, and I have no doubt they'll try to do something about it, but I can take them." Luther squeezed Josiah's hand. "I promise I know what I'm doing. I don't expect any of this to be easy, but I'm willing to do it because I love you, and I want to be with you."

Josiah nodded. It was what he'd wanted to hear, and even though his shoulder hurt, he'd never been so happy. "What if you're not allowed to stay?" he asked because he needed to know that, too.

Luther sighed. "Well, there are a few possible scenarios here. I might be allowed to stay by the council but not by my superiors. I might be allowed to stay by my superiors, but not by the council. That last one would be the worst option because it would be easy for the council to find out if I'm around. But if it's a problem with humans, I don't care. I'll quit my job and just move. I'm quitting my job anyway, because I don't like what it's become."

"What will you do?"

Luther smiled gently. "Well, I thought that for a start, I could focus on you and our child. You might be pregnant, but you're still the alpha, and I know that as soon as the baby is born, you'll have to go back to work, or at the very least, that you'll need someone to help with the baby and the job. I want to be there for the two of you."

"That sounds . . ." It sounded perfect, but Josiah couldn't imagine Luther being a stay-at-home father. Luther was always on the move, and he was great at his job. Surely Josiah or someone else in the forest could find him a job he would be happy to do.

"Boring, I know," Luther said with a smile. "But that's what I want. Over the past couple of years, I've been sent all over the country. I'd like some time to put my feet down and not have to think about work. Once the baby is a bit older, I'm sure I can find something to do around here."

They were planning their future together, but Josiah wanted to kiss Luther. Was that something Luther would want? They were both hesitant, and Josiah wanted to break that. He wanted them to go back to how they'd been with each other before.

He reached for Luther, praying Luther wouldn't move away. He could have sobbed in relief when Luther didn't, instead gently taking Josiah into his arms, careful of his shoulder.

Josiah didn't know how long they stayed that way, and he didn't care. He was safe and he belonged. That was all that mattered.

Someone knocked on the door a little while later, and Arlene looked in. She beamed when she saw them still wrapped around each other. "You made up. Good. Luther, your team is here, and they want to talk to you."

Luther got to his feet, and Josiah followed. It was obvious from Luther's expression he wanted Josiah to stay where he was, but Josiah wasn't going to allow that. He was an alpha, and he'd been shot. He should know what happened, even though his shoulder hurt like hell.

He followed Luther out of the bedroom, but Arlene stopped him before he could walk down the hallway. "I'll be with Kari if you need me. Come talk to me before you leave. I want to get an ultrasound and see how your baby is."

Josiah wanted to do that right now. He needed to be sure his baby was okay. There was Kari to think of, though, and of course, the shooter. "I'll be there as soon as I can."

Arlene nodded. "Good. You know where to find me. And if you don't come, I'll hunt you down."

That made Josiah smile. The coyotes might still be angry at him, and they might still hate him, but he wasn't alone anymore.

Luther's team was gathered in Thomas's office, along with Thomas, Alex, and Raven. Everyone looked pissed, which told Josiah that they probably hadn't found the shooter. The thought made him angry and worried. He was hoping the shooter hadn't been aiming at him personally, but rather, at him as an alpha, but he couldn't be sure, and he couldn't help but wonder if maybe a coyote had tried to kill him.

"We couldn't find them," Dean said.

Josiah was starting to get to know the people who worked with Luther, and he liked all of them, although some of them more than others. Dean was one of those.

Luther swore while Thomas nodded. "I'm organizing a council conference call. Everyone on the council needs to know what's going on." He looked at Luther. "This is what you were afraid of."

Luther pulled Josiah closer. "It is. Hawley targeted another alpha, and we're lucky Josiah didn't get killed." His gaze drifted to Raven. "Thank you."

"Don't bother with the thanks. I would have done it for anyone," Raven said. "But we have to find this asshole. There's a killer on the loose, and they're going to try to kill someone else if we don't stop them."

Josiah had been lucky. If Raven hadn't been there, he probably would have died, and his child along with him. There wasn't much he could do in this situation, but as everyone settled around the office for the video conference call, he stayed beside Luther. He might not be a council member, but this involved him, too, and he wasn't going to be left behind.

Luther was so angry he could have punched someone, but he was used to keeping control of his emotions. The fact that Josiah was staying close helped a lot. That way, Luther was sure he was safe, but he couldn't wait to get Josiah home anyway.

As strange as it was, the band felt like the safest place for Josiah to be. If a stranger tried to sneak in, the coyotes would no doubt notice, and it would help keep Josiah safe. Of course, the coyotes themselves could be a danger for Josiah, but Luther would have to deal with that later. Right now, the biggest danger was the shooter who was sneaking around the forest, and something had to be done about them.

Once every council member was in on the conference call, Luther told them what had happened. Thomas didn't intervene except to give them a few details Luther hadn't noticed because he'd been so focused on Josiah. Once they were done explaining, the council members were silent.

"Something needs to be done," Thomas said.

He was standing in for Calder, who was with Kari right now. No one expected Calder to leave Kari alone to give birth to their child.

"I agree," Josiah's mother said.

She kept staring at him as if she wanted to ask if he was okay, but thankfully, she hadn't. She was focused on the job, but Luther had no doubt that as soon as she could, she would make sure her son was fine.

"What, though?" Marjory asked. "It's true we need to do

something, but can we really find one person in the entire forest? Your people weren't able to do it, Thomas. I don't think that adding more people will help, although of course, we will. But we don't even know if this person is a human or shifter."

Luther had thought about that, and he realized how big a problem it was. "I want to try calling Hawley's superior. He needs to know about this, and he might be able to tell us something. He promised he would do everything he could to find a way to get rid of Hawley, and this could help."

"You should put him in on the conference call," Marjory said.

"I'll let him know about it." Luther took his phone out and stepped away from the conference call. He could still hear the council members talking to each other, but he wasn't about to leave the room, not when Josiah was still here.

He called Gerald's private number, wondering if he was still allowed to call the man Gerald.

"Luther. I didn't expect to hear from you today," Gerald said when he answered.

Luther took that as permission to call Gerald by his given name. "We have a bit of a problem. Another alpha was shot."

Gerald swore. "Who? How are they?"

"Josiah is fine. He could have been killed, though. The only reason he wasn't was that someone was near him and pushed him to the ground. He was shot in the shoulder, and he's pregnant, so it could have been so much worse."

There was a pause before Gerald answered. "I don't think I've ever heard about a pregnant alpha."

He no doubt knew about carriers. Luther had mentioned it in a few reports, and Gerald read them. He wasn't sure if telling Gerald he was the baby's other father was a good idea, but maybe it would help him get permission to stay more easily. "Josiah's pregnancy is young, but we're both happy about it."

"When you say you're both happy, do you mean that you're the father?"

"We both are."

"I see. So he's the man you want to stay in the forest for."

"He's one of the reasons I want to stay, yes, and having a baby makes it even more imperative."

"I still haven't found a solution for you, but I promise I'm looking. Now, let's focus on the shooter. Did your team manage to apprehend them?"

"We haven't, and there's a conference call with all the council members happening right now. They'd like for you to be brought in."

"Of course. I should have met them a long time ago."

Luther was relieved Gerald was so eager to participate. Working with him was nothing like working with Hawley, and he wished Gerald could have been his superior all along.

Gerald didn't act any differently with the council members than he had with Luther. They might be shifters, but it didn't seem to make a difference to him. They talked about what happened, but they didn't find a solution. None of them could, not when they didn't even know if the shooter was human or a shifter.

If the person was human, it should be fairly easy to find them. Luther suspected they were a shifter, though. It would be easy for one to disappear in the forest and go home. No one would notice, and they wouldn't think of being wary of a shifter.

So Hawley was working with someone in the forest. They had to find who that someone was, but they didn't have a way to do so. The easiest way to deal with the situation would be to get rid of Hawley, but that wasn't something the council could do.

"You focus on your people and on trying to find the

shooter," Gerald said. "I'll take care of Hawley. I'd been planning on doing that anyway, and this is one more reason to do it quickly."

"You don't have proof he's behind this," Thomas pointed out.

"But I can find it. I'm already working on it, and I have been since Luther mentioned it could be a problem. You won't have to worry about him after today, but you'll still have a traitor in your midst. Unfortunately, that's something you'll have to take care of."

"We'll find them," Thomas promised.

"Good. Luther, I'll call you as soon as I have news. I'd tell you not to worry about Hawley, but we both know that's not going to happen until he's behind bars. Stay with your man and keep him safe. Leave the rest to me."

Luckily, Luther wasn't one to blush easily. He could feel every council member's attention on him, though, and it made him want to squirm.

Thankfully, no one asked what was going on, and they started hanging up one by one until only Josiah's mother was left. She was staring at him, smiling. "I take it the two of you talked?" she asked.

Josiah nodded. "I'll tell you everything once I'm home."

"All right. Are you sure you're okay?"

Josiah grimaced. He was still bare-chested, so the bandages on his shoulder were obvious, and he couldn't lie to his mother. I've been better, but I'll be fine. I promise."

"All right. Come home soon, please."

"I will."

He looked at Luther as he said so, and Luther wondered if he wanted him to come along. Hopefully, he did.

"You should head home," Thomas said once Josiah's mother hung up, too. "Nothing else can be done for today, although I'll send a team into the forest to try to find a trail.

I'll let you know if we find something, but I doubt we will."

"If this is a shifter, wouldn't they have left a scent trail?" Luther asked.

"Possibly, but there are ways to hide it. Maybe now that we're not in such a rush, we'll find something."

"We have to see Arlene again before we go," Josiah said.

Luther instantly turned anxious, but he waited until they were out of the office to ask him, "What does Arlene want?"

Luther smiled. "To give me an ultrasound to make sure the baby is fine."

Luther's gaze moved down to Josiah's stomach. "She said the shoulder wound shouldn't be a problem."

"I don't think it is, but I've needed to see a healer for a while now. I should have done it sooner, and she's angry at me because I didn't. You don't have to stay if you don't want to."

"Unless you ask me to leave, I'm not going anywhere."

Josiah smile. "I don't think I'll ever ask you to leave. Not again, anyway."

"Then that means I'm here forever."

Josiah's smile was brilliant. "Forever sounds perfect to me."

EPILOGUE

Luther couldn't stop staring at Josiah's stomach. He still had a hard time wrapping his mind around the fact that his baby was growing in there. Josiah was as beautiful as ever, even with the bulge becoming bigger and bigger seemingly every day—maybe especially with it. Luther suspected he would find Josiah beautiful even when they were seventy and walking around with a cane and white hair.

But there was something glowing about Josiah as he was now, naked in bed with Luther, the sunlight kissing his pale skin, his stomach obvious. Josiah looked happy, and in turn, that made Luther happy, too. He wanted this to never end, but he still didn't know if his superiors would allow him to stay.

Not knowing was only one of the problems he had to deal with right now. No one had been able to find the shooter, but Luther was convinced that person was a shifter. It was the only thing that made sense. A human would have been found by now, especially a human who didn't belong to Luther's team, and Luther didn't want to think about the possibility that one of the people he trusted with his life could be behind this.

Luther and Josiah's phones started ringing almost at the same time. They both shot up in a sitting position and looked at each other. Josiah's eyes were wide, and Luther knew exactly why. Their phones ringing like this could only mean trouble, and neither of them wanted any more than they already had.

They couldn't ignore the calls, though, so Luther took his phone and stepped into the bathroom to give Josiah space. He was still getting used to the thought of becoming an alpha mate and helping Josiah make decisions when it came to the band, and he would have stayed if he hadn't had to answer his own phone call.

Gerald's name flashed on the screen, so Luther answered. "Hello?"

"Have you seen the news today?" Gerald asked.

Luther frowned. "Not yet."

He could almost hear the smile in Gerald's voice. "Busy with your man?"

"Well, I haven't been given orders, so my team and I have been at a loss. There's not much to do here when you're not working, and we've been taking it as a vacation."

"You're right to do that. You really should turn the TV on, though."

Luther peeked into the bedroom, not wanting to bother Josiah, but Josiah had already turned the news on, and he was staring at the screen with wide eyes. His phone was in his lap, so Luther went to sit next to him.

Breaking news: government official had plans to decimate the shifter population.

Luther held his breath as he watched the lady on the screen explaining that one unnamed government official had plans to kill as many shifters as possible and give the forests back to the humans.

"Someone leaked Hawley's plans," he told Gerald.

"Someone did, yes. My superiors aren't happy about it, but at least they had to do something about Hawley."

Luther suspected Gerald had been the one to leak it, but he wasn't about to ask. "What did they do?"

"Fired and arrested him. He's in a cell right now, and I've been tasked to investigate what he's been doing. As of right now, I am officially your superior."

"I can't say I'm sorry to hear that."

The news of what Hawley had been planning had caused an uproar, and apparently some government officials were using that to push equality laws for shifters. Luther didn't know if they would succeed, but he hoped so. If the shifters didn't want to leave their forest, that was one thing. Forcing them to stay if they didn't want to was another entirely.

It would take work, but maybe this time, the shifter freedom movement would finally succeed. Humans and shifters had been separated for too long, and now that Luther had spent time in the forest, he knew shifters weren't any more dangerous than humans. They probably hadn't been before, either, but that was in the past. They needed to look at the future, and as far as he was concerned, the future was a mix of shifters and humans, both in the forest and outside of it.

"Do you need me to come back?" he asked Gerald. Now that Hawley wasn't in charge anymore, there was no doubt his team would be assigned a new job. Luther would have to quit before that happened, but he already knew he would have to visit his old office and get everything in place. He also had to sell his apartment and pack his things, but he didn't want to leave Josiah on his own.

Not that Josiah would be alone. He was healing well, but Arlene was keeping an eye on him. The baby was growing as they were supposed to, and the band had thankfully calmed down a lot after both Stephen and Josiah's mother had yelled at a few members. Gordon still grumbled every time he saw Josiah and Luther together, and Luther suspected they were going to have to take care of him. But for now, things were as peaceful as possible in the forest considering the traitor was still running around with no consequences.

"Well, I have a new assignment for you, so you'll have to come back soon."

Luther sighed and leaned back against the headboard.

"You already know I want to quit. I can't accept a new assign-ment."

"Why don't you hear what I have to say first?"

Nothing would take Luther away from the forest, but he owed at least this to Gerald. "I'm listening."

"Good. With everything happening, both the government and military agreed that there needs to be an oversight when it comes to relationships between us and the shifters. Every-one can see that eventually, the forests will be open. There's no way to know when, and it's not going to be anytime soon, but it *will* happen. People want to know more about shifters, and they want to have better relationships with them. I've been ordered to select a team that will move into the Alle-gheny forest permanently. They will act as a communication team between the government and the shifters who live there, especially the council."

Luther had a hard time wrapping his mind around what Gerald was saying. "So that team would have to live in the forest?"

"It would, yes. I already talked to the council, and they've agreed. They also agreed to have you as the team leader. You made quite an impression on them, and they are more than happy to allow you to stay."

Luther couldn't believe it. "Not all my team members will want to stay."

"And that's fine. Only those who want to should do this. You'll have the power to select your own team, so I'll leave that to you. Does this mean you accept the job?"

Luther looked at Josiah, who was staring at him instead of the TV now. "You want me to accept a job that would allow me to continue working but also to live in the forest? Of course I'm accepting." At least for now.

Eventually, Luther would have to accept his role as an al-pha mate to Josiah. That would mean quitting his job and focusing on the coyotes and the band, but he had a lot of work to do before he could do that, and not just for Gerald. He'd agreed to spend time with Thomas's wife to see what being an alpha mate entailed, and while he knew it would be complicated, he was eager to start.

"Good. Since it'll be a permanent post, you should probably come back to the city and pack your things. I need to see you face to face anyway. Unfortunately, your Josiah won't be able to come, but I'm sure we can organize something to have you back with him before he gets too far along with the pregnancy."

"Give me a few days, and I'll be there."

"I'll see you then, Luther. It'll be a pleasure to work with you."

"Same."

They hung up, and Luther couldn't help the beaming smile that spread on his lips. "I'm staying," he told Josiah. Forever, if he was allowed, and if he wasn't, well, he would find a way around it.

He wasn't going anywhere.

Josiah threw himself into Luther's arms as soon as Luther hung up the phone. Luther wrapped himself around him, and Josiah could have cried from happiness.

Luther would be allowed to stay. Hell, he was being *asked* to stay, and Josiah couldn't think of a better outcome. They'd both been worried that he wouldn't be allowed to stay, but that wouldn't be a problem now, and Josiah could relax.

"Does this mean you're moving in with me permanently?" he asked once they were done kissing and hugging.

"Do you want me to? Because I'm sure Gerald is already planning on renting an apartment for every team member."

"I wouldn't ask if I wasn't sure. I want you to move in with me. You're staying. Why should you rent an apartment when you don't have to?"

Luther kissed Josiah again. "I'll move in, then. I'll have to go back for a bit to choose my team members and pack my things, but I'll be as fast as I can."

Josiah wished he could go with him, but it wasn't possible, not yet anyway. One day, though, he would be able to go outside of the forest with Luther. They would visit his family, and they would get to know Luther's child.

Josiah touched his stomach. It would be several months before the baby was born, but they would be born in a different world than Josiah had been. Things wouldn't move so fast that shifters would already be free by the time the baby was born, but it would happen. Josiah knew it.

Things weren't perfect by any means, but then, they never were. Josiah was fine with his life being perfectly imperfect, as long as Luther was in it.

ABOUT THE AUTHOR

Catherine is the creator of several series, most of them paranormal, including the Whitedell Pride Series and the Gillham Pack Series. While she graduated in translation, she decided to go the writer's way because it was more fun to create her own stories and characters.

She's been living in Italy for more than twenty years, but she's a daughter of the North—Belgium to be precise—and she misses it so much that she's already planning to move back.

She loves pizza—probably too much—her son, her pets, and of course, books. She sneaks some reading time into her schedule every time she has five minutes free from writing, demands from her various pets and son, and lastly, housework.

Connect with her:

lievens.catherine@gmail.com
BookBub: https://www.bookbub.com/authors/catherine-lievens
Website: https://authorcatherinelievens.com/
Facebook: https://www.facebook.com/catherine.lievens.9
Facebook Group: https://www.facebook.com/groups/411788002341528/
Twitter: https://twitter.com/authorCLievens
Newsletter: https://authorcatherinelievens.com/newsletter/